STORM STORIES

A SECURITY SPECIALISTS INTERNATIONAL BOOK

MONETTE MICHAELS

ISBN-10: 149059423X
ISBN-13: 978-1490594231

Cover artist: April Martinez

Stormy Weather Baby, first published in e-Book by Monette Michaels, December, 2011.

Second e-Book edition published by Liquid Silver Books, an imprint of Atlantic Bridge Publishing, April, 2013. Copyright © 2011, 2013, Monette Michaels.

Storm Front, first published in e-Book by Monette Michaels, January 2013.

Second e-Book edition published by Liquid Silver Books, an imprint of Atlantic Bridge Publishing, April, 2013. Copyright © 2013, Monette Michaels.

This is a work of fiction. The characters, incidents and dialogues in this book are of the author's imagination and are not to be construed as real. Any resemblance to actual events or persons, living or dead, is completely coincidental.

Stormy Weather Baby

Keely Walsh-Maddox is eight months pregnant and feeling boxed in by Ren's over-protectiveness. So, when Price Teague's doctor sister, Fiona, calls and says she's in Idaho and needs a ride, Keely takes the opportunity to escape her velvet cage and drive to Grangeville to pick her up.

Keely never expected to place her unborn child in danger, but that is exactly what happens when the women find themselves pursued by mercenaries. Normally, bad guys following her home wouldn't faze Keely—she'd just turn the tables and shoot them. But this time, she's in early labor and doesn't want to mess with them.

At least she has a doctor riding shot gun…

.

DEDICATION

To my fans.

ACKNOWLEDGEMENTS

To Holly, Cherise, Ezra, and Tracey for helping me polish this gift for my fans. And to Sharis for the clean-up read for posting at Liquid Silver Books.

CHAPTER 1

June 15th, 8:30 a.m., Sanctuary.

Keely Walsh-Maddox entered the kitchen at the main lodge. Gathered around the table in the breakfast nook were Quinn Jones and his wife Lacey and Scotty, the SSI cook and a second father to Keely. The three looked up and smiled.

"Hey, princess," Scotty called out. "How're you feeling today? I made your favorite egg dish. It's in the warmer. Your orange juice is here on the table."

"Thanks, Scotty. And as to how I feel? Stir crazy." She walked to the warming drawer and pulled out a plate containing a goat cheese, spinach, and mushroom frittata.

"You were just out yesterday." Quinn pointed his toast at her for emphasis. "You can't be stir crazy."

Thus speaks another overprotective male.

"Quinn, shut up." Lacey tapped a finger on her husband's mouth and then lovingly wiped away a crumb that had caught on the corner of his lips. "I told you Ren is smothering her. He's operating under the misconception that pregnant women are invalids."

"Ain't that the truth." Keely sighed, put her food on the table, then slid onto the bench seat built into the breakfast nook. "I feel like one of those frou-frou, yappy, little dogs. You know the ones. Their owners take them to the doggy beauty parlor and carry them around in a special doggy purse. All I need is a collar and a leash. It's like Ren thinks I'll hurt myself if I walk across the floor." She waved a forkful of egg and cheese around. "Do you know what he told me this morning before he left to go to the ranger station outside of Coeur d'Alene?"

Lacey smiled. "No, what?"

"To stay in bed!" The three laughed. "It's not funny. He wanted me to rest after the arduous journey to the obstetrician's office yesterday." Keely slapped the table with her free hand, rattling the silverware. "The most stressful thing I did yesterday was stand up and sit down. He barely let me walk on my own—Arrgh! The man is driving me frick-fracking nuts!"

"He wants to protect you," Quinn said. "I felt the same way when Lacey was pregnant. Of course, my lovely wife," he turned and placed a kiss on Lacey's cheek, "soon showed me the error of my ways."

"And he kept on protecting me anyway." Lacey's tone was teasing and affectionate. "My advice is to do what you need to do until you can't do it anymore."

"Exactly!" Keely smiled at the other woman before shoveling some eggs into her mouth.

"What did the doctor say, Keely?" Scotty asked. "Did she tell you and Ren something that set him off again?"

"Again? Scotty, the man has never stopped since he learned I was pregnant."

That had been back in November. The actual "deed" had been done in late October after Ren had returned from South America via Boston. Once Ren had gotten over his fears about her small size, they'd made love night and day. A few missed birth control pills and an extremely virile man, and *voila*, one pregnant Keely.

Scotty chuckled. "I stand corrected. But what did the doctor tell you? I haven't had *my* report yet." He winked at her.

Keely giggled. "The doctor said she'd see me next week for the regular checkup. That I was still on schedule for the C-section in three weeks, which is still one week shy of my due date. And that Riley is head down and everything looks good." Keely ran her fingers through her mass of red-blonde curls. "Ren heard every single blessed word the doctor said and then completely disregarded them."

Ren had also refused to make love to her last night and this morning, even though the doctor had said love-making was fine as long as Keely was comfortable and the act wasn't too vigorous. Hell, she didn't blame Ren. What man wanted to make love to a waddling cream puff?

"Ah, yes, the selective listening capabilities of the alpha-male," Lacey said. "I know them well." She patted Keely on the shoulder. "What do you want to do today? The men are all gone…"

"Hey, two males present here!" Quinn protested.

"Sorry, my love. I meant the three primary males who have made it their duty to keep Keely penned up at Sanctuary—her hubby, her brother, and her hubby's brother—are gone."

"Well…" The phone rang before Keely could reply. Being closest, she picked it up. "Sanctuary, Main Lodge. Keely Maddox speaking."

"Oh, Keely. Um, this is Fiona Teague, Price's sister. Is he there, please?"

"Oh, Fiona, I'm sorry. He isn't here. In fact, he's in your neck of the woods. The U.P. in Michigan. Hasn't he called you?"

"No. Well, this is a hell of a mess." The woman sighed loudly. And was that a sob?

Keely had never met Fiona, who was Price's youngest sister and an emergency room doctor in Detroit, but it was obvious the woman was upset. Keely put the call on the speaker so the others could listen in. Something was wrong and she might need Scotty's and Quinn's advice on how to handle it.

Price was part of the SSI family; that made Fiona family too. Family helped family.

"What's a mess? Are you in trouble?" At her mention of "trouble," the other three stopped their quiet conversation and listened intently. "Call Price on his cell. He can be in Detroit in a matter of hours."

Fiona choked out a hesitant laugh. "That's the problem. I flew to Idaho for a surprise visit. I'm in Grangeville at a diner called Ma's. The Greyhound bus from Boise dropped me off here. I was hoping Price would come pick me up since there isn't a taxi service to Sanctuary or a rental car agency."

"I'll come get you," Keely offered, waving off the beginnings of protests from the two men seated at the table. "It'll take me about fifty minutes to an hour to get there. So, sit and enjoy some of Ma's good food."

"Oh, Keely … that's … that's too much trouble. Price told me you were pregnant and…"

"I'm pregnant," Keely snarled. "Not disabled. I'll pick you up. Just hang tight."

"O-o-okay. See you soon." The call ended from Fiona's end.

Keely put the phone back in its charger and turned a smiling face to the others. "Well, that's just what I needed—a good excuse to get out of the house and off Sanctuary. What?" Scotty and Quinn glowered at her while Lacey hid her smile behind a hand.

"You can't pick up Fiona. Ren will kill me," Quinn said bluntly. "He told me to keep you safe."

"From what? It's just a two-hour round trip to Ma's and back. It's not like I'm hopping in the Hummer for the six-hour drive to Boise and the mall or something. And if you mean potential danger from the Department of Defense traitor? Well, he hasn't sent anyone after me since March. I can't live my life worrying whether or not someone might be coming after me someday in the future. I refuse to live my life in fear." She reached across the table, grabbed Quinn's hand, and squeezed. "If I thought there was real danger out there, I wouldn't leave. I would never expose my unborn child to danger."

Quinn frowned. "Jesus, Keely, I know that, but…"

"There's no but about it. I'm picking up Fiona." Keely wanted to scream in the face of Quinn's continued stubbornness, but knew it wouldn't faze him. Rational arguments with lots of back up from Lacey would. "Lacey? Am I asking too much here? I'm an adult. I'm not sick or disabled or mentally defective."

"Nope, you're exactly right. You are none of those things. I think you should go if you feel like it. Eight months pregnant is far enough away from your due date to still live your life as you wish," Lacey said. "But Quinn is correct on one point. Ren will ream him a new asshole if he finds out you've left the premises."

"Call and tell him after I've gone," Keely said. "That way you'll have done your duty in reporting my break for freedom and Ren can be mad at me. See? Easy solution." She turned to Scotty. "Fix me a Pepsi to go, please? I need to get my snow gear. The wind is from the north and really cold. The predicted weather front should hit just about the time Fiona and I are heading home."

The Weather Channel had talked about a late spring-early summer snowstorm for this part of the Bitterroots. Mother Nature's one last joke before milder weather set in for the summer. She wasn't worried. The Hummer could handle the roughest weather, as could she.

"Are you sure about this, princess?" Scotty asked.

"Abso-fricking-lutely. This is just what I needed. A road trip—alone. I love my husband, but he needs to understand that I need my space from time to time."

One hour later, Grangeville, Idaho.

AFTER AN UNEVENTFUL DRIVE TO Grangeville, Keely entered Ma's Bar and Grill and looked around. She nodded to the owner, a large, burly, bald guy named Nick. "Ma" was his mother and she told anyone who'd listen that she'd earned her retirement. Of course, she came in every day to watch over Nick to make sure he didn't let her high standards down.

Ma waved at her from the pass-through to the kitchen. Keely waved back.

As usual the place was packed even with the threat of snow. Late spring into early summer in northern Idaho was not for the faint of heart. This year especially had been one for the record books as winter did not want to give up its hold on the Bitterroots. But not even the threat of thunder-snow, sleet, hail, and gusty winds stopped an Idahoan from going where he wanted.

She paused once she moved farther into the room and away from the door and rubbed a hand over her stomach where her son, Riley, was doing jumping jacks in her womb. God, she could hardly wait to hold her baby in her arms instead of on her bladder. She would also like to see her feet again.

Keely walked the perimeter of the small eatery, nodding at patrons. She recognized most of the people eating Ma's delicious home cooking. Not much of a surprise since there weren't many residents in this part of Idaho and very few places to eat and socialize.

When she'd almost finished one full circuit of the restaurant, Keely spotted the only female who looked out of place. The curly-haired redhead sat in a corner booth and was not dressed for the inclement weather. Fiona Teague was so short the booth in which she sat almost swamped her. She looked as if she was barely sixteen years old and a strong wind would knock her on her butt. Her hair was secured into a high, messy ponytail and added to the look of youth. Her striking blue-green eyes were almost too large for her face, with long lashes matching her hair. Her skin was pale—and bruised.

Some son of a bitch had hit her—and recently. Keely's intuition during their earlier phone conversation that something was wrong in Fiona's life had been proven correct.

Keely rushed to the booth. "Fiona?"

"Keely? God, you're almost as short as me. From the stories Price has told me about you, I expected an Amazon." Fiona frowned and her gaze strayed to the obvious baby bump under Keely's Navajo-woven, wool coat. "How far along are you? Price never gave me details, just said you were pregnant." The woman's trained medical eye assessed Keely from top to bottom.

"I have about another month, but I'm scheduled for a C-section in three weeks."

"Really?" Fiona scowled. "You look full term. Your baby has obviously dropped … uh, sorry, professional habit. You might just carry low, some women do. I'm sure your OB knows what he or she is doing." She slid over and made room in the booth. "Here, get off your feet. You look as if you could use a warm drink. This weather is nuts." Price's sister shivered visibly, dressed only in a light-weight, denim jacket, T-shirt, and jeans.

Keely slid into the booth, drew off the scarf around her neck, and then unbuttoned her much more practical winter-weight coat. She rubbed a hand over her belly, soothing the baby who had switched from calisthenics to playing drums on her spinal cord.

Not much longer, Riley, and mommy will play with those little kicking feet and hands.

"I could use a cup of tea." Keely signaled Nick who nodded.

The owner knew what she liked well enough. She and Ren drove through Grangeville on the way to and from the OB visits in Coeur d'Alene. Ma's was always a stopping place on one side or the other of the now weekly visits. For a period in the middle of her pregnancy, Keely had craved Ma's meat loaf. Ren had made the one-hundred-mile round trip several times a week just to get it for her.

Fiona picked up Keely's wrist and took her pulse. Several seconds passed before Fiona spoke. "Too rapid. You're grimacing from time to time. What's going on, Keely? Why did the men let you pick me up when you look as if you'll pop within the next ten minutes?"

Keely didn't know whether to laugh or be insulted by Fiona's forthrightness and take-control attitude. For someone who looked like a pixie in a Disney movie, the woman was assertive. But then she was an emergency room physician and the attitude probably went with the territory. "Fiona…"

"Call me Fee, please. Only my mother calls me Fiona, usually when she's bitching about my career choice and her lack of grandchildren." She sighed. "Sorry, I guess I can come across kind of strong. But Price told me how protective your husband and the other men are."

"Yeah, they've been somewhat vigilant." Keely snickered. "Ren just looks at me and gets this expression of horror on his face. It's as if he's thinking 'My God, what have I done?'" She shook her head. "Even with the doctor—and my mother who's my size and had six kids including a set of twins, all vaginally—telling Ren I'll be fine, he still has nightmares. Plus, for a while, we were dealing with mercenaries sent to kill me; that situation didn't help his mental health either."

"Jesus … and I thought I had problems." Fee frowned and looked around the crowded restaurant. She leaned closer to Keely and spoke in a lower tone of voice. "Is it safe for you to be here? Do you know all these people?"

"It's safe. I wouldn't endanger my baby. Besides, you're the only stranger here. I also have a sixth sense about trouble. My spidey senses are all good at the moment." She smiled at Nick as he delivered her usual snack. "Hey, Nick, thanks for the tea and blueberry scone."

"Anything for you, Keely. When you're ready to throw that asshole Maddox over, you just let me know." The gentle giant smiled and gave her a naughty wink.

"You're so sweet, but I think I'll keep the asshole for a while longer." Keely fluttered her lashes. "I'm just getting him broken in."

Nick barked out a laugh and lumbered toward his counter, greeting regulars as he made his way.

"Everyone seems really friendly." Fee heaved a sad-sounding sigh as she glanced around the noise-filled room.

"Idahoans for the most part are very friendly." Keely blew on her steaming green tea and then took a cautious sip. Her gaze never left Fee's very expressive and bruised face. She wondered where else the doctor was bruised—or worse. "I'll apologize in advance for being nosy, but since you're Price's sister that makes you one of the family. So … who beat on you? And why hasn't Price frick-fracking killed the bastard yet?"

"I, uh … I can't … talk about … just can't." Fee shook her head, hating the tell-tale quiver in her voice. *Control, Fee. Control.* She gripped the glass of watered-down cola until her knuckles turned white, fighting to hold back the tears she'd refused to let fall ever since she'd given notice at her job in Detroit. She refused to revisit the memories of what had driven her to Sanctuary. If she did, she'd start crying, screaming—and never stop. She let out a shuddering breath as she beat her demons back.

Keely patted Fee's arm. "Are you here to ask Price for

help? And don't deny there's a problem, because I can see there is." Keely traced a gentle finger over Fee's bruised jaw and cheek.

"Price can't fix the problem." Fee had attempted to deal with the situation herself and had been stone-walled every step of the way. Power and money always trumped justice. Lesson learned. And while the thought of Price beating the crap out of her nemesis sounded good, it wouldn't solve the problem and could only cause trouble for her beloved brother. Her leaving Detroit had been the only solution.

"Wrong answer."

Fee shot her an incredulous glance. She couldn't believe the woman who looked like a pregnant fairy princess wouldn't leave it alone.

"Yeah, yeah, I know, I'm pushy." Keely grinned cheekily and rubbed Fee's arm. "O-o-kay, if you aren't here to ask for help then why the surprise visit? Not that you aren't welcome, like I said, you're family, but I'm damn sure your brother wouldn't have taken off if he'd known you were coming for a visit."

Fee sighed. "I didn't call him, because this trip was a spur of the moment thing. Since he's not here, I can leave tomorrow. If you could just put me up for the night?" She swirled the remnants of her cola, wondering if she needed another one. The altitude was making her damn thirsty. Water would be better, but her energy hadn't been good lately and the caffeinated sugar kept her going.

"Of course you can stay. Price has an apartment in the main lodge you can use. And no, you will not leave tomorrow. We can get Price back here in less than a day. He'd be pissed if he missed you. He'd planned on stopping by Detroit to see you before heading back to Idaho."

"Price was planning on seeing me? When? What did he hear?"

God, had someone called him? Did he already know what had happened? She'd hoped he would never have to hear about the whole fucking mess. He'd be so disappointed she'd run instead of taking on the big boys.

She heard their father's voice, *"You can't be my child. Teagues do not run. Teagues stand and fight."*

Keely leaned over the table. "Fee? You just went white." The other woman's voice had softened, become gentler. "What's going on, sweetie? Hey, you can tell me. We height-challenged gals have to stick together in a world of big, bad-ass men."

Keely wasn't going to give up. Better to give her something and then move on to the bigger issue in the room—why Keely was denying she was in early labor.

Fee took a bracing sip of her cola. "I've left my job in Detroit. I've asked to be sent to another under-served hospital, preferably in a rural area, so I can finish paying off my medical school federal loans. I had some down time so I decided to visit with Price until the Feds tell me where they're sending me."

"Uh-huh, and pull my other leg, why dontcha?"

Jesus, Keely was like one of those yippy, little, ankle-biting dogs who sank in their sharp little teeth and didn't let go. "That's the truth. It's why I'm here."

Keely snorted. "Price told us you loved that job. That you planned to stay there even after you'd worked off those loans." She gently squeezed Fee's fingers. "Are you running from the bastard who hurt you?"

Fee choked back a sob. "No."

Way to control your emotions, Fee. The cat is out of the bag now.

Keely would persist until she had the whole story—and then she would tell Price.

Fee didn't plan on being around when that happened. She didn't want to see the look on her brother's face. He would be so disappointed she hadn't called him to "fix" things. The one thing she hated most in the world was disappointing the only male who had ever stood up for her.

"Liar." Keely scooted around the booth and then hugged Fee. "Shit, sweetie, we kick butt on a regular basis at SSI. If the asshole follows you, he's toast. Or, better yet, Price and some of the guys can go to Detroit and pay the abusive jerk a visit. Teach him a lesson."

"No … no … that won't help." Fee took a panicky breath. Despite her resolve, tears streaked down her cheeks. She swiped at them with the cocktail napkin.

"He won't follow. And I don't want anyone going to Detroit. I've handled the situation." She wiped her eyes on the back of her sleeve after the napkin shredded from too much moisture. "God, look at me! I'm a fucking mess. I'm an intelligent twenty-nine-year-old doctor for chrissakes. In my ER, I've dealt with shot-up and knifed gang members, drunks going through DTs, junkies coming off drugs, and abusive men demanding to see their beat-up women. And I let one overly aggressive ER doctor scare me away from my home and the job I loved."

Fee looked Keely in the eye. "I was doing some fucking good in that hospital and the bastard took it away from me."

"You're running from a fellow doctor?" Keely asked.

Shit, she had just told the woman too much.

Fee stiffened as Keely grimaced and let out a little gasp. "You okay, Keely?"

"Fine. Don't change the subject. Who are you running from?" Keely nibbled on her scone and made a face. She shoved the scone toward Fee. "Here, eat something to soak up all the cold caffeine you've been drinking. Looks like all you had to eat or drink during the hour you waited on me was cola. You need real food and hydration so you don't get sick at this altitude."

"Talk about changing the subject. Aren't you hungry?" Fee shoved her distress over the past aside. She straightened in her seat and scrutinized Keely with a clinical eye.

Keely waved off the concern. "I ate before I drove here. I'm good. Go on, tell me about the A-hole who beat on you."

"Persistent cuss, aren't you?" Fee's lips twisted into a reluctant smile.

"Takes one to know one," Keely retorted. She clenched her jaw as a wave of nausea came and went in an instant. She rubbed her stomach where Riley was bouncing around like a Mexican jumping bean. "Now talk to me. Maybe I can help."

"No. It's over. He's not worth another second of my time or yours—or my brother's." Fee's mouth had a mulish twist to it. Keely had seen the same look on Price's face. Like brother, like sister.

While Fee was good at changing the subject, Keely was damn sure Price would get the full story from his sister. Charm and good looks aside, he was a force to be reckoned with when he chose, as were all the SSI operatives. His sister wouldn't leave Sanctuary until her safety had been assured. Big brothers were very protective. Keely should know; she had five of them.

"Can we get started?" Fee looked around. "Your health and that of your baby is far more important than sitting here and revisiting my problems with Dr. Adam-fucking-Stall. I think we need to be heading back to Sanctuary."

Woot! Now Keely had a name. Good. By nightfall, she and Tweeter would know whether Dr. Adam-frick-fracking-Stall wore briefs or boxers and whether his dick dressed right or left.

Keely tossed a ten on the table and shoved Fee's money toward her. "I've got this covered." She signaled Nick and then pointed to the money. He smiled and waved her on. Scooting out of the booth, she joined Fee and led the way to the door.

Maybe Fee had a point about her health, but she didn't think so. Still, it wouldn't hurt to head home. If Quinn had called as soon as she'd left, and she bet he had, Ren was probably about halfway home by now. And her brother and Trey would be heading back to the Lodge with orders from Ren to fetch her ass home.

Keely rubbed her lower back through her thick coat as another mild twinge made itself known. She was pretty sure she was having another round of Braxton-Hicks. The cramping in her stomach had moved to her lower back and seemed regular, but then so had the false labor she'd experienced several times over the last few months. Plus, her OB had been darn certain Riley would not come early and cited all the statistics about first births. Keely, as a numbers kind of person, had been reassured by the stats. Ren had just snorted and said FUBAR happens.

At the moment, the sensations were like really bad menstrual cramps and more than tolerable.

Fee followed on Keely's heels with an attitude like an overprotective mama grizzly. As if a woman two inches shorter who weighed about one hundred pounds could protect her.

Keely snickered silently. Even pregnant, Keely was more lethal than four out of five of the people in the restaurant.

"Looks like the weatherman got it right for once." Leaving the steamy warmth of the diner, Keely drew her scarf more closely around her neck.

"I can't believe it's snowing in June! It was sunny when I arrived here." Fee's teeth audibly chattered as she pulled the collar of her spring-weight denim jacket up closer to her ears. "Brrr. Don't you people have spring? And I thought Michigan had crazy weather."

Keely laughed. "Just winter's one last hurrah. I have some warmer clothes you can borrow once we get home."

The predicted snow had begun to fall since her arrival at Ma's less than twenty minutes ago. The flakes were large and wet and coming down steadily. The snow covered the ground and vegetation like slushy mashed potatoes. The winds gusted upwards of thirty miles an hour, making visibility semi-lousy. The really bad news was as they climbed in altitude on the way to Sanctuary, the conditions would be worse. The snow could be blizzard levels and the roads icier. The trip home would be dicey, but she'd driven in worse.

"Where did you park, Keely?" Fee hissed as a particularly vicious wind gust hit them. Keely grabbed Fee's arm to steady her.

"We're heading for the black Hummer at the far end of the front row." Keely pointed to the big, armor-clad behemoth which the men insisted was the only vehicle she should drive. It had every safety feature imaginable and some she and Tweeter, her alpha-geek brother, had designed. She could survive on the moon in that vehicle.

At the Hummer, Fee stopped on the passenger side and sent her a sideways glance. "Um, is there a drop-down ladder so we vertically challenged types can climb up?"

Keely laughed. "Nope. But there are built-in steps—two of them—and the hand-holds. It's sort of like mounting a horse. Grab the hand-hold, place your foot on the lower step and sort of spring up and grab hold of the other hand-hold and pull yourself in." Keely held her hand out for Fee's bag and tote. "Give me your bags. I'll place them in the back."

"Maybe I should stow them," Fee said.

"Give me the damn bags, Fee." Keely stared until Fee handed over the luggage.

"Here goes nothing," Fee said as she opened the door.

Keely smiled when the woman made it on the first try. The doctor had some upper body strength and a good sense of balance.

After stowing the bags, Keely went around, opened

the driver's door, and then paused. Something niggled at her senses besides the aching in her back and stomach.

She casually swept some snow off the side mirror and looked around as she cleaned the windshield with the scraper. She saw nothing out of the ordinary and shrugged. Maybe it was the drop in air pressure from the storm causing the feeling.

After slapping the snow off her gloves and kicking slush off her boots, Keely climbed into the vehicle, shut the door, and engaged all security.

Ren had hammered home many a time that engaging security was rule one when Keely was out driving alone. "No use having the systems," he'd said, "if they aren't used." The one time she'd forgotten and he'd caught her, he'd swatted her ass. The light spanking had led to sex— and it had been some of the best sex she'd ever had. While she liked pushing Ren's buttons from time to time, now, while she was hugely pregnant and couldn't enjoy the side bennies of it, was not the right moment.

Keely looked at Fee and noted she was all buckled in. She started the engine, shifted into first gear, then pulled out, quickly picking up speed. The heavy vehicle handled the almost two inches of slushy snow like a thoroughbred.

"How long will it take us to get to Sanctuary?" Fee asked.

The doctor's tone was too casual. Keely eyed her but saw nothing but polite inquiry on Fee's face. "About fifty minutes on a good day. Maybe more like an hour and fifteen minutes on a day like today. I don't want to push too hard through some of the S-curves in these conditions if I don't have to."

"So, where is the nearest hospital?" Again, Fee's tone was even, no inflection at all.

Keely would play along. "If you're asking where Riley is to be delivered, we're talking Coeur d'Alene. That's an almost six-hour drive. We'd use the helicopter in an emergency. Boise is a six-hour or so drive to the south. Sanctuary is pretty isolated and the surrounding area as a whole is sparsely populated."

"Jesus! There's nothing closer?" Fee's voice held emotion now—shock and maybe a tinge of fear.

"Well, there is the regional medical center near Elk City, which is on the other side of Sanctuary by about twenty minutes. But Ren ruled it out. Not modern enough for his wife and son. It's more like a clinic than a hospital. Serious cases are medevaced to Coeur d'Alene or Boise."

"This really is the middle of nowhere." Fee sounded worried.

"Welcome to the wild west." Keely chuckled. "Why are you asking, Fee? I told you what my OB said."

Keely eyed her mirrors as she routinely did and noted a silver-gray Escalade as it pulled out of a little-used side road. The SUV was about a quarter mile behind them and shortening the distance quickly. She'd seen the car before—on her way to Ma's. The rental car plates on the front gave it away; it was the same SUV which had followed her part of the way to Grangeville from Sanctuary.

She'd thought nothing of it at the time since Ma's was a popular destination and this road led to the interstate. But the vehicle was definitely following her once more. Her internal warning system went to red alert.

God! She'd endangered her baby by leaving Sanctuary. Ren would freak. Hell, she would kick her own butt once she was able. Right now, she had to take all the precautions she could. Nothing and no one would hurt her baby.

Fee had been mumbling something Keely hadn't caught as she'd assessed the situation. Whatever was bothering the doctor wasn't as urgent as the current state of affairs.

"Make sure you're buckled in tightly, Fee." Keely hit a combination of key codes into the on-board communications system. Any SSI operative within one hundred miles would respond to the call for help and track to her position using GPS.

"What's wrong?" Fee's gaze assessed Keely as if looking for a medical issue. God, the doctor thought it was the baby.

"It's not the baby." Keely angled her head toward the back of the Hummer. "Looks like I picked up a tail. We can't go back to Ma's because it's safer to outrun the bastards."

Going back would make them more vulnerable to an attack by their pursuers; the bad guys would love for her to play into their hands by slowing down and turning around. So, she would force them to play catch up.

She also needed a back-up plan. There was a high likelihood her pursuers had buddies up ahead on the road to Sanctuary. She didn't want to chance a full-out gun battle if she didn't have to. She had the baby to think of—and a civilian.

"Fee, I might have to take us off-road before we get to Sanctuary in order to elude them—and whoever they might have in front of us."

"A tail? Who? Where?" Fee looked in the passenger side mirror. "And how do you know they aren't just lost or something?"

"The fact the Escalade followed me part of the way from Sanctuary toward Ma's and that they just pulled out behind us once we cleared Grangeville's city limits. Fee, there's nothing in this direction but the Nez Perce National Forest, lots of mountains, and Sanctuary." Keely looked in the rear view mirror and grimaced. "Plus, my shit detector is going off the charts."

Fee took in and let out a deep breath. "So—what are we gonna do?" She looked in the passenger side mirror. "Jesus, Keely, they're staying awfully close. Will they try to ram us?"

"They could try. I almost wish they would. I've been

taught by the best. And if they decide to play bumper cars with that piece-of-shit street vehicle against my armored, military-grade Hummer, I would win that game." She pushed the powerful vehicle up to seventy miles an hour from the far safer fifty she'd been doing. She noted with a smile the guy behind her didn't seem comfortable driving that fast on snow-covered roads. Good, she had an advantage and would milk it for all it was worth.

"As to your other question, I've already sent an SOS to all SSI operatives in the area. And in a second, I'll notify the Idaho County Sheriff. Law enforcement out here is spread thinly over a vast area and I ain't holding my breath anyone can get to us in time." She took a deep breath and turned to look at Fee whose formerly pale face had gone somewhat green. "My guys aren't close. We might have to play hide-and-seek with the bad guys until help arrives."

Keely used the cell phone plugged into her car's blue-tooth system and put the County Sheriff on alert to the situation. The sheriff's dispatcher would notify the State Police. But as Keely had thought, it would take time to get someone to their position. The weather had grounded the law enforcement copters and the road patrols weren't anywhere near her current position.

The weather wouldn't stop Ren from flying, though. She prayed he'd be careful, but knew he'd push it to get to her. She'd expected to hear from him and the others as soon as the alert had gone out. Obviously, the weather had affected SSI's communications satellite signal. She'd barely gotten the emergency call out to the sheriff; her cell signal had gone in and out.

"What do you mean by not close?" Fee asked after Keely had ended her call to the sheriff. "Where are they?"

"Ren travelled to a ranger station near Coeur d'Alene." Keely heaved a big sigh. "He's flying in this mess."

Fee looked out the window at the swirling whiteness and swore under her breath. "Will your husband be horribly angry that you picked me up?"

Keely heard the worry and what sounded like dread in Fee's voice. Obviously, Dr. Adam frick-fracking Stall had really done a number on her. Not all men were abusive and Fee needed to know that. "He'll be upset, but he won't hurt me. Good men do not beat on women."

"Okay … good. I'd hate for you to … be chastised because of my surprise visit."

"No punishment. Just a few snarls and growls and a look of disappointment. After which, he will lecture me and then take me to bed." Keely winked at Fee. "A win-win all around. He gets to reinforce he is the man and I get hot monkey sex and lots of orgasms out of it." She glanced at Fee whose eyes held disbelief. "Sweetie, only lame-ass cowards beat on a woman when they're angry."

Fee choked back a laugh. The mood in the car lightened for the moment.

Mission accomplished. She needed Fee's head in the present, not the past or the possible future.

Keely slowed to sixty miles per hour for a particularly sharp S-curve. Their pursuers, she noted, slowed far more than she did, so she was able to pick up some precious yardage coming out of the curve. Her knowledge of the roads and area was a tremendous tactical advantage.

Fee looked in the side mirror, her left hand grasping the armrest between her and Keely. "So, Ren is out of the picture for now. Anyone closer?"

"My brother and Ren's brother were working on Sanctuary's northernmost perimeter security. They took ATVs," at Fee's frown, she clarified, "all-terrain vehicles with special all-weather tires. They are almost certainly heading back to Sanctuary at Ren's urging to come get me." Fee still had a confused look on her face. "Oh, God, I didn't tell you. When your call came in, Quinn, Ren's third in command, heard it. I told him to tell Ren where I was going. So, my guys could've been travelling for almost an hour when the emergency signal went out. Things aren't as dire as they could be."

Fee half-laughed, half-choked out a breath. "Thank God. You aren't totally without common sense."

Keely sniffed. "I think I might be insulted. And why are you worrying so much? I can handle those guys behind me."

"God, Price did *not* exaggerate. And I didn't believe

him. I'll apologize to him—if we survive." Fee pointed toward the back of the Hummer. "Keely, you've exposed your very pregnant self to danger for me. If something happens to you or the baby, I'll never forgive myself."

The stern doctor Fee was now present in the car. The scared, abused Fee buried in light of the current danger. Keely really liked Price's sister—she had guts.

"Nothing is going to happen," Keely told her as she increased her speed to eighty on the straight-away. The Hummer handled like the expensive dream it was. "If we can't lose them, I'll take them out."

"With what?" Fee shook her head. "Jesus, Keely, you're only slightly bigger than me and most of that is baby weight. And if I'm not mistaken, you're in the early stages of labor. You're grimacing. Your stomach is moving like something out of a horror movie. And you keep arching your back."

"Not labor, just Braxton-Hicks." Keely inhaled sharply and gripped the wheel tightly. As if Fee's words conjured it up, an extremely sharp pain shot through her pelvis. Its origination? Her lower back. "Damn, that one hurt. I think Riley just jabbed a nerve with his hand or foot. I swear this kid is going to grow up to be a kick boxer."

She smiled thinly at Fee who didn't look at all convinced. "Trust me. I've had several bouts of false labor off and on starting several months ago. Ren has flown me to the hospital in Coeur d'Alene three times on false alarms."

"That was the past. Let's deal with the now. I bet the baby is head down, bouncing on your pelvis, ready to come out. If your water breaks, I don't care if you're dilated or not, you would be quickly enough." Fee let go of the armrest to touch Keely's arm. "Honey, you're in the first stage of labor and will have this baby in the next twenty-four hours more or less. I've delivered a lot of less than full-term babies in the ER. I know the signs. So, fighting? Out of the question."

"Don't bet your retirement plan on that." Keely gritted her teeth against the pain in her lower back. She had some tricky driving ahead, a series of four sharp S-curves, and needed to concentrate. She planned to gain some mileage and not just yardage on their pursuers. "Hold on, because I'm about to show the guy behind me he shouldn't mess with an angry, pregnant woman."

CHAPTER 2

"What are you talking about?" Fee held on to the sissy bar above the passenger door as Keely punched the Hummer's speed even higher. She was shocked to see they were now traveling over eighty miles an hour on slush-covered roads she'd hesitate to drive forty on even with a heavy four-wheel-drive vehicle.

"Are you nuts?" Fee noted the pursuing SUV was now a mile or so behind them, taking the curves at a much slower speed. Damned if Keely wasn't leaving the bad guys behind!

Keely emitted a sound somewhere between a snort and a laugh. "Nope. Just determined to put enough space between us and them so I can lose 'em on a ranger access road. With luck, they'll lose control of that piece of crap and crash."

"If we don't crash first," Fee muttered after she stifled a girly screech as Keely took a curve at sixty-five miles per hour. The right-side wheels left the road and traveled the slush-rough shoulder until they came out of the bend.

"I heard that." Keely chuckled. "I'm a much better driver than the guy behind us. And this is a better engineered vehicle. We'll be fine." She patted Fee's knee.

"Keely, for chrissakes!" Fee shoved the hand back. "Keep both hands on the wheel. Ten and four, please, for these types of conditions." She remembered Price telling her ten and four was better than ten and two for hazardous driving.

"I'm fine. Now reach under your seat and pull out the submachine gun for me, would ya?"

"Gun?" Fee got a sick feeling in her gut. Now she wished she'd allowed her brother to teach her how to handle one. But she'd seen too many results in her ER of what guns could do. She hated guns. "I don't know how to shoot a gun."

"You don't have to use it." Keely's tone was humoring. "Just pull it out so I can access it if needed."

"God, help me. I'm riding with a pregnant Rambo-ette," grumbled Fee as she pulled the ugly-looking weapon from below the seat. "Okay, now what?"

Keely looked over and grinned. "Just keep it close."

"Close. Right." Fee nodded and gave the black gun in her hands a frowning look. God, she hoped she wouldn't accidentally shoot the both of them.

"Keely, what the fuck is going on?" A male voice rumbled around the interior of the Hummer. An angry voice.

Fee started. Flashbacks of Adam raging at her assaulted her mind. His face, distorted by fury because she'd reported him as a stalker, because she'd rejected his sexual advances. The beating he'd administered right before he'd raped her.

She wrapped her arms around her waist and moaned low in her throat.

"Keely, fucking answer me!" the male voice ordered. "Are you in pain? Is it the baby?"

"That wasn't me, Trey." Keely shot Fee a concerned look.

The voice belonged to Trey Maddox, Keely's brother-in-law. Fee shook off the horrible memories. The here and now was more important. She'd survived Adam's abuse. The jury was out if she would survive the current predicament.

Trey snorted loudly, forcing Keely to add, "I'm fine, Trey. That was Fee making the noises. Some bad guys tailed us out of Ma's. I've already notified the sheriff's dispatcher who'll notify the State Police."

"Fuck!" Trey groaned. "Ren will go fucking nuts."

There was a pause, and the sound of low male voices came over the speakers. Fee couldn't make out what they said, but the conversational tone wasn't a happy one.

"Tweeter said to tell you he'll spank your ass if your hubby doesn't."

The man's voice was a low growl and once again Fee had to steal herself against bad memories. Clinically, she knew she was suffering from post-traumatic stress disorder; emotionally, she was still a victim.

God, would she ever be able to hear an angry male voice again without having flashbacks? How could she work in an ER where all sorts of angry males visited every day? She had to hope that time and sheer Teague stubbornness would get her through the next days, weeks, possibly even months.

"Him and what army?" Keely snorted, a cute and disdainful sound.

Keely was nuts and without fear which probably explained how she could live in a male-dominated household. The petite woman wasn't afraid of the men on the other end of the call or her husband. Fee envied her unconcern.

"Goddamn it, Keely. This is not the time to joke." Trey sighed, sounding much put-upon. "I know you have a plan. So, what is it?"

Fee noted Keely's hands tightening on the wheel. Shit, another contraction. Fee checked her watch. Keely's last contraction had ended about five minutes ago, right before Trey had connected with them.

Get with the fucking program, Fee. Keely and that little baby need you at peak performance.

"I figure our pursuers have friends between me and Sanctuary," Keely said. "So I need to go off-road and find a place to hide until you big, strong men can come and take care of the badasses."

"Sounds good. Tweeter has a fix on your GPS. We'll find you."

"I'll be stopping soon. I'm less than five minutes from the ranger access road leading to Cave A-5. I plan on getting far enough ahead of my tail so we can abandon the Hummer and hike to the cave."

"Keely, tell me the real reason why you aren't heading straight for Sanctuary?" Trey's voice was rough and snarly. Fee couldn't decide if he was mad at or just exasperated with Keely, but he seemed to understand his sister-in-law's actions and could read between the lines. "Quinn and Scotty can head out now and clear the road from that end."

"Trey, I can't outrun them to Sanctuary." Keely grimaced and bit her lip.

Besides the telling facial contortions, for the first time, Fee noted a hint of fear and worry in Keely's voice.

"It could prove to be dangerous for the baby." Keely's breath hitched on a sob and she visibly controlled the weakness to continue, "Talk to the doctor for a few seconds. I need to concentrate on the next set of S-curves. It's damn treacherous up here and I'll be doing seventy through them."

"Doctor? What fucking doctor? Baby, answer me, damn it!"

The voice was male but a different one. This had to be the husband, Ren Maddox, and Price's boss and former SEAL team buddy.

"This is Fee Teague, Ren. I'm Price's sister. And your wife is in labor. How she's handling contractions that are five minutes apart and driving like a bat out of hell, I'll never know."

"Keely!" The male roar was full of gut-wrenching anguish—and love.

Keely gave Fee a nasty look. "You didn't have to scare him." She heaved a shaky sigh. "Ren, I'm fine. The contractions aren't all that bad right now…"

Fee pinched Keely's arm. When Keely glared at her, she mouthed "liar."

Keely stuck her tongue out and continued to placate her husband. "…and feel like really bad menstrual cramps. My water hasn't even broken. Heck, I'm not even convinced I'm in real labor. But I'm playing it safe by getting us to a secure place as soon as I can."

Fee closed her eyes in horror as Keely took a particularly nasty set of S-curves with the panache of a driver at Monte Carlo. With deep drops on one side and sheer mountain walls on the other, she prayed silently and held on until Keely accelerated out of the last curve.

Chancing a look back, Fee didn't see their pursuers.

"You lost them?" Her words came out on a squeak, her throat still tight with the fear of imminent death in a car crash. She coughed and cleared her throat. "Uh, nice driving."

"Thanks. But they're still back there. I just bought us some time. I'm turning off just ahead. With any luck they won't follow, but I ain't holding my breath."

"If they do follow?" Fee asked and was ashamed to hear a quivering in her voice.

"If they do," Ren's voice boomed across the speakers, "Keely will do what is necessary to protect all of you." It sounded more like an order than a statement of confidence. "It's a good plan, baby, considering the circumstances. But you're in big trouble for leaving Sanctuary without an escort."

"Ren … I'm so sorry, but I felt hemmed in and…" Keely's voice was all soft female and placative with just a slight hint of tears. Fee checked and saw no indication of extra moisture anywhere in Keely's eyes.

"Hell. We'll talk later, baby. I love you." Ren's voice sounded almost as pacifying as Keely's. He paused, coughed, and reverted back to his previous all-knowing male tone. "Now, describe the fuckers' vehicle."

Fee's lips twisted with wry amusement. Maybe she needed to study at the hands of a master manipulator of alpha-maledom. Keely had taken one outraged male and had twisted him around to her way of thinking and back to the business at hand in less time than Fee could think it … with just her voice!

Keely answered, "A silver-grey Escalade, dark tinted windows. Nevada plates, Zulu-four-four-four-Charlie."

Fee was amazed that Keely had gotten the plates. She hadn't even thought to look. She checked the side mirror, something she found herself compulsively doing every few seconds, and still didn't see their pursuers. But with all the curves in the road, they could be just one curve behind them and blocked by the mountainside.

"Got it, sprite. I'll get the description out to the Sheriff and the State Police."

"You do that, big guy. I expect you to come get me at A-5." Keely actually smiled at Fee and winked. "Just think of the stories we'll tell our grandchildren someday about how their daddy participated in a high speed chase while still in the womb. Not many kids can tell that kind of story. And, Ren, don't worry. *If* I'm in labor, at least I have a doctor with me. Fee has assured me she's delivered a lot of babies in her ER."

"God, sweetheart. You'll be the death of me." Keely's husband sounded scared but affectionate. "I love you. Don't get you or the baby dead—or Fee either, for that matter. Take the sat phone with you and leave it on so I can monitor you."

"Love you back, Ren."

Fee noted Keely purposely ignored responding

to Ren's order. She was beginning to understand how Keely survived surrounded by all that protective male testosterone—the little minx complied with the orders she wanted and ignored the rest.

"No messing around, baby." Ren was obviously aware of his wife's *modus operandi*. His voice held sternness moderated by amusement. "I'll head straight for the cave once I land."

"Be careful," Keely said. "And I'm not messing around. I'm taking this threat to me, our baby, and Fee very seriously."

Ren's aggravated sigh came loudly over the car's communication system. "Keely, do not engage the enemy. You hear me? Do not stop to take them out. Just get your sweet ass to safety. Let Trey and Tweeter carry the load with the bad guys. Tell me you heard me."

Keely stiffened at her husband's tone. Fee had to smile. So there was a tipping point when Ren pulled the dominant-male card.

"Give me some credit, Ren. I'm pregnant not brain dead."

Keely's sigh held the same amount of aggravation in it as her husband's had. Fee choked back a laugh. If they hadn't been in a life-and-death situation, she would have enjoyed observing the couple's relationship dynamic— maybe she could learn something. Keely continued in a slightly affronted tone of voice. "I hadn't planned on a pitched battle … but I can't promise not to engage. If they shoot at us, big guy, I will shoot back."

"Well, my brother and yours had better get a move on then … because I won't be happy if I find out you got involved in another gun battle while carrying our son. The last time still gives me nightmares."

"Me, too, Ren. I promise to do all I can to avoid a gunfight."

"God, baby, please stay safe—I can't lose you."

"You won't lose me, I promise. Just come get me."

"Damn right, I will."

The resolve in Ren's voice was convincing. Nothing would stop him from getting to Keely's side. Fee wondered what it would be like to have a man love her that much. And would she recognize the right man if he appeared in her life?

After the number Adam-fucking-Stall did on her, she wasn't sure she'd ever be able to trust a man again. Hell, who was she fooling? It was herself she didn't trust. She'd had a horrible track record with men even before Adam.

Fee checked Keely's condition and noted no grimacing at the moment. The contractions seemed to be regular, for the time being, at about five minutes apart. She prayed that would hold until they got to the promised safe place or the men reached them. She checked the side mirror again, keeping an eagle eye out for their pursuers. At the moment, Keely was in control of their future; the least Fee could do was watch their behinds.

CHAPTER 3

Keely chanced a glance at Fee. The doctor gripped the sissy bar so hard her knuckles were white. Her general color was ashen, making the bruises look that much worse. Even without the actual details of the abuse Fee had suffered, from her own past experiences Keely had a fairly good idea what might be concealed by Fee's clothing. The current predicament had to be exacerbating Fee's already fragile emotional state. All things considered, Price's sister was holding up really well.

Since the situation was bad and would probably get worse before it got better, Keely needed Fee to continue functioning to the best of her ability. Price had once told her all of his sisters were extremely A-type and dedicated to their professions. What she needed to do was to keep

Fee focused on her and the baby as patients.

"Uh, Fee, do you really think my contractions aren't Braxton Hicks this time?"

Fee stared at the side mirror, turned, and blinked as if she were coming out of a daze. "Um, yes. From what I can read from your facial expressions, the hitches in your breathing, and your convulsive gripping of the steering wheel, you're experiencing contractions every five or so minutes, and they seem to be lasting anywhere from thirty to forty-five seconds. This is typical of early labor."

Keely held back a smile. Price knew his sister well. Fee was now all clinical concern—right where Keely needed her.

Angry male grumbling told Keely the men were still monitoring them.

"How long until the more active and painful parts of labor?" Keely thought about cutting the communications until she glanced in the rear view mirror and became distracted by a glimpse of the SUV pursuing them. They weren't as far back as she would've liked. "Damn, those assholes are taking chances. Ren? Trey? Tweeter? You guys need to get a move on. The guy driving the SUV is better than I thought."

"We're coming, Keely," Trey said. "Tweeter and I are using old logging trails to intersect your destination from the Sanctuary side. We should be able to park and then hike the footpath down from A-5 as you girls make your way up. Just stick with the plan, little sister. We'll be there to cover you."

Keely let out a breath and barely managed to stifle a gasp as her entire lower abdomen and back seized with a huge cramp. She eased off the accelerator and corrected for an inadvertent swerve. Good thing her exit was coming up soon, because this contraction was unlike the previous ones. She was afraid it was a harbinger of what was to come, and she didn't want to be driving when the next one happened.

Fee took her pulse and laid her other hand on Keely's baby bump. Her gaze was calm as she mouthed, "you'll be fine." And Keely hoped Fee knew what she was talking about since this was strange territory for her.

"Baby, I should be landing in the next ten minutes. How close behind you are the bastards?" Ren's voice soothed her just as it had done that time in Argentina when they'd first met. It was his voice then and during the months they'd been together since that drew her from the nightmares of the abuse she'd suffered, the kills she'd been forced to make.

"They're maybe four or five minutes behind." She managed to keep the pain out of her voice. She didn't want her hubby freaking out while he flew a helicopter in the mountains in high, gusty winds. "Ren, I can't count on them missing the turn-off. There's not enough traffic out here to hide my tracks. I'll be leaving an easy trail to follow."

"Understood. Can't be helped. Getting to safety is paramount." Ren paused. "Sprite—go straight to the cave. No detours."

"I hadn't planned on giving Fee a tour of the sights, big guy."

His amused snort was a good sign he hadn't heard the fear or pain in her voice. But she wasn't sure how much longer she could breathe normally and not moan. This last contraction had lasted for what seemed like hours, but she knew it had to have been under a half-minute.

"Fee?" Ren's voice sounded grim. "Answer Keely's last question, please. How long until she's in more active labor?"

Keely looked at Fee. "And don't sugar-coat it. I don't want to be caught in the open giving birth in the snow with those murderous assholes on our butts. I would need time to make us a snow shelter we can defend if we can't make it to the cave."

If birth were imminent, then no matter what she'd promised Ren, all bets were off. She'd find a place to make a stand and shoot the men following her before they shot at her. She wasn't in the mood to mess around with them. And she wasn't sure how much longer she'd be able to control her pain. Excruciating pain and shaky hands did not make for accurate shooting.

"Jesus, are you for real? We're not planning to go to war here." Fee waved off any answer Keely might have made. "Sorry, the stories Price told me are beginning to make sense. You are a warrior sprite." Fee rubbed a hand over her eyes before looking at Keely. "Okay, looking at the averages, you could go for hours before giving birth. Since your OB didn't tell you to stick close to home, I assume you had no dilation and had not started to present?"

"Are you asking me or telling me?" Keely sighed. "Sorry, little tense here. No dilation. The baby had not entered the birth canal as of yesterday at 0900." She checked the rear view mirror and couldn't see the SUV, but knew it was hidden because of the sharp curves in the road. The bad guys were back there and maintaining their distance—for now. She'd gain time once she hit the ranger access road. The pursuer's SUV wouldn't be able to handle the rutted dirt road as well as the Hummer; the driver would bottom out the street vehicle if he drove too fast.

"That's good." Fee looked as relieved as she sounded. "In theory, you could be in this stage of labor for a while. First births tend to take longer. Once your water breaks, though, the contractions will get closer together and be much stronger as you dilate fully for the birth. At that point, we need to be in a safe and preferably warm, dry place. A snow shelter doesn't float my boat, by the way. A nice modern hospital would be the best, but from the sound of things, I've deduced that isn't happening any time soon." Fee grabbed the sissy bar as Keely quickly decelerated. "Why are you slowing down?"

"We're getting off here."

Keely made a sharp right onto a snow-covered, dirt road which led to the ranger station. They wouldn't make the full trip to the top of the mountain, but would turn onto an even worse road or more like a track leading to a break in the thick forest where they'd leave the Hummer. From the clearing, it would only be a short hike to the cover of rocks and the hiking/climbing trail to Cave A-5. The cave was on Sanctuary land and completely defensible.

With any luck, she'd lose their pursuers during the climb. They had to be strangers to the area and would get lost easily. With Fee's assistance and Mother Nature providing enough snow and wind, she'd cover her and Fee's back trail so as not to give the bad guys anything to follow.

"Ren, I'm on the ranger access road. And FYI, I counted only three heads in the SUV."

"Roger that. I'll be setting the bird down in the meadow not far from A-5 on national forestry land. I'll be there as fast as I can, but you know as well as I that the climb to the cave could take some time in this weather."

That was a hell of an understatement, since Ren would be making a difficult-even-on-a-mild-day climb in blowing snow. After first arriving at Sanctuary, she'd made the same climb to work on the perimeter security system. But she'd had Tweeter spotting her as they'd traversed the sheer mountain faces like spiders on a web.

"God, Ren, please be careful."

"Count on it." His beloved voice was calm and sure. "Nothing will stop me from being with you and our baby."

The certainty in his voice lulled the fears roiling in her mind. A determined Ren was a force to be reckoned with and she knew she'd see him soon.

Keely steered the Hummer onto the smaller track which led to the clearing where she'd park the vehicle. The narrow lane was uneven and tricky to drive in the best of conditions, and these weren't. The wide vehicle brushed the trees lining the route and bounced like a bulky pogo stick on the washboard texture of the snow-covered, packed-gravel-and-dirt track. The strain on her arms, legs, and lower back as she attempted to keep the Hummer out of the trees was tremendous and exacerbated the now dull but building contraction she sensed coming.

Shoving her discomfort to the side, she fought the vehicle, the crappy road, and the elements. "Fee, after we stop, we won't have a lot of time. We'll need to exit the Hummer quickly. Keep the machine gun you're holding with you. I'll get a couple of other packs we'll need from the back." She chanced a quick glance away from the lane to look at Fee's feet. "I'm sorry I don't have any other winter clothing in the back. But I do have some rain boots that might fit you. What kind of boots are those?"

"Doc Marten Motorcycle boots. They're comfortable and warm, thank God. This weather is nuts!"

As if to underline the fact, a particularly strong gust of wind shook the Hummer. Keely swore under her breath and tightened her grip on the steering wheel. Pain shot from her hands to her shoulders, adding to the pain gripping her back and pelvis.

"They have rubber soles and some tread?" Keely gritted out the words. Her jaw clenched against the pain shooting up and down her body as if the Marquis de Sade played the xylophone on her spine with knives. Every muscle in her body seized in sympathy.

"Yeah, why?" Fee scowled. "Don't answer that. We're going to make like mountain goats, right?"

"Yep. Your boots should do fine." Keely gasped and had to force her eyes to remain open as the agony threatened to rip her insides apart. She could not afford to crash. They had another quarter mile to her planned parking spot. She needed to get them as close to the cover of the rocks as she could.

God, please let me get through this without killing my baby.

"How was that pain?" Fee reached over and felt Keely's wrist. "Tell me."

Keely pulled her hand from under Fee's light touch to flick off the communications system just as Ren started to roar her name.

"He doesn't need the distraction." Fee looked at her as if she'd grown an extra head. "He's flying a damn helo, okay? In treacherous conditions. Besides, the pain's bearable. He doesn't need to be freaking out over my minor aches. Um … I've had worse menstrual cramps."

What a liar. The cramping—and that was too innocuous a word for what she experienced—was excruciating. It felt as if someone simultaneously raked her insides and stuck a poker in her lower back while squeezing the air out of her lungs. She'd had less pain being shot.

Fee arched a brow and sighed. "He can't hear now. So tell me the truth. I need the truth so I can help you—it hurt like a son of a bitch, right?"

Keely choked back a laugh. "Pretty effin' much. I might need you to help me up the last fifty or so feet to the cave. But I can do this. I will do this. I have to."

"I'll do whatever I can, Keely. But the last two contractions were closer together and noticeably stronger. You're progressing rapidly for a first-timer. You might be one of the infamous outliers in the birthing statistics. How long were your mother's labors, if you know?"

With an audible sigh of relief, Keely pulled the Hummer into the small clearing and shut off the engine.

If she'd had to drive farther, she might have wrecked the Hummer.

She turned to look at Fee as she opened the driver's side door. "All five deliveries including the twins were less than three hours from the time her first contractions started—"

Fee muttered "oh shit" under her breath.

"—that's why Ren flew me to the hospital for every blasted set of false labor and why he's scared out of his mind now. My mother and her sisters are the queens of the short and quick labor."

"Well, hell, now you tell me." Fee opened her door and looked down. "Jesus, with my luck the gun will go off as I get out of this monster car." She looked over her shoulder at Keely. "Go on, get out. I'll figure it out and meet you at the rear of the car."

Keely laughed as she heard Fee mutter, "I fricking hate tall cars." Keely's exit was not as graceful as usual, but she managed to get to the ground without falling face first into the knee-deep snow. She slammed the door and moved to the rear where Fee stood, shivering in silence, the H&K cradled awkwardly in her arms.

"Let's get what you need from the back." Fee's teeth chattered. "The sooner we walk, the warmer I'll be."

Keely had to brace herself against the vehicle for a second. Between the wind gusts and weakness from the pain, she wasn't as steady on her feet as she would've liked. But she'd be damned before she gave up; they had to get to cover. She had to protect her baby.

"Keely? You okay?" Fee had the machine gun hanging from her shoulder, freeing up her hands. She rubbed Keely's back.

"Been better, but I'll deal. Watch out for the door." After opening the rear of the Hummer, she retrieved the extra sat phone and the medical kit and handed them to Fee. While the cave was fully stocked for most medical emergencies, Ren's paranoia had been instrumental in the creation of a field medical kit for a FUBAR-birth scenario.

God, she was lucky her husband was an overprotective control freak. Not every mother-to-be had a Marine field medical kit with diapers in it—maybe she'd set a new trend? They could package and sell them to the survivalist market over the Internet. She snickered at the idea.

Fee shot her another worried look.

"Inside joke. Tell you later," Keely said.

The doctor had shifted the medical kit to one small shoulder and now awkwardly cradled the machine gun once again in her arms. The sat phone was stuffed in a pocket of Fee's denim jacket. Between the gun and the kit, Fee was carrying at least an extra twenty pounds, about one-fifth of her body weight. The doctor was stronger than she looked.

"Just need to get one other thing and we'll move out." Keely opened her sniper rifle case, quickly assembled the

Lapua, and pocketed several extra magazines. Her hands were steady despite the cold and the lingering discomfort from the last powerful contraction. She mentally thanked the men in her life that had her keep her weaponry training up-to-date. Not even impending birth disturbed the familiar routine of assembling her rifle and loading it. She'd fall back on that training for as long as she could. She had three lives dependent on it.

Less than two minutes had passed since they'd stopped. They had maybe four or five minutes on the bad guys.

Keely could feel the ache preceding the next contraction simmering low in her back and wanted to be in or as close to the rocks as possible before it took her breath away.

"Okay, let's go." Keely reached for the H&K Fee held, shouldered it, and carried the sniper rifle, allowing Fee to carry the medical kit and the phone. "We have about a five-minute walk through the woods before we hit the rocks and start climbing."

Keely set a rapid pace. She walked a zigzag trail through the trees, using as many of the areas without snow as possible so as not to leave an obvious trail. She backtracked several times in order to leave deliberate prints in the deeper snow, hoping to confuse the men following them.

"Keely." Fee had followed wherever she led without

complaint. "Your husband said to have the sat phone turned on."

She spoke over her shoulder. "Leave it off. The GPS works either way."

"But your husband said…"

"Fee, if we don't make it to the cave, I might have to take the assholes out. Ren does not need to hear that. Trust me." She stopped, bracing her hand on a new-growth tree. Gasping for breath, she hunched over the rifle she cradled one-armed against her distended belly. Fee grabbed her around the waist and supported her. "Um, he'll be landing soon … and then he has … shit … to climb … climb's a bitch … in good weather. He can't effing hear me like this … okay?"

"Okay. You're doing fine. Keep breathing." Fee rubbed Keely's lower back.

Keely grimaced as the contraction took her over. She bit her lips and refused to scream. Noise carried far in the mountains. But she couldn't stay completely silent; she'd never felt this kind of pain before. "God, oh, God … uh, shit … he heard what I didn't say … he knows … hell that hurts…" She panted through the contraction as Fee continued to support her. "He knows I'll shoot the asses to save our baby."

"Shoot the asses!"

Fee's voice was shrill—with concern or fear, Keely couldn't tell. Probably both at this point and she didn't blame the doctor. The conditions were not optimal for delivering a baby.

"Keely, for the ever-loving hell of God, you can barely stand … how on earth—"

"You'd be surprised…" Keely took several cleansing breaths as the sharp pain receded to a threatening simmer. "…what I can do when needed. Let's get moving."

Fee shook her head but kept quiet and walked. She stayed by Keely's side, an arm around her waist.

They broke trail together now. No use trying to lay any more false trails—they needed to get to cover in the rocks ASAP. Keely wasn't sure how much longer she could go on with the strong contractions coming more closely together. Fee was a babe in the woods and could not find adequate and defensible shelter without Keely's assistance.

"How long was that last one?" Keely concentrated on putting one foot in front of another on the uneven ground.

"Forty-five seconds or so. And before you ask, it was less than four minutes from the last one you had in the car. Did your water break this time?"

"Nope. All dry. But Riley is pounding his head on my pelvis and thumping limbs along my back. This is one active kid I'm bearing." Keely would've chuckled, but she needed to focus on the deep breathing the maternity nurse had taught her in pre-natal classes. "I'll start panting at the beginning of the next contraction instead of in the middle. Also just realized I can't pant and talk at the same time."

"Yeah, funny how that works. And you're doing super on the deep breathing. For the life of me, I don't know how you can. It seems to me we're walking straight uphill. The altitude is making it hard for me to breathe normally."

For the first time, Keely noted that Fee panted and wheezed like an asthmatic puppy. The woman's color was more green than the earlier ashy gray and made her bruises look even more grotesque. What a pair! If the situation hadn't been so dire, she'd laugh.

"I'm used to the altitude and climbing. You're not." Keely was concerned Fee would collapse before they made it to the cave.

God, she needed Fee whole and healthy for the impending delivery. Maybe it was time to go to Plan B.

"Um, Fee, this is the easy part of the climb. You're already having difficulty and showing symptoms of altitude sickness. I think we'd better look for a place to build a snow shelter."

"Jesus Christ, Keely! If you can fricking climb while in labor, I sure as hell can climb with a little nausea." Fee gasped like a guppy and held more tightly onto Keely's waist.

Under the current circumstances, who supported whom would be a toss-up.

"Okay, but let me know if you get dizzy." At that point, Fee wouldn't be getting enough oxygen to her brain and would be in serious, and potentially life-threatening, danger. "No matter where we are, we'll stop and find a place to defend."

As Fee opened her mouth to argue, Keely growled, but it came out more like a groan. "Listen, Fee. I'm scared. I need you clear-headed and strong—not lying on the ground unconscious. My baby needs you ... besides, Trey and Tweeter will follow the GPS signal from the sat phone. They'll find us no matter where we end up. There's no use making yourself sicker."

"You're right. That makes sense. I forgot about Trey and your brother. Not sure where my brain went," Fee muttered.

Keely looked up the trail and spotted the distinctive bush Ren had planted to indicate the entrance to another and less obvious trail leading to the cave. "See the holly bush?" She pointed with her rifle.

Fee followed Keely's finger. "Yeah." The word came out on a quavering breath.

"That's our first objective. We'll stop there. I can see the parking area and most of our back trail from that vantage point." *And put the fear of God into the bastards with my sniper rifle.* "Can you make that?"

Her dad had always said, "Little girl, small achievable goals boost morale."

A pale, sweaty-faced Fee nodded.

A warm, wet gushing between Keely's legs had her swearing silently. Now was not the time to tell the struggling doctor her water had just broken.

Taking slow and deep breaths, Keely trudged forward with Fee at her side.

CHAPTER 4

In the air.

When Keely switched off the communications in the Hummer, Ren wanted to hit something, but he had his hands full keeping the Bell jet helicopter from meeting up with the side of a mountain. Adjusting for another sharp change in the swirling winds, he spoke into his headset. "Trey! Where in the hell are you?"

"Tweeter and I just parked the ATVs above A-5. While the weather is absolute crap, we can still be at the cave in four or five minutes and down the trail to intercept the ladies shortly after that." His brother's confident, calm tone went a long way to steadying Ren.

"Good … that's good." He maneuvered the copter through a narrow opening between two mountains and spotted the meadow where he wanted to set the Bell down. He'd have to test all the approaches. With the wind gusting and eddying, it might take him two or three tries before he could land safely.

He made one pass and then another. Over the Motorola communications system, he was vaguely aware of Trey and Tweeter's muttered conversations and heavy breathing as they pushed themselves to get to the women. It was all white noise. His focus had to be on figuring out the bitch winds that threatened to toss him into the side of the craggy mountains. He wouldn't do his wife and baby any good dead.

Then it hit him. "God, I'm going to be a father."

Trey's and Tweeter's laughter came across his headset.

"Jesus, Ren. I figured you knew that already," Tweeter said. "It's not like the Imp hasn't been carrying an extra thirty pounds around for the last month or so."

"You okay, brother?" Trey's baritone rumbled in his ear. "You need to stop worrying and pay attention to landing that bird and then getting your ass up and over the mountain to A-5."

"Well, start praying for me." Ren assessed the way the trees blew and made a decision. "I'm landing now. My gut is telling me those fuckers chasing my pregnant wife are far too close. And I didn't like the sound of the last conversation we heard before Keely cut us off."

"Neither did I," Trey said. "We're at A-5 and no one's home. After we weapon up, we'll head down the mountain and find the girls. Tweeter has Keely's GPS signal. They're at the base of the trail leading to the cave and not moving."

"Let me know the sit rep." Ren paused and took a deep calming breath as he made his approach to the meadow. "And Trey—get her into that cave no matter what. Tweeter can handle the fuckers until you get back to him."

"I'll take care of it."

Tweeter chuckled evilly. "I'll be more than happy to take care of the assholes. Trey will be lucky if I leave him one."

"I want at least one of those bastards alive, Tweeter. I want to know who in the hell sent them after my wife."

He was fairly sure the culprit was the DoD traitor. The fucker was still in the wind. No matter what Tweeter and Keely had done in their many attempts to track him down and lure him into a trap—the slimy turncoat had managed to slide under the radar. In the game of chasing shadows, victories never came easily.

"I'll do my best." Tweeter chuckled. "Give my sister credit, she does nothing in the normal way."

"Isn't that the truth. After she recovers from the birth, I'm beating her sweet little butt for leaving Sanctuary to pick up Price's sister. She could've called you two. Price's sister wouldn't have died waiting at Ma's for one of you to pick her up." Ren settled the helicopter onto the snow-covered meadow. His tense shoulders and clenched jaw relaxed as he took a full breath and let it out. "I'm down. I'll get geared up for the climb. Tweeter, which route should I take up the mountain? Didn't you and Keely set some new pitons out this way last October?"

"Yeah. From the meadow, take the northern route. It'll put you on the mountain farther from A-5, but it will be the safest route and has some shelter from the winds." Tweeter's voice was all business now. "You should be able to handle the climb without a buddy. I've done it."

"Thanks. See you soon."

"Safe climbing, bro," Trey said.

Ren heard the concern in his brother's voice, but that was because Trey hated mountaineering even on a calm, sunny day. His brother normally let Tweeter, Keely when she wasn't hugely pregnant, Ren, and a couple of the other SSI agents do the climbing necessary to check on Sanctuary's complex security array and the solar-powered batteries that kept the system running. Trey could hike all day long, up and down the trails, but climbing sheer, vertical mountain walls with ropes and safety harnesses was not his brother's idea of fun. Today's outing had been necessary because no one else had been around to spot Tweeter.

"I'll be fine, Trey. I'll maintain silence unless you need me."

"Roger that."

Ren geared up for the arduous climb with only the sounds of his brother's and Tweeter's even breathing and the whistling of the fierce mountain winds coming over his headset for company.

Trey turned to Tweeter who kept pace immediately behind him on the narrow hiking trail leading down the mountain from A-5. The ice and snow made the rocky path slipperier than shit and potentially life-threatening. The sooner they got the women up it, the happier he'd be.

Something about Price's sister just showing up in Idaho with no advance warning bothered him. Price hadn't said anything about a sister visiting and, in fact, had planned on visiting his family in Michigan while he was there helping Risto Smith finish outfitting SSI-East.

"Tweeter, you ever met Fiona?" Trey stared down the path and only saw snow. The conditions were nearing blizzard levels. Worry for his brother ate at his gut, but if it were his pregnant woman being harried by mercenaries, he'd be taking the same risks Ren was. A man protected his family ... period.

"Nope. She's the youngest. An ER doc, I think. All three of his sisters are very talented. Too bad Price didn't get any of the smarts."

Trey barked out a laugh. Price was intelligent in his own way—and a damn good soldier. "Has Price mentioned anything about her? Is she in some sort of trouble?"

Trey didn't do small talk about personal things like families with the other operatives. He didn't consider himself stand-offish or even uninterested. He liked to think of it as respecting a person's privacy. If the operatives wanted him to know something, they told him.

"Well, she owes a lot of money if you want to call that trouble. Ticked Price off she wouldn't accept a loan from him to pay her federal school loans." Tweeter came alongside Trey as the path widened. "She has to work in underprivileged or under-served areas of the U.S. to pay back her loan. For each year she works, they forgive a portion of the money owed." Tweeter took a deep breath. "Price doesn't like his little sister working in an ER in the inner city of Detroit."

"Fuck, neither would I." Trey glowered.

"I've seen pictures. She's smaller than Keely." Tweeter snorted back a laugh. "Price told me Fee has the heart of a lion. She loves her job and told him to take a long walk off a short pier when he forbade her to work in the inner city."

"God save us all from tiny women with more courage than strength. Keely has put so many gray hairs on my brother's head, I'm going to start buying him Grecian Formula."

"You are so jealous." Tweeter socked him in the arm. "Ren has no gray hairs, but you do, old man."

Tweeter dodged Trey's retaliatory head slap.

As they turned to follow another jag in the zig-zagging trail, Trey spotted the parking area through a break in the blowing snow. The lot was about a hundred feet down and just east of his and Tweeter's current position. He pulled his binoculars out of his parka pocket and zeroed in on the activity below. "Shit, there are two vehicles besides Keely's Hummer."

"Ren, do you copy?" Trey spoke urgently into the headset. "We have two sets of bogies in pursuit. Both vehicles just pulled into the clearing. Six, I repeat, six bogies are exiting their vehicles. They are heavily armed men, dressed in white snow gear." Keely and Fiona were in more trouble than previously thought. The men geared up like a well-trained unit. "Tweeter's updating the Sheriff and the State Police."

Ren replied, "Do what you need to do."

Trey understood that to mean "don't worry about keeping any of the bastards alive. Keeping the women safe is more important."

"Roger that," Trey said as Tweeter put in, "You got it, boss."

"Since there are more bad asses than we thought previously, it's a good thing we decided to pick up some extra ordnance." Trey's lips quirked with amusement. "With me and Tweeter on one side and the local law enforcement blocking them from the highway side, these bogies aren't going anywhere, brother."

"Figured that. I'm about a quarter of the way to the top of the mountain. See you soon. Out."

"Steady climbing, Ren. Out." Trey turned and looked at Tweeter. "Shock and awe?"

"Oh hell yeah. Flash bangs are just what we need to send the a-holes scurrying. However, I bet by the time we get to the ladies, my baby sister already has her Lapua trained on those fuckers and is taking them down."

"Not taking that wager. I always bet on your sister when it comes to sniping." Trey shook his head, an unholy smile on his lips for the first time since Keely's SOS signal had gone out. "Those bastards didn't understand what they'd gotten themselves into. No way the DoD traitor is paying them enough to get killed. Let's go."

CHAPTER 5

Fee couldn't remember the last time she felt so horrible. Well, she could, but she didn't need to fall into that dark and hellish abyss at the moment. They were in serious danger. Keely needed a competent partner, not a hysterical albatross.

Damn, it was cold. Her teeth chattered and she swore every muscle in her body trembled. She wasn't dressed for this kind of weather and thought fondly of her down-filled coat back in her apartment. She hadn't counted on June in the Bitterroots to feel like November in Detroit. At least her feet were warm and dry.

"Fee?" Her name was gasped out on a breath filled with pain.

"What's going on, Keely? Talk to me. Describe what

you're feeling." Fee pulled Keely the last few steps to the holly bush and then behind it. They were now partially sheltered from the wind and the sight of anyone coming up from the clearing where they'd left the Hummer. The trail leading up and to the promised safe haven tantalized just ahead.

"Pain…" Keely moaned and bent over, clasping her abdomen while leaning against a rock.

The laboring woman still managed to hold on to her weapons, the automatic weapon hanging over her shoulder and the sniper rifle hugged against her distended abdomen. Fee knew if push came to shove, Keely would use the guns in order to protect them. She was frickin' amazing—a prime example of women being the stronger sex.

"Pant through it." Fee panted along with Keely while rubbing the tightened muscles of Keely's lower back. "Good girl. Keep panting. Heh, heh, heh…"

As Keely huffed and puffed through the contraction, Fee did a surreptitious check to see if Keely's water had broken. It had.

"When did your water break?" Fee smoothed hair out of Keely's face as the younger woman straightened and took several deep breaths to cleanse as the contraction receded.

"At the beginning of the path leading here." Keely turned what appeared to be totally unapologetic eyes toward Fee. "You weren't looking so hot. What could you have done anyway? We needed to get to shelter and you don't know where it is."

Fee sighed and hated that Keely was correct. What could she have done? She felt useless. She was not an outdoorswoman and had been counting on Keely to get them to safety. Fee hated feeling helpless.

All that aside, she *was* the doctor and needed to take charge—beginning *now*. She had a patient—soon two—to care for.

"Forget how I look. You're getting ready to have a baby. Let's get moving before the next contraction hits."

Keely nodded, turned, and led the way.

Fee was happy to follow since the trail through the rocks was too narrow at that point for them to walk side by side. Plus this way she could always catch Keely if she fell.

However, Keely seemed to be moving just fine, slower, but still moving. Fee felt as if she could lie down and sleep curled into a ball for a week. She couldn't be that out of shape; she ran and did Pilates and yoga. It had to be the altitude. She prayed the medical kit had both acetaminophen and anti-nausea meds. She needed to be alert for Keely's sake and the way she felt right now, she wouldn't be without chemical assistance. Altitude sickness was extremely debilitating and could lead to hypoxia and dehydration and ultimately to death if not treated properly and as soon as possible.

After five or six minutes of climbing, they reached a flat area where Keely stopped and braced her rifle on a rock, the barrel cushioned by a bean bag she'd removed from her pocket. Fee leaned against another rock and watched as Keely placed her eye to the scope. Fee dripped with sweat, which meant Keely had to be damp and overheated also. Although, other than panting through another contraction about a minute ago, Keely looked as if she could climb Mt. Everest.

Fee could easily despise the younger woman. She felt like a wimp.

"What do you see?" Fee placed the medical kit on a hip-high rock and opened it. Eureka! The kit was neatly and logically organized. She easily found the compartment with all the meds and located acetaminophen and nausea meds. Because her symptoms had increased incrementally as they'd climbed, she dry-swallowed a double dose of each. Even if Keely hadn't needed this rest, Fee had.

"Bad news." Keely kept her eye on the scope and flexed her finger, lightly touching the trigger, and then let up, adjusted the aim of the barrel, and chambered a bullet before fingering the trigger once more.

"What kind of bad news?" Fee watched as Keely took several deep, slow breaths and pulled the trigger. The sound was louder than she would've expected and echoed off the rocks. A split second after the first shot, Keely ejected the casing, chambered another round, and fired again.

Keely looked away from the scope. "Six bad asses instead of three. Two are now down—injured but not dead 'cause I rushed the shots—and the rest scrambled to hide like the frick-fracking rats they are. I just bought us some respect and time. Let's go." She pocketed the bean bag and stood up, cradling her rifle.

"Shit … shit…" Keely gasped and panted as she moved to lean against the rock behind her. "The contractions are coming closer together. Pain is stronger too. Doesn't that mean the birth canal is widening?"

"Yes." Fee frowned and timed the contraction. And yes, it still lasted approximately forty-five seconds, but this one had been far closer to the last one. "Tell me about the pain," she demanded as Keely struggled to take a full breath after the contraction ended.

"Like I'm splitting in two. My back hurts as much or more than my pelvis." She hitched a breath. "I can barely concentrate on breathing. I feel as if I'm hyperventilating. Even now, the pain is there, just bubbling and ready to explode."

"Shit, sounds like they're overlapping." Fee braced Keely as the woman dropped her rifle on the rock and bent over, both arms holding her stomach, as another contraction piled right on top of the previous one. "Damn, I hate it when I'm right."

Keely moaned and gasped. "Fee … help…"

"Shit, shit, shit. Fuck. Just fuck." Fee placed an arm

around Keely's waist in an attempt to keep her from falling to the ground. Because if that happened, Fee would never get her up and they'd be delivering the baby here, in the open.

"Is that any kind of language for a doctor to use?" A deep male voice came from behind her. "What's wrong? Is Keely ready to have the baby?"

Fee slipped the machine gun from Keely's shoulder and managed to keep an arm around the woman's waist as she turned to point the weapon at the man. He was tall with dark hair and piercing pale eyes. He had an ugly-looking gun, but it was aimed at the ground. The look on his face was a mixture of affection and concern for Keely.

"Who are you?" She was pretty sure this was Keely's brother-in-law, but it didn't hurt to ask. If he gave the wrong answer, she'd figure out how to use the damn machine gun if it killed her.

"Trey Maddox. We heard Keely's shots. Tweeter's moving down the path to provide some interference so I can get you ladies to the cave. Here," he held out the gun in his hand, "hold this for a second so I can pick up the little warrior. Do you know if she hit any of the fuckers?"

"Um, two, she said. Not dead, just injured. There's six total." Fee found herself holding yet another gun as she relinquished her hold on Keely.

"Yeah, I saw that from above." Trey pulled Keely into his arms and held her against his chest as if she weighed nothing. "Stay close. I might need that gun. Leave her rifle here. Bring the field kit. The assholes won't make it this far to steal the Lapua. I'll be lucky if Tweeter leaves me any bad guys to tromp on."

Normally, Fee would've refused being bossed around on principle. Trey Maddox reminded her too much of her brother and father, but oddly enough not of Adam or any of the other losers she'd dated. Plus, she was out of her element, and not being stupid or suicidal, she'd follow his instructions and take whatever help she could get.

She and Mother Nature would be in charge once the baby started coming. Although, she had a sneaking suspicion this man could deliver the baby if she weren't around. He looked immensely competent and confident. It was in the way he carried his large body and in his calm demeanor. And, yes, in the gentle way he spoke to Keely, soothing her as he carried her laboring body up the mountain.

Fee followed Trey as he set a brisk pace. She panted and wheezed as silently as she could. She didn't want him to slow down on her account. Keely was in pain and her contractions were overlapping; she was obviously dilating quickly. And, Fee suspected, Keely had back labor, a situation in which the baby's hands and feet were facing too far toward Keely's spine. Thus causing more pain than normal—and normal was bad enough.

Fee would have to turn the baby more sideways before delivery. At least the baby was not breech. As soon as the head crowned, she should be able to maneuver the little guy into the proper position to ease the shoulders, the widest part on a newborn, through the vaginal opening.

After several minutes of a grueling pace, he finally spoke. "What's wrong with Keely? You were cursing up a storm when I arrived." His voice was low, but it easily carried to her position behind him. And he wasn't even out of breath, damn him.

"The labor went from slo-mo to fast forward in the blink of an eye." She panted and concentrated on putting one foot in front of the other. She was miserably cold and damp and would kill for a hot cup of anything. The meds, while she knew they had to be working, had been taken too late to stave off most of the symptoms of mountain sickness. Her head throbbed and her vision blurred from the pain. At least the nausea had subsided to a dull simmer rather than a full-out boil.

"Well, then it's a good thing I'll get you both to safety in a couple of minutes. The cave is dry and can be warmed up quickly." Trey muttered something she couldn't hear and she realized he was talking into a headset.

"Are you talking to Keely's husband?" Fee stopped abruptly so she wouldn't run into the man. "We're here?" She looked around. "Where is this cave Keely spoke of?"

Trey turned, cradling the pain-wracked Keely in his

arms. He rubbed his cheek over her hair. "Hold on, little sis." While a tinge of panic was in his voice, the look he turned on Fee was calm. He was scared for Keely but he would never admit it. "Yeah, Ren has landed and is making tracks for us now. He has some heavy climbing to finish first. And we are here. Push on the spot that looks darker than the rest of the rock face, would ya?"

Fee did as he asked. Her mouth formed an "o" as a futuristic panel appeared in the rock wall. "Holey moley."

Trey snorted his amusement. "Punch in 8-9-9-2-4-6 and hit enter."

She did so and a door slid open. She followed him into a dimly lit antechamber which led to another door in another rock wall just ahead. The door to the outside swished closed behind them. Fee let go of some of the tension in her jaw and neck now that they were inside and away from the pursuers. "Now what?"

"Step aside. I'll use the retinal and palm scans."

Fee moved and watched as he leaned over just enough so his right eye could be scanned. Holding Keely against his chest with one muscled arm, he placed his right palm on a small pad and the door opened, smoothly and quietly. Inside, the space was one big black hole, but heat seemed to rush out at them. She sighed, happy at the evidence of warmth.

"Where do I find the light switch?" she asked.

"Lights will come on as we move into the space.

They're on motion detectors." Trey adjusted his hold on a squirming Keely and strode into the space. "Come on, don't dawdle, doc. I need to get you ladies set up and then go help Tweeter exterminate the roaches."

"Lovely image." Fee walked behind Trey and was pleased to find the place clean, well-lit, and dry. "I want to get Keely into something loose and dry. She'll need to be on a flat surface. I'll need blankets for warmth and lots of pillows or something similar to prop her up for delivery."

"We can do all of that." Trey led her farther into the cave and stopped in what looked to be a sleeping area. "Pick the bed you want. They're all clean."

Keely moaned, groaned, and panted in Trey's arms. His face was grim as he muttered soothing nonsense against her hair. He turned tortured eyes on Fee. "Hurry, doc. I've never seen her like this before."

"She's doing fine. Tell her that. She's having a baby, not dying." Fee hurried and arranged a bed to her satisfaction. "Hold her so I can strip her pants off, and then you can lay her on the bed. I can handle the rest. I'll need it warmer in here, if possible. I could also use hot water and soap to scrub my hands and later to clean the baby."

"On it." Trey helped her get Keely to bed.

Keely turned onto her side and curled into a semi-fetal position. The pain now rolled over the laboring woman in huge swells, each contraction crashing into the next with very little respite.

Trey swore under his breath. His voice when he continued to address Fee's requests displayed none of his emotions, but his distress at Keely's condition was present in his light green eyes. "There are clean T-shirts and ski underwear in that cabinet at the end of the row of beds. I'll take care of upping the heat some more. Hot water is instant and in the bathroom," he angled his head to a door in the rock wall, "and in the kitchen, which is in the main area we walked through."

"Good." Fee looked around as she rubbed Keely's back through another contraction. "Pant, Keely. That's a good girl. Keep panting. It's easing some, take a deep breath. Good. You're doing well."

Pale under his tan, Trey muttered into his headset.

"If that's her husband you're talking to—tell him he'd better hurry. This baby is on a fast clock."

Trey nodded and whispered into the microphone. After he'd finished relaying her words and the situation, he turned toward her. "The other medical supplies are in the cabinet by the door to the bathroom." He retrieved the medical kit from where she'd dropped it and brought it to her.

"Thanks. Now go help Keely's brother. Keely and I've got this. We women will do just fine."

"Bossy little thing, aren't you?" Trey moved around

the room, adjusting electronic panels. The heat, she assumed.

"Yes, I am—so don't forget it." Fee briskly removed Keely's coat, sweater, and bra. Trey handed her a T-shirt. She slipped it over Keely's head and then tucked the blankets around her.

Keely's brother-in-law had a worried look in his eyes but he kept the conversation light. She suspected he didn't want Keely to see or hear his fear. "I like bossy little women. My brother did just fine by finding himself one."

Fee almost laughed when he winked at her outrageously. But she shook her head. "Stop flirting. So not in the market." At a strangled gasp from Keely, she shooed Trey out of the area. "Go. I need to take care of Keely."

"I've turned the sat phone on." He placed the phone on the night stand. "Punch one and then the pound sign and someone will come running. You're safe here—no one can get in but one of the SSI operatives."

"We'll be just fine. We bossy little women are tough— and I have delivered babies before. Once I did triplets in an elevator. So this is a piece of cake. Now go."

Trey's lips thinned. He swept a trembling hand over Keely's sweaty hair. Then he leaned over and kissed Keely's forehead. "That was from Ren, sprite. He told me to tell you he loves you."

Keely looked at Trey through obviously pain-glazed

eyes. Speaking with a clenched jaw, she said, "Tell him not to get dead … and I love him, too."

Trey, a grave look on his face, left.

When Fee heard the outer door shut, Keely let out a guttural scream. How the woman had held in all that pain while her brother-in-law was present, Fee would never know.

"Go ahead. Scream all you want. It's just us women now." Fee stroked a damp, golden-red tress off Keely's face. "Now, let's see where you're at. Can you hold your legs apart for me, Keely? Bent at the knees?"

CHAPTER 6

Keely panted through another excruciating contraction which threatened to tear her body in half.

"Keely? Hon? Can you hear me?" Fee was directly in her face, stroking it with a cool, damp cloth.

"I thought … there were … supposed to be … uh, plateaus." Her words were punctuated with gasps and groans.

"Yeah, but you breezed through early and active labor and went straight to transition." Fee's eyes held sympathy and concern. "All you can do now is take each contraction one at a time." Keely grimaced and Fee chuckled. "Yeah, I know, easy for me to say, huh?"

"Yeah … too close … hard to control … breathing." She moaned low in her throat, bottling up the scream threatening to erupt. She was not a screamer and refused to start now.

Fee rubbed Keely's abdomen and murmured soothing nonsense throughout the back-arching pain.

"Want Ren." Keely hated the pathetic whine in her voice but couldn't help it. If Ren were there, he'd fix this—he'd never stand for her being in pain. Somehow, some way, he'd take care of it.

"I know, sweetie. He's coming as fast as he can." Fee touched Keely's face lightly. She struggled to concentrate on what the doctor said. "Keely, I can give you Tylenol. A mild analgesic won't hurt the baby and might help. This very well-equipped facility has IV-setups."

Biting her lip, Keely shook her head. She remembered the no-drug lecture the birthing instructor had given. She was pretty sure that had included all drugs. Riley would come into this world drug-free. She hadn't taken even an aspirin since before her last bullet wound back when she'd found out she was pregnant.

"Okay, then." Fee patted her shoulder. "Let's check to see how dilated you are and if you're ready to push this little guy out."

Fee moved out of Keely's direct line of sight. She sensed the doctor's hands between her legs, but wouldn't swear to it since every nerve in her body protested the agony pulsating through her. It was as if all her body parts had morphed into one—and they all hurt like hell.

When Fee came back into Keely's eyeshot, the doctor's face was a mask of neutrality.

"What?" Keely attempted to control her breathing as a sharp pain shot from her lower extremities to the top of her head. "What's wrong?"

"Good news is you're fully dilated and are able to push. Bad news is the little guy is facing fully backwards."

"What does…?" Keely grabbed her abdomen and felt the huge moving bulge as it seemed to shimmy and shake just under the surface of her skin. The image the motion evoked was Sigourney Weaver's character giving birth to the alien. "Riley wants … out."

"Yeah, he does." Fee's lips quirked. "But we need to make it easier on you both. I have to turn him to the side so his head and shoulders can be delivered."

Fee cupped Keely's face between her hands and stroked Keely's cheekbones in a soothing manner. "Keely, this means you'll have to resist the urge to push when I say so. At a certain point, your body only wants to push. So, you'll need to resist. Understand?"

Keely nodded. She wasn't sure why this was a problem. Whatever it took to take this pain away and put little Riley in her arms was fine with her. She hissed and panted rapidly and then groaned. "Oh God … bad one."

Fee gently removed Keely's hand from where she had gripped the doctor's arm. "Ready to do this?"

"Just … do it."

Keely grimaced and uttered another guttural moan. She was so ready and hoped the stories about women not remembering the pain were true, because if she remembered, she'd never get pregnant again. Ren would just have to settle for one natural heir and adopt any more kids he wanted. She couldn't believe her mother had done this five times!

Fee chuckled. "Let's prop you up so gravity will help." She arranged several pillows behind Keely's back, elevating her upper torso.

If it had been hard to catch a deep breath before, it was worse now. With her knees bent and her stomach pressing into her diaphragm, it was difficult to do anything but gasp for breath.

"Not comfortable." Fee rubbed Keely's stomach. "I know, but the angle will help push the baby out more easily."

Keely had an image of a toothpaste tube and rolling the end to get the last bit of paste. She snickered and then groaned.

"During the next contraction, Keely, pant until I tell you to push. Okay?"

Keely scowled. "Only having … contractions."

"Yeah, I know. They're overlapping, lots of peaks. Just pick a point where it hurts the most and start panting."

The doctor must not be paying attention since that was the only way Keely could breathe now. But she couldn't get enough air to call the doctor on her inattention.

Keely huffed and wheezed like a hippo in respiratory arrest as the pain became unbearable. The urge to push was great, but Fee said Riley wasn't ready, so she resisted the urge—and it hurt, dammit! "How long … now?"

"Varies…" At Keely's snarl, Fee laughed. "Nature has her own schedule. Remember, one contraction at a time. The baby's head is almost down far enough for me to turn him. Once I do, we'll try for three good pushes per contraction. We want to work with the contraction, Keely. Understand?"

No, she didn't, but she nodded anyway. Anything to keep Fee on task and to bring Riley into the world safely. She closed her eyes. Pain was a color now—all red, orange and yellow lights behind her lids. Her body was putting off heat like a nuclear reactor—and her body and everything around her was wet and uncomfortable. She wanted this done … now!

Fee's soothing, calm voice and gentle, cool hands were the only anchors in the sea of agony ebbing through her body.

"Okay, sweetie." Fee gently nudged Keely's knees farther apart. "Hold this position if you can. I can see lots of lovely dark hair." Fee's hand had moved to Keely's abdomen. "I feel a contraction building right on top of the one that just finished. We need to work with them even though they're close together … ah, there it is … lovely, strong one … Keely, pant for me. Push when I tell you."

Keely panted for all she was worth. If there was a blue ribbon for panting, she'd effin' win it.

Then the blessed words she had been waiting to hear. "Push, Keely."

Keely stopped panting, gritted her teeth, and bore down. A stinging, burning pain shot up her spine from her pelvis. For the first time since she'd been tortured in a Boston warehouse, she screamed. And screamed. And screamed. She was very glad her mother wasn't there because she uttered several loud "fucks" to punctuate the cries.

"Keely! Stop! Stop pushing."

Fee's shouts finally reached her through the inferno of pain permeating every cell in her body. Keely panted for breath, realizing she needed air.

"Whoa, there, hon." Fee's voice seemed muffled and Keely looked down to see the top of Fee's head still between her legs. "Man, you've got strong abs. You almost shot Riley out before I got him turned. That would've torn you up badly."

Keely watched Fee's messy, red ponytail bob as the doctor continued to work between her sprawled legs. "Is … baby okay?" She panted. "Need to … push again."

Fee looked up. "Not yet. You're doing great. Get some air into your lungs. Breathe slowly. In and out. In and out." Keely forced her breathing into compliance. "Good girl." Fee smiled. "On the next contraction I want you to push for all you're worth."

Closing her eyes against the distracting lights, Keely laid her head back against the mound of pillows and concentrated on controlling her breathing as she began to list prime numbers in order. But that took too much concentration, so she worried about her brother and Trey fighting the mercenaries and Ren making the climb to reach her side.

All too soon her worries were buried under an avalanche of pain. She was also light-headed from the combination of pain and the lack of breath. The world behind her lids was chaotic, filled with swirls of hot, angry colors and flashes of heat lightning. She refused to succumb to the darkness that beckoned; she needed to be conscious to push Riley out. So, she attempted to breathe between the ebb and flow of waves of pain.

She was about to ask Fee if she could push again when large, cold masculine hands cupped her face and Ren's unique scent and that of clean mountain air cut through the miasma.

"Baby, I'm here." His lips brushed hers lightly before he kissed her. With long, slow breaths, his tongue and lips took her away from the real world for a short time, breathing for her. When his lips left hers, she moaned. Her eyes opened. His stormy blue gaze filled with concern and love strengthened her.

But her respite was short-lived as pain pounded her body once more. She screamed.

"Keely!" Ren's voice was filled with panic. "What's wrong, Doctor?"

Keely couldn't worry about soothing him now—the urge to push battled her eroding self-control. All she wanted now was one little word—push.

Ren held her shoulders. His hands were a welcome support, a focus for her willpower. Her big strong man paled, his concern turning to fear right before her eyes. She wanted to reassure him but she didn't have the breath.

"Doctor! She's in pain. What do I need to do?" he asked Fee without turning his gaze from Keely.

"Your strong wife—man, she has abs—has almost done it all." Fee paused and grunted. "There we go, little man. Just needed to make sure the cord wasn't in the way."

Keely moaned as anguish shot up her spine and wreaked havoc with her pelvis.

"Hold her up just like you are and massage her abdomen when I tell her to push," Fee instructed.

With one arm around her shoulders, Ren braced her even farther upright. His other hand covered both hers on her abdomen. He brushed a kiss over her sweaty brow. "Ready, love?"

Keely turned her face into his shoulder and inhaled his scent, letting it soothe her. The pain was still there, a mixture of stabbing hot pokers and rending and tearing, but she felt more in control. Ren's presence was better than drugs. "Yes … ready."

CHAPTER 7

On the mountain.

Trey reached the lookout where he'd found the women. The mountainside was quiet except for the sounds of the wind blowing through the pines. Too quiet considering the weapons Tweeter had on him.

"Tweeter?" Trey spoke into the headset. "Sit rep?"

"Keely's two shots hit major organs and those fuckers are bleeding out. I sort of slit another guy's throat. The other three are hunkered down by the vehicles, having a little conference." Tweeter grunted with disgust. "Looks like they're making some phone calls. Guess they didn't expect a pregnant woman to fight back."

Trey chuckled. "Nope, your sister is one of a kind." He picked up Keely's rifle and adjusted the sight and the shoulder-butt pad. He checked the magazine and found

94

three of the five bullets remaining. After springing open the bipod, he rested the rifle on the flat rock. Through the sight, he checked out the area where Tweeter said the three remaining killers lurked. Unfortunately, no heads popped up, but there was always time.

"How's Keely?" Trey could tell Tweeter was moving.

"In pain. Lots of pain." He gulped, his stomach churning at the helplessness he'd felt. "I've seen gut-shot guys feel less pain. How in the fuck do women do it?"

"Hey, they are the stronger sex, just ask my mom and sister." Tweeter sang under his breath, "One little, two little, three little Indians."

Trey chuckled. "You have a shot, Kimosabe?"

"Nope, but I can lob a little flash bang and flush them out for you. We need to take care of them before the locals get here. Dan just radioed on the alternate frequency that he has the ranger access road blocked and his team and a State Police SWAT team are heading up the mountain."

"Well, hell. Flush the fuckers out." Trey put his eye to the scope. "Let's see how many little Indians I can take out before Sheriff Dan comes riding in to ruin our fun."

"I'll clean up any you miss. Let's get this done. I want to see my sister and, I hope, my little nephew."

"I'm with you there." Trey smiled.

And he would never admit it out loud to Tweeter who would tease him mercilessly, but he'd like to get more closely acquainted with one bossy little doctor. He'd always liked red-heads. He smiled as he imagined all that fiery temper tamed and in his bed. If Price didn't kill him first, that is.

When Tweeter shot the flash bang into the midst of the vehicles, Trey only had to wait a second or so for the three men to run away from the shock and awe. They were temporarily blind and deaf—and soon-to-be permanently dead. It was like shooting fish in a barrel.

———

"CONTRACTION'S COMING. OOH, A NICE big one. This is it. Keely—pant for me. Push when you feel like it," said Fee.

Again the contraction ate away at Keely's control. The urge to push was a prime imperative. But she refused to lose face in front of Ren. The torment continued and grew until it engulfed her. She bit her lip, holding in the screams. The taste of blood was coppery in her mouth.

"God, baby, let go." Ren's voice cut through the tsunami of pain sweeping through her mind. His lips brushed her forehead, her eyes, her lips. "Let go and push, sweetheart."

No! If she pushed, she'd scream. She refused to scream. She was embarrassed she'd screamed earlier. What must Fee think? What would Ren think? Only cowards screamed.

What the hell, Keely Walsh-Maddox? You were tortured in Boston and you screamed. So what? Doesn't make you a coward. And if you let go and scream now? Still doesn't make you a coward. It makes you human ... and in pain. Ren would be the last person to judge you. Scream and push that baby out!

The dam to her subconscious shame broke, releasing all the pent-up feelings of disgrace she hadn't even realized she'd held inside.

Keely screamed and screamed and screamed some more—and pushed for all she was worth.

This time Riley was coming out. Enough was enough. She reached deep and pushed with everything in her.

Ren's voice cut though the noise of her shouts. His tone and what he said gave her the extra strength to deal with the agony ripping her apart.

"God, baby! You are so beautiful. So strong. I love you." His voice hitched. Her big strong man was crying. "Sprite, he has dark hair like mine. One more push, sweetheart." His hand massaged her stomach as he peppered kisses and words of praise and love over her face and hair.

After one huge burning sensation tore through her pelvis, the pressure, the pain, lessened—so much so that she could breathe again without screaming or gasping. She took several deep breaths and relaxed into Ren's supporting arm.

"God, look at him, Keely. Look at our son." Ren kissed the top of her head and continued to massage the area over her now empty womb.

Keely opened her eyes as Fee held up a messy little bundle that kicked and flailed. His strong cries echoed off the cave walls. She cried and laughed at the same time. Riley was strong and vocal and a miracle. She looked at Ren whose teary eyes held love for her and the child they'd created.

He kissed her lips gently, reverently. "God, he's so beautiful. You're beautiful."

Keely scrunched her nose. "He's gunky … and loud."

Ren barked out a laugh. "Jesus, baby. Only you would point that out."

Fee, looking as exhausted as Keely felt, smiled broadly and reassured her. "Keely, Ren is correct. Your son is beautiful. He has all his fingers and toes and other assorted parts right where they should be." The doctor wiped the white, cheesy-looking stuff off Riley with a wet towel. The baby screamed even louder than before, his little fists looking for a target.

"What's wrong? Is he hurt?" God, what if he was hurt inside and they didn't have the equipment to figure it out?

"He's fine, Keely." Fee's tone was confident and humoring. Keely imagined the doctor had a lot of practice calming patients and their families. "Since he's an early baby, we'll do some tests when we get you both to the hospital. But he looks to be just fine. He's big for his gestational age. I'm not sure you could've delivered him vaginally if he had cooked a little longer."

"That's what my OB said. Which is why we'd scheduled a C-Section." Keely ached to hold Riley, but Fee was taking her damn fine time bringing him to her. Ren patiently waited by her side, but she felt the tension in his body as he watched the doctor like a hawk. "You didn't answer my question. Why is he crying?"

Fee smiled. "Wouldn't you cry if you were jerked out a skinny tunnel from a nice warm, dark place and ended up cold and wet with bright lights all around you?"

"Yeah, guess so." Keely felt so stupid, but since she'd never been around babies much, how would she know? Well, there was a learning curve in everything she'd ever undertaken. She had the books she'd bought and she'd figure out how to take care of this precious little life. Plus, she wouldn't be doing it alone—she had Ren, her family, and the SSI family to help. Riley would probably turn out to be the most-loved baby in all of Idaho.

"Ren, would you like to cut the umbilical cord?" Fee held Riley with one arm, cradled securely against her chest. Her other hand held surgical scissors.

"Yeah." Ren moved away from Keely. She immediately missed his warmth and nearness. But he'd be back—and he'd better bring their son with him.

Keely watched as her big strong man swept a gentle hand over his son's head.

The breadth of his palm completely encompassed Riley's skull. She bet Riley's length wouldn't even fill the space between Ren's elbow and the tip of his fingers. Their son was so tiny.

Ren took the scissors Fee held. His hand steady—hers would've been shaking so badly she wouldn't have trusted herself—he cut the cord. He didn't take the baby from Fee but moved back to Keely's side.

"Um, why didn't you bring Riley with you? I want to hold him."

"Fee's still cleaning him up, love." He nuzzled the top of her head as he sat on the edge of the bed. The look on his face made her insides turn to goo. She'd known he loved her, but this look was a combination of love, awe, and adoration. "Thank you for our son." He kissed her lips, his hand cradling her face.

When he broke away, she whispered against his mouth, "You're welcome."

Keely lay back and let Ren fuss with her blankets. She vaguely sensed him putting something warm and dry on her and changing the soiled linens around her. Fee's soft voice and Ren's rumbling one surrounded her in a pool of calm.

Everything was a blur now that the horrendous pain was gone. Though, she still felt some abdominal cramping and had a raw feeling around her vaginal opening. She was so tired but refused to sleep. Instead, she floated in a fugue state. She needed her son in her arms, and then she could sleep.

Riley's cry startled her from her drowse. She focused on the doctor as Fee did whatever doctors do after a baby's born. Ren watched Fee also. They were two of a kind. Nothing and no one would ever get within a mile of their child without them knowing it.

Finally, Fee wrapped Riley in one of the fluffy blue blankets Keely had put in the field medical kit. "Here, I swaddled him. Now hold him on your chest so he can hear your heart beat. The sound will soothe him. Talk to him. He knows your voice. He's been hearing it for months." Fee laid Riley on Keely's chest.

Ren held Keely against his side as she held their son, his body angled to cover them in case of danger.

Keely cupped Riley's head. His dark hair was soft and silky. She looked into his sapphire blue eyes. He stared at her. "Hey, Riley, welcome to the world." She placed a kiss on his little scrunched forehead, then his nose. He smelled unlike anything she had ever scented before. His skin was so fragile she was afraid to touch him.

And his reaction to her attentions? His lips made sucking motions, little bubbles forming on his tiny rosebud mouth.

Ren laughed and kissed the top of Riley's head.

"That's my boy, wanting to kiss the girls already."

"I think that means he's hungry, big guy." Keely swept a finger over Riley's lips and he tried to capture it. She and Ren looked at each other and laughed.

"Well, that's like me, too." Ren nuzzled her cheek and whispered against her ear. "I love to suckle your breasts almost as much as I like kissing you."

Keely snorted and would have made a teasing remark when another contraction, albeit a much milder one than those earlier, moved through her body. "Fee? I…"

"It's okay, Keely. Just the placenta and umbilical coming out." The doctor was between her legs again. "Ren, could you massage Keely's stomach gently for me? It will help deliver the after-birth."

"On it." Ren kissed Keely's cheek and nuzzled her ear as he massaged her stomach. "Feeling better, sprite?"

"Sort of shivery, but this is mild compared to earlier." When Ren frowned and swore, she hurried to reassure him. "Ren, I'm fine. Although you might have to do some mighty fine persuading to get me pregnant anytime soon."

"God, baby, I should have been with you."

"You were with me when it counted. You helped immensely. Just knowing you were here and safe was better than any pain medicine." Keely reached for him as she cuddled Riley with her other arm. "Come here, big guy. I need you to hold me."

Ren looked at Fee. "Is that okay, Doctor?"

Fee turned from whatever she was doing on a side table and smiled. "Yep, you can hold her. But let's get the bottom half of the bed and Keely cleaned up again. She needs warm, dry layers around her for when we transport her and Riley to the hospital."

Ren nodded. "Hold on to Riley, sprite. You don't have to move a muscle. Let me do all the heavy lifting while we swaddle you just like our son."

Keely yawned. "So tired. Need to rest now." She rubbed a hand over Riley's back. He was asleep, snuggled on her breast, his mouth pursing and blowing baby bubbles. Her son was clearly more tired than hungry. Being born was hard work. "Don't want to let him go."

"You don't have to," Fee said. "I think your big strong husband can lift you two. Just rest. If you feel me checking you from time to time, that's normal. I need to make sure your uterus is contracting and no excessive bleeding occurs."

"'Kay." Keely closed her eyes to the murmurs of Ren and Fee. She felt as if she floated on a cloud and was quite willing to hover in this warm, comforting world for as long as she could.

"Doctor … Fee… tell me the truth. Is everything all right with Keely? She seems so out of it."

Fee had to laugh at the big, dark male looming over

her, watching her every move like a predator ready to pounce. He was a protector just like Price.

"She's fine. She's exhausted. Having babies is hard work normally. Keely had a rapid progression, skimmed through a few steps, and had overlapping contractions—and no drugs. So, she is more tired than most." Fee tucked the blankets around Keely's waist and then stroked a hand over Riley's back as he lay nestled on his mother's chest.

Instinctively, Keely's hand moved to hold her baby closer.

Fee smiled and pulled the blankets up and over the baby, stopping them at the base of his head now covered in a little baby cap of the softest blue cashmere. "You have a beautiful family, Ren. If you can move them without waking them, go on and hold them like she asked. I'll just clean things up around here and package what the hospital lab will need to test."

"Ren, hold me … won't sleep fully until you do." Keely peeked at them through her lashes as she stroked Riley's back.

Fee watched in amazement as Ren managed to lift Keely without disturbing the baby or the nest of blankets. He settled on the narrow bed next to his wife, pulling her into his side, one arm under and one arm over her and the baby. He literally surrounded them with his strength and protection.

Sighing at the sight, Fee wondered if she'd ever find

a man who'd put his body between her and the world. Who'd ever look at her as Ren did Keely? God, what was she thinking? It must be exhaustion and the altitude sickness making her so maudlin. Men like Ren and her brother were rare.

A rumbling male voice came from behind her. "Look at that. I'm an uncle."

Fee turned. "You're all right?"

Trey Maddox turned away from staring at his new nephew and smiled down at her. "Yep. The motherfuckers didn't have a chance." He turned back toward his brother. "Man, Ren, the little guy looks just like you."

Ren grinned and stroked a gentle finger over the baby's cheek. Riley made little sucking motions and the men laughed quietly.

"What's so funny?" Keely's brother had entered the cave just as quietly as Trey. His gaze drifted to the loving scene on the bed. "Damn, look at that. My baby sis has a baby." Tweeter pulled out his phone. "I need to send pictures to the folks and the brothers."

Trey nodded. "Good idea. I'll send pictures to our sister and parents."

Fee was floored by what big softies these macho men were at heart. Then she realized they were looking at her. "What?"

"Are they okay?" Tweeter asked, holding his smart phone up. "My family will want to know. Riley was a month early."

Trey frowned and nodded. "Do we need to get them to a hospital to be checked out? We might be able to get the medevac helicopter to lift them out."

"They're fine at the moment. And, yes, a medevac would be good. I don't see us carrying them down that treacherous hill. I would like to get them to the hospital. There are tests that need to be done on Riley and other things." Like a circumcision, if requested, but she never mentioned that in front of men since they seemed to get queasy just thinking about it.

A wave of dizziness swept over Fee. She wobbled and braced herself on a table. "Plus, there's always the potential of Keely continuing to bleed. I would feel better if we were in a medical facility…" She looked around the cave and the well-supplied medical cabinet. "…although, if needed I could start a saline IV here if she required fluids."

"I'm her blood type," Tweeter offered. His gaze took in the bloody bedding Fee had kicked out of Keely's sight. No need for a new mother to see how messy the birthing process was. Experiencing the pain was bad enough.

Fee patted his arm. "Good to know. Let's not worry yet. Your sister did a super job and is very healthy—as is the baby. Everything went extremely well considering the circumstances."

The men smiled and some of the tension went out of their bodies.

Fee looked Trey and Tweeter over and noted both were disheveled, bruised, and bleeding. All she wanted to do was get warm, lie down, and sleep for a week, but if she had patients still, she would find the energy to take care of them. While she had been safe inside this cave, the two men had risked their lives for her and Keely.

"Do you two need medical care?" asked Fee.

"We're fine, little doc," Trey said. "You need to sit down. You look like someone dragged you through a keyhole backwards and then pulled you back through again."

Fee glared at him. "I'm fine."

"Trey! Stop teasing Fee and make a full report." Ren spoke in a soft, but authoritative murmur. He soothed his son's back as the baby whimpered in his sleep.

Trey turned from her and approached the bed, but Fee sensed he knew exactly where she was and what she was doing as she cleaned up after the birth.

"Keely had already gotten the numbers down to four. By the time I got back to pick up Keely's sniper rifle, Tweeter had taken out one more. The remaining three made it easy by gathering near the vehicles. One flash bang and three .338 caliber bullets later, the battle was over. The Sheriff and the State Police are doing clean up. Dan wants to talk to all of us—tomorrow. I told him about Keely being in labor. He asked me to convey his best wishes." Trey glanced with what Fee would call fondness at his sister-in-law. "Keely wounded the first two. The fuckers are in serious condition, but probably will survive for us to question them at their hospital bedsides."

Tweeter approached the other side of the bed, his gaze never straying from his sister and nephew. "Like Trey said, we didn't suffer a scratch. The torn clothing is mostly from scrambling over rocks while checking security arrays earlier today."

"And the blood?" Fee asked. They had too much blood on them for scratches from climbing rocks.

A wicked smile appeared on Trey's face as his green eyes sparkled with malicious glee. "Not our blood, little doc. But if you want to kiss the bruises I got bouncing off mountain walls earlier today, checking out electrical conduits, I wouldn't mind."

How could they be so relaxed after taking on hired killers? And how had she never known this was what her brother did? If she'd realized, she would've worried about him all the time.

She snorted. "In your dreams."

Trey laughed and winked at her.

"Stop flirting with Price's baby sister, Trey." Ren stroked his wife and child.

"I'm not flirting. I'm dead serious." Trey turned toward Fee and his warm smile took her breath away.

God, he was handsome, this big, tall hunk of male. Too bad just the thought of any man touching her made her want to gag. Adam-fucking-Stall had broken her. How could she have been so wrong about him? Adam had looked to be everything most women wanted—urbane, intelligent, highly educated, rich, and GQ good-looking. But he'd turned out to be a crazy stalker and an abusive thug. It would take a long time to get over him and what he had done to her—if she ever could.

"Still not interested," she said.

Trey's answering frown made her stomach hurt. Or, was it still the altitude sickness? Why did she feel as if she should apologize to this man for disappointing him? She didn't even know him—and he sure as hell didn't know her or what she'd gone through in the last week or so.

Changing the subject, Fee turned toward Ren. "You live a dangerous life." She looked at the baby. "You think you can protect your family from people wanting to hurt them?"

"No one will hurt my wife or my child. No one." Ren's words were delivered in a fierce tone of voice that made Fee a believer.

Fee felt like a stranger in a strange land. She needed to get back to her world—the world of healing, preferably unpopulated by predatory, stalking peers like Dr. Adam-fucking-Stall.

She nodded. "Okay, got that. And from what I've seen of Keely, I know she'll protect her baby. Hell, she protected me and she was the one in labor."

With shaking hands, she busied herself cleaning up surfaces she'd already cleaned. The world began to swirl around her. *Uh-oh.* Whatever reserves she'd been operating on had just run out. She was sliding downhill fast.

Through what sounded like a vast, echoing tunnel, she heard Keely, "Trey! Catch her. She's had altitude sickness since we left the Hummer."

Trey put his arm around her waist. Fee gasped out "no" and tried to pull away. The last man who'd grabbed her had hurt her. The nightmare in her mind, which she'd so successfully sublimated for the last few hours, rose to the surface with a vengeance. She whimpered, pathetic mewling sounds, and scratched with clawed fingers at the man holding her.

But he didn't let go. "Stop it. Shh, little doc. I'm not hurting you. You're sick, Fee. Shh. I won't hurt you. No one will hurt you while I'm here, sweetheart."

Fee heard Trey's next words as if from a distance. "What the fuck, Keely?"

"Not now, Trey," Keely's soft voice replied. "Just don't let her hurt herself. I think she needs to see a doctor more than I do."

Fee almost laughed. Keely was more right than she knew. Fee hadn't let anyone see her bruises. She'd treated herself and then left Detroit.

The arms around her tightened and lifted her. She

cried out and resumed her struggle. "Don't hurt me anymore, please!"

A man's voice, not Adam-fucking-Stall's, swore colorfully under his breath, but his arms were gentle. He wasn't hurting her.

This is Trey, dummy. Not effin' Stall. Plus, there's a room full of people. You look like a crazy woman. Chill.

Trey pulled her gently against his big, broad chest. Her hands went to the solid slab of muscle and shoved. "Calm down, little doc. Everything's fine." He soothed her in a crooning tone of voice, his breath whispering past her ear. "It's over. Whatever happened—it's over. I won't let it happen again."

"Let go. I don't like being held." *By a man* went unsaid. Fee met his smoky green eyes.

"I like holding you—and you need to be held." He frowned as his gaze traced the bruises on her face. He opened his mouth and she shook her head frantically. She couldn't answer questions about who had hurt her. It was bad enough she'd let too much slip to Keely. "Okay, little doc. We'll save the questions about who beat on you until later. Once you're rested and Price is back."

"No." She turned her head away from his suddenly piercing stare and found Tweeter and the others watching them. She buried her burning face into her newfound nemesis's chest. Her body shook harder—the altitude sickness was making her weak. She was also experiencing an adrenaline crash.

"You're one of those people that holds up under fire and then slowly dissolves into quivers once the battle is done, aren't you?"

"I'm a coward through and through—just ask Price. I couldn't even watch scary movies as a kid. Noises in the night had me screaming the house down. Your world scares me." She wanted to shove out of Trey's arms but knew she'd fall on her face if she tried to stand. She'd reached her physical limits. So, to keep from freaking out again, she pictured him as a hammock, a warm, muscular, firm hammock, and relaxed into his body with a sigh.

"No, you have quiet courage when it's needed, little doc. Now just let me hold you until you stop shaking." He pulled her even closer.

Sighing in capitulation, she laid her cheek on his chest and let him warm and soothe her. She inhaled deeply as she attempted to get her racing heart back under control.

Trey smelled good—right. His scent was healthy male sweat and a tinge of lemon with an overlay of pine and clean mountain air. His body was a blast furnace pouring off heat. She hadn't realized how cold she was until he held her.

She ignored Trey's concerned gaze and turned her throbbing head so she could watch Ren and Keely show Tweeter their son. She wanted what they had—love, a family. Her lips trembled and tears filled her eyes. She was so damaged—she might never be able to "be" with a man again after what had been done to her.

Trey must've sensed her upset, because he whispered soothing nonsense mixed with vows to make it all right and promises of vengeance against the bastard who'd hurt her. She couldn't help it, some of the punishments he mentioned were so similar to those she'd dreamt of doing to Adam-fucking-Stall—she had to laugh. The sound came out on a hiccup and sounded a little watery, but it was a laugh.

God! A man could make her laugh. Yesterday that would not have happened.

Too bad she hadn't met someone like Ren or Trey or Tweeter a long time ago. Maybe time would heal all wounds, wasn't that the saying? For now, her path lay elsewhere. She had at least two more years of work in under-served areas to pay off her medical school loans. She'd bury herself in her work—and hope she would heal.

EPILOGUE

Forty-Eight Hours Later, on Sanctuary.

Keely stroked the soft dark hair on her son's head as his little mouth sucked away at her breast. Riley's cobalt-blue gaze was fixed on her face as if he was afraid she might disappear, taking his mid-afternoon meal away from him.

She chuckled and stroked a finger down his little nose. "Don't worry, little guy. Mama won't deprive you of your food."

A sound at the door to the master bedroom had her looking up. Ren stared at her and Riley. The look in his silver-blue eyes made her melt inside. He'd always looked at her with love, but now it seemed multiplied by a factor of ten.

"Hey," she husked, "how did things go?" He'd gone to the regional hospital to assist in interrogating the two mercenaries who'd survived.

"They never met the guy who hired them. Their payment was wired from a numbered account to their handler's numbered account who in turn paid them. Your brother is already on the electronic fund transfers." He moved across the room to sit on the bed by her legs. His hand covered hers as she held Riley to her. "How are my beautiful wife and son?"

"We're fine." At his snort, she narrowed her eyes. "We're fine. It would take more than a little loss of blood to knock me on my butt. I'll have you know that your son and I had a bath today. We splashed and had a good time." She nuzzled the top of Riley's head. "Didn't we, little man?"

With his mouth full of nipple, Riley continued to suck and stare. Silence was assent in most cultures.

Ren laughed, the concern in his eyes gone as quickly as it had appeared. "Okay, so you're fine. Fee said as much…" he leaned over to kiss her forehead and then the top of Riley's head, "…but I was worried. She told me to grow some balls." He snorted. "Sounded a lot like you when she said it."

"About Fee." Keely scrunched her forehead. "Did she tell Price about what happened in Detroit to make her quit her job and drop in here so unexpectedly?"

Price had arrived less than eight hours after they'd made it to the regional medical center. Fee hadn't wanted to chance the longer trip to Coeur d'Alene after Keely's bleeding hadn't slowed.

"Not that I heard. Trey might know if Fee talked to her brother." Ren grinned. "My brother is attracted to the little doc as he calls her. Price is having fits about it, warning him off."

"And Price can fuck himself. If the little doc and I want to see each other, we will." Trey spoke from the doorway. "May I come in and see my nephew?"

Ren pulled the baby blanket up over Riley's head, covering Keely's breast. She frowned at him and then said, "Come in, Uncle Trey. Your brother is getting territorial about a small amount of exposed breast."

Ren growled. "He doesn't need to be seeing your breast."

Trey laughed. "I won't look. I promise. Thought I'd offer to burp the little guy and take him on a walk-about so you two could have some quiet time. Things have been hectic."

"That's so sweet." She shot a glare at Ren. "Isn't it, big guy?"

"Yeah, sweet." Ren crossed his eyes at Keely and she giggled. He turned as his brother sat on the other side of the bed. "So? You and Fee Teague?"

"Not just yet. The little doc is making things difficult," Trey replied, a grim look on his face.

"About time some woman gave you a challenge," teased Ren.

"Eff you." Trey gave his brother the finger and then shot an apologetic glance at Keely. "Sorry, Keely."

Trey was steaming mad and attempting to control his anger around her and the baby. She punched Ren. "Stop it, big guy." She turned to Trey. "How is she making it difficult?"

Trey's face went from mad to grim. "The maddening woman ran. Left Sanctuary before dawn to go to Boise for a flight to Santa Fe." He wiped a hand over his face. He looked and sounded weary, defeated. And Keely had never heard either of the Maddox brothers ever sound that way before. "Scotty fed Fee and Price breakfast and overheard them talking. Fee has her new orders from the Feds. Seems she'll be working in New Mexico, close to the border with Mexico.

"I'll be borrowing the jet from time to time." Trey skewered his brother with a piercing glare as if daring Ren to argue with him. "Fee could be the one, ya know? Like Keely was for you. Little doc needs to give me a chance to see if this would work out for us."

Trey sounded hurt. But Keely understood why Fee had run and he didn't. If he'd known even a small part of what had happened to Fee, he and Price would've been on a plane to Detroit to get Fee some justice—and Fee would still be at Sanctuary.

"Damn it!" Keely said. "She got away before I could twist her arm into telling Price and you guys about the a-hole who hurt her."

Trey scowled. "You know what happened? Who beat her?"

Before Keely could answer, Riley unlatched from her breast and looked at her expectantly. She shifted Riley to her shoulder for a good back rub and burp. Fee's problems forgotten for a split second, the men watched with silly looks on their faces as Riley let out two loud baby burps and then fell asleep, his little mouth blowing milk bubbles. "God, he's so cute," she whispered.

Ren used a soft cloth to wipe his son's mouth, taking the opportunity to kiss her on the lips. "You're both cute."

"You're all cute." Trey's voice was a low snarl, ending the intimate moment. "Now, what should Fee have told Price—and me?"

Keely sighed and continued to rub Riley's back. "Some asshole she worked with in Detroit attacked and abused her. And, I suspect, raped her."

Ren stiffened and swore under his breath. Trey stomped around the room, swearing a blue streak. His hands fisted at his sides.

Keely, used to such alpha-posturing, waited them out. Someday the little bundle lying against her shoulder would probably act the same way. She smiled. God, she loved her men, so predictable.

Fee didn't realize it yet, but she now had the protection of every SSI operative at her back. The woman wouldn't know what hit her.

"Okay, sprite, fess up. Who's the asshole?" Ren asked.

Trey approached the bed and stared at her. "You do know who the bastard is, don't you?"

"Of course she does." Ren shot his brother a nasty look. "She's a protector like us. She wouldn't let Fee get away without telling her, even if she was in pain and having a baby."

"My man knows me well." She nuzzled Riley's head. "The creepazoid worked with her in the ER. His name is Dr. Adam-fucking-Stall. Fee's words not mine."

Trey grunted. "Good, at least the fucker…" He cast a guilty look at the baby. "…oops, sorry … the effing coward, didn't break her spirit."

"Trey," Keely spoke softly, "she's lost her confidence when it comes to trusting a man. She didn't want to tell Price or you guys. She chose to run instead. She's suffering. She needs time and space…"

"She needs someone to hold her and help her work through the nightmares. To show her that not all men are abusive, raping shitheads." Trey turned his back and swore colorfully. When he ran out of steam or breath, she couldn't tell which, his shoulders heaved as he let out a despondent sigh. "Sorry, Keely. I want that little woman. I fell like a frigging ton of bricks for her. Even when she was sick and scared, she came through for you. The woman has grit and is the sweetest little armful … well, enough of that."

"Yeah, I could tell you liked her," Keely gently teased, and then she sobered. "You'll have to be patient. She'll shove you away if you let her."

"I'll be as patient as she needs me to be." He turned and looked at them. "But first, Price and I need to go kick us some Stall butt. I figure if I help Price beat the shit out of the man who hurt his baby sister, he might put in a good word for me."

Ren barked out a laugh, startling Riley, who whimpered. Ren stroked his son's back. He turned to his brother. "Lots of luck, brother. Price knows you. I mean you two cut a swath through the women in Idaho County and the surrounding environs."

"That's in the past. Fee is it for me." A lost look came into his eyes. "What if she never lets me woo her? God, she was so scared of my flirting, she ran clear to New Mexico."

Keely shook her head and smiled. "Well, we could use another doctor in this part of Idaho. I do believe we classify as an under-served rural area. Or at least Tweeter said so after I had him look up the program she's in."

"And that kind of thinking and planning is why I love you so much." Ren kissed her nose. "Well, that and a lot of other things. Great idea, baby."

"Thank you." She smiled at her husband. "I also thought after she finishes paying off the student loan, she could come to work for SSI as our resident doctor. Our operatives and employees deserve the best medical care. Fee is super-smart and damn good in a crisis. Plus she has a way that just makes you want to trust her."

Trey muttered something and Ren laughed. Keely frowned and looked to her husband. "What did he just say?"

Trey snarled "no, Ren, don't" as her loving husband replied, "He said Fee had a way which made him want to fuck her."

Keely giggled and covered Riley's ears. "Guys, watch your language. Riley is far too young to hear such talk."

"I figure it's too late, sprite. He's been hearing it in the womb since he was conceived."

Keely sighed. "Yeah, well, try to control it. I might have to follow my mama's example and charge per f-word."

Ren leaned over to kiss her. "We'll put the money in his college fund."

"Good idea, big guy. MIT costs a lot of money. By the time he's ready, we should have enough with the way y'all swear."

THE END

STORM FRONT

Less than one week after Earl Blackhawk helped Risto
Smith and Callie Meyers fight off a Colombian drug lord in
Osprey's Point, Michigan, he travels to Idaho to act as Risto's
best man at his marriage to Callie. There he meets Callie's
friend, Tessa Andrews. When he'd asked Callie to find him a
woman just like her, he'd been teasing ... sort of. But Callie
had taken him seriously and he was glad she had.

Tessa comes to Idaho with a problem dogging her
heels. A cyberstalker has resurrected a past she thought
deeply buried. A past any man, a man such as Earl, would
take one look at and run the other way.

But then, Tessa has never met a man like Earl. He's more
than attracted to Tessa, feels instantly protective of her, and
nothing and no one will harm her while he's around.

Tessa doesn't believe she deserves a happy ever after,
and when Earl and some others see the damaging images
her cyberstalker sends her, she runs into the teeth of a
storm front and deadly peril.

ACKNOWLEDGEMENTS

I would like to thank my beta-readers and critique partners for taking their valuable time to read and comment on this manuscript. I couldn't have done this without you—Cherise, Ezra, Valy, Debbie, Shannon, and KaLyn.

I also want to thank my fabulous and very busy cover artist, April Martinez, for another fantastic cover.

Most of all, I want to thank the loyal fans and readers who have made it a joy for me to write these books. There would be no SSI series without you—I would have stopped after Eye if you all hadn't demanded more. I hope Storm Front meets your expectations.

CHAPTER 1

***Monday, December 5th, 6:00 a.m. (MST), Sanctuary,
Idaho.***

Earl Blackhawk leaned against the doorway leading
from the Lodge's great room into the kitchen and
enjoyed the view.

Tessa Andrews stood at the center island, doing prep
work for breakfast. Her thermal, long-sleeved shirt clung
lovingly to her full, and if he wasn't mistaken, braless
breasts. Like Callie Meyers, now Smith as of yesterday,
Tessa had been a super-model, recognized by only her
first name. Her skin-tight jeans displayed the heart-
shaped ass that had been featured in his and probably
a lot of other men's sexual fantasies over the years. Her
long, dark hair was pulled up into a ponytail; let loose
he'd bet the hair reached her butt.

Tessa leaned over the chopping board and the quick knife action set her breasts to jiggling. He stifled a groan and adjusted his cock into a more comfortable position. He'd been in one stage of erection or another since Tessa's arrival on Saturday morning for Callie and Risto's Sunday afternoon wedding.

When Callie had introduced them, it had been all he could do not to stammer and blush like a thirteen-year-old. Earl had fallen a little bit in love and a lot in lust with Tessa because of a perfume ad she'd done with Callie years ago. Whoever had crafted that promotion knew what made men tick.

Tessa was night to Callie's day. Dark to Callie's light. Sultry, Eurasian heritage to Callie's sweet, All-American sensuality. The ad campaign had made the women instant super-models. Both had been discovered by the world-famous photographer Evan—Callie in the Chicago diner where she worked as a waitress to support her twin brothers and herself while she attended college, and Tessa on the streets of Chicago where she'd lived after escaping some sort of abusive home situation.

"Are you going to stand there and stare at me all morning," Tessa's low, sexy voice tinged with amusement resonated in the empty kitchen, "or, are you going to tell me what you want?"

What he wanted was her, but she wasn't ready to hear that—yet. He'd never believed in love at first sight before, but it had happened to Risto with Callie, Ren with Keely, and now, it seemed it had happened to him.

Call it fate, karma, kismet, or destiny—or even Callie's obvious attempt at match-making—he and Tessa were meant to be. He believed it with everything in him. Now, he needed to convince Tessa to believe in it—to believe in him.

Tessa turned her head and looked at him over her shoulder. Her almond-shaped eyes, the color of aged whiskey, held curiosity—and exhaustion.

"Did you even go to bed last night?" Earl asked before he could stop himself.

When he'd turned in, she'd been sitting in the great room with Callie's brothers watching the *Rocky Horror Picture Show*, along with Loren and Paul Walsh, Keely Walsh-Maddox's twin brothers. The five had sung along with the musical numbers and seemed to have been having a good time.

Tessa scowled and turned her attention back to chopping onions. "Yes, I went to bed, Mr. None-Of-Your-Business. I couldn't sleep. I have a deadline on my book, so I worked on line edits." She shrugged. "Besides, I don't sleep much."

She was lying.

Editing might have been what she'd done when she couldn't get to sleep, but the book deadline wasn't the cause of her insomnia.

Something else was.

Callie had confided her concerns about her friend at the same time she'd fed him background on Tessa. "I'm worried about her, Earl. Someone's bothering her, but she won't give me details. For her to mention it at all, means it's bad news. Take care of her for me, please."

Callie hadn't needed to beg. He'd already determined he'd look Tessa up when they both got back to the Midwest. He'd decided he would need to ease into a relationship with the beautiful Tessa. He was more than ready to settle down and get some of what his best friend Risto had found with Callie: a loving wife and a baby on the way.

But Callie's words had chilled him to the core and then made him see red. Nothing and no one were allowed to scare Tessa. He wouldn't allow it. As far as he was concerned, Tessa was his responsibility now—whether she liked it or not.

One thing he knew—if he were in her bed, he'd make sure she slept. The thought of lulling Tessa to sleep with lots of sex and then holding her all night, cuddled against his naked body, made him smile and his cock twitch.

"Earth to Earl. What do you want?"

Tessa scooped the perfectly diced onions into a small bowl and then pulled a green pepper over and began to dice it when her cell phone lying on the island rang. She startled and nicked her finger. "Dammit."

Sucking on her finger, she threw a frightened look at the phone and didn't answer it. The look of fear was gone in a split second. If he hadn't been observing her so closely, he would have missed it.

He'd seen the same expression before. Put on alert by Callie, he'd kept a close eye on Tessa the whole weekend. Six times on Saturday and four on Sunday, and now this time—and who knew how many times when he hadn't been around?—when her cell phone rang, she'd startled and fear crossed her beautiful face. Then she'd check her smart phone with trembling fingers and whatever she read or heard would leach all the color out of her face.

By the third call on Saturday, he'd barely resisted the urge to snatch the phone out of her hand and demand what was wrong.

Today, somehow, he'd get his hands on her phone. Once he checked the messages and found out who or what had caused the look of abject fear on her face, he then could set about taking care of the problem.

Tessa moved to the sink and stuck her bleeding digit under running water. The phone finally stopped ringing.

Speaking over her shoulder, her voice strained, she said, "You never answered my question—did you want something? Breakfast won't be ready for another forty-five minutes or so."

Yeah, he wanted answers, but she wasn't ready to confide in him—yet.

Swearing under his breath as Tessa's finger continued to bleed, Earl straightened and stalked into the room. He skirted the island and stopped next to her. He pulled her bleeding finger from under the frigid water. "Jesus Christ, Tessa." He grabbed a paper towel.

"What do you want, Earl?" She sighed with just a hint of exasperation and a lot of exhaustion and tried to pull her finger away from his grasp.

"I don't want anything." *Liar.* He wanted to take her upstairs and make love to her all day so she wouldn't hurt herself and so she'd get some much-needed sleep. Sex was a great stress relief.

But instead, he wrapped the paper towel around the cut and raised her arm above the level of her heart. "Hold that there and keep the pressure on. I'll get the First Aid kit."

He waited until Tess's gaze met his, and she nodded. Satisfied she'd follow his instructions, he strode to the pantry, pulled the kit from the wall, and took it back to the kitchen island.

"Come here and sit." He pulled out a stool at the island and waited.

Her eyes sparked fiery gold. She heaved a loud sigh, but complied. "You're a very bossy man, Earl Blackhawk. Does that come from owning most of Osprey's Point, Michigan, or because you were a hot-shot Army Special Forces guy?"

Sometime over the past two days, Tessa had gotten an earful about him from someone. He'd place money on Cupid Callie being the source. Bless her little match-making heart.

"No, being bossy, as you call it, came naturally and led to those other things." He laid out the supplies he'd need and then took her hand gently into his. Her fingers were long and graceful; her hands, small compared to his. "Now, let's see how much damage we have here."

As he unwrapped the blood-soaked paper towel, Tessa hissed as some of it stuck to the gaping wound. Her finger still bled rather freely when it should've begun to slow.

Worried about the poor coagulation, he frowned. "Do you have some sort of blood problem? You should've started to clot by now."

"No-o-o. I'm perfectly healthy." A look of confusion crossed her exotic face.

Damn. He wanted to howl or hit something. He hated seeing her upset, tired, hurt, bleeding. He wanted her laughing and enjoying life or, better yet, dreamy-eyed and satiated after he'd given her a few orgasms.

"Are you taking any medications? Even over-the-counter ones?" After cleaning the cut, he placed a gauze pad over the wound and applied more pressure, while keeping the finger elevated above her heart.

"Um, aspirin." Her expression lightened somewhat,

and she let out a sigh of relief. "That has to be it. I never thought…"

"Why are you taking so much aspirin?" Because it would take more than a casual intake to compromise her coagulation factor. She was too young to be on a preventive dose for heart disease. He lowered her hand, removed the gauze. He grunted his satisfaction. "It's slowing down."

Earl looked up and resisted the urge to release her hand so he could soothe away the crease marring her forehead. "Tessa, sweetheart…" she gasped and looked at him with something akin to shock in her oh-so-expressive eyes, "…answer me. Why are you taking so much aspirin?"

Tessa shook her head and muttered something he couldn't quite make out, then said, "Not that it's any of your business, but, um … I've been tired, achy … have killer headaches … ouch, dammit, that hurt." She glared and tried to pull her hand away. "Why are you pulling my skin like that?"

He held on. "Stop fidgeting. I need to make sure I line up the edges properly so the scar that forms isn't all jagged."

"Like my finger is some damn jigsaw puzzle," she grumbled, but stopped fighting his hold.

He quickly and efficiently applied the steri-strips, covered the area with antibiotic cream, and proceeded to wrap the wound with gauze and then a self-sticking wrap.

"There," he placed her hand gently onto the island countertop, "it might not look like much, but it'll do the job."

"It looks fine." She drew back her hand. "Thanks."

"You're welcome." He packed away the first aid supplies and then cleaned off the counter with an antiseptic wipe. "Don't get the bandage wet."

He was highly aware Tessa's gaze followed him in his tasks. He could almost feel her irritation at his "bossiness." He grinned. At least when she was pissed off at him, the sadness was gone from her eyes and replaced by fiery golden glints.

As he walked to the trash can to get rid of the wipe he'd used to clean the island, she stepped in front of him. He managed to stop in time to avoid treading on her feet shod in what looked to be Hello Kitty slippers. The top of her head came to just below his nose. Her hair smelled like flowers and vanilla and made his mouth water. He wondered if she smelled like that all over, and once again the thought of taking her upstairs and stripping her naked zoomed to the forefront of his mind.

Get your head out of your pants, Blackhawk. She's nowhere ready to hop into bed with your ass.

As tall as she was, she still had to angle her head to look him in the eye. "How in the heck am I supposed to clean and chop veggies for my western-style scrambled eggs if I can't get my hand wet?"

"You don't." He swept a finger down her dainty, straight nose and tapped the tip. "I do."

He took in her wide-eyed look of disbelief mingled with a goodly amount of annoyance and barely kept from laughing. His Tessa had a temper. *Good.* He liked women who gave as good as they got. A timid woman wouldn't make it in his world.

"Sweetheart…" his lips quirked as she uttered a kittenish growl, "…back in Michigan, I run a diner and do most of the cooking in the off-season. I've been known to chop more than a few vegetables. You can watch me work. You're so tired you might cut off a finger."

"I'm fine," she huffed. But she clearly wasn't. She had lines of pain around her mouth, dark circles under her beautiful eyes, and the muscles in her neck were taut.

Earl couldn't stand seeing her in pain, so he turned her around and massaged her neck and shoulders. She moaned. "God, that feels good."

Her moan turned into a shriek when Earl let go of her shoulders and picked her up, cuddling her to his chest. He walked the few steps to the island and set her down on a stool.

"Stop touching me and carrying me and … um, just stop it."

"For now." Earl leaned over and touched his forehead

to hers. "But I reserve the right to continue working the kinks out of *all* your tight muscles … later. It'll help you sleep."

"I can't believe…" she sputtered. "I'm not a … a … parcel to be placed somewhere. And I told you to stop all the touching stuff."

"Tessa, you're definitely not a parcel." He shot her a sexy grin. "But I did place you where I wanted you." His voice was husky as he added, "And I like touching you."

Her little snort and fiery-eyed glare made him want to chuckle. Time to change the subject. At least, she wasn't pale-skinned or sad-eyed any longer.

Earl grabbed an apron hanging on a hook by the kitchen door; it had a Navy insignia on it. He grimaced, a knee-jerk reaction since he was Army all the way, but put on what had to be Scotty's apron. "By the way, where's the old salt? Shouldn't Scotty be making breakfast, and you, a guest, be in bed sleeping and not risking your precious fingers in his kitchen?"

"Precious fingers, my ass." Tessa sniffed. "The old salt, as you call him, is hung-over. He looked pretty pathetic when I came down to get some coffee at five-thirty, so I sent him to bed. I have Cordon Bleu training—I don't normally cut my fingers."

The sound of her cute little sniff had his cock stiffening to steely hardness once more, just as he'd thought he had the unruly appendage under control.

All this inflation and deflation of his dick couldn't be good for his health. The situation was totally out of his control. He'd jerked off last night and again this morning, but it hadn't helped. He had a constant hard-on around the little darling. This level of intensity had never happened with any other woman. The only satisfactory solution he could think of was to take Tessa to bed and make love to her, but he couldn't, not yet anyway. So he'd continue to use his hand.

Sooner or later, Tessa would be sure to notice the large bulge he constantly sported around her. He didn't want to scare her off. At least, for now, the apron would cover his predicament.

"Drunk? Scotty looked sober when I turned in." He finished chopping the green pepper she'd been working on and pulled another from the colander of rinsed vegetables. He cored it and then quickly sliced and diced it into pieces.

Tessa hummed approvingly under her breath. He grinned. Good, he'd impressed her with his culinary skills. They shared an interest in cooking, one area of common ground he could use to court her. Their shared friendship with Callie was another such area.

Tessa stood.

"What the hell?" Earl put the knife down and prepared to plant her sweet butt back on the stool. "Sit. Rest. Watch."

"No." She went to the refrigerator and pulled out eggs and milk. "I promised Callie's brothers I'd make them *pannekuchen*. They love my *pannekuchen*."

"German, Swedish or Dutch?" he asked as he turned back to dicing potatoes for hash browns. He'd have to pick his battles with sweet Tessa. Plus, he'd keep an eagle eye on her. At the first sign she might injure herself, her ass would be back on the stool.

A look of pleased surprise crossed her face and lingered in a slight smile on her full lips. "German."

Earl nodded. "Do you separate the eggs and then add the beaten egg whites to the pancake batter right before you put them on the griddle?" That was how Earl's Swedish mother had done it; he knew Germans often did it the same way. He craved the resulting fluffy pancakes, especially with fruit and whipped cream on top.

"Is there any other way?" Tessa smiled at him fully for the first time since he'd met her. A smile that acknowledged they shared a common life experience.

He wanted more smiles like that from her. Smiles just for him. It was all he could do not to walk over, take her into his arms, and put another kind of smile on her face.

Instead, he stayed where he was and replied to her quick quip. "Not in my book, there isn't. But then there are a lot of cooks who are plain ignorant and not savvy like us."

Tessa laughed, a deep-throated, sexy sound that caused his heart to stutter for a split second. He now made it his life's goal to make her laugh a lot in the future. Although he wasn't sure his over-active libido could handle any more Tessa-stimulation.

Earl coughed to clear a boulder-sized lump of desire from his throat. Changing the subject, he said, "So... Scotty got drunk? Does that mean we're doing lunch, too?"

He hoped so. It would be a perfect opportunity to continue to gain her trust and woo her as they shared cooking chores.

"Most likely." Even with a bum finger, she expertly broke and separated the eggs into two bowls. "He was sloshed." She chuckled, a sound he liked almost as much as her laugh. "After you turned in, Scotty joined us to watch the *Rocky Horror Picture Show*. He challenged the Walsh twins to a drinking game to demonstrate the superiority of the regular Navy over the SEALs. They did shots of top-shelf tequila. The twins won, I think—or, at least, they aren't as hung-over since they went out about an hour ago to help clear paths to the main buildings and plow the entrance road. The snow just doesn't seem to want to stop."

Earl glanced at the window in the breakfast nook area and saw white upon white as far as he could see. Looked to be near white-out conditions at the moment. No one would be leaving Idaho anytime in the next day or so. He probably should go out and offer to help dig the facility out, but he was a damn good cook and didn't want Tessa to chop off a finger in her exhaustion.

Plus, he wanted to be with her.

They worked companionably and silently for several minutes. Earl finished off the vegetables and then went to the refrigerator and pulled out two dozen eggs to start a western-style egg scramble for the buffet table. He checked on Tessa from time to time to make sure she wasn't overdoing it.

Somehow, he would convince her to take a nap after breakfast. He and some of the others could do clean up and start lunch.

A clattering sound had Earl looking up from his eggs.

Tessa had dropped her spoon on the granite island. She visibly swayed and then leaned on the counter for a few seconds. Her head bowed as if it was too heavy for her neck to hold up. After a second or so, she straightened and resumed working on her batter.

Earl growled in the back of his throat and viciously rapped an egg against the island countertop. He didn't say anything, nor did he intervene. She wasn't in danger of injury at the moment, and he didn't want to spoil the camaraderie he'd managed to establish. But later, after breakfast, Tessa would rest if he had to tuck her in bed himself.

Tessa turned to look at him; her eyes widened either at the noise he made or maybe it was the way he attacked the eggs. "Um, Callie told me about you."

Earl stopped breaking eggs and returned her look. From the way she chewed her lower lip, he could tell she was nervous about whatever Callie had shared. "She did?"

Tessa heaved out a huge breath and looked anywhere but at him. "Um, she thinks we should date—or something."

God, Callie had not only fed Tessa his background, but the minx had also out-and-out plowed the field and sowed seeds for his pursuit. He didn't know whether to applaud or curse Risto's new wife.

"And what do you think?" He kept his tone neutral and his voice low and soft so as not to frighten her with the strength of his interest.

When she didn't say anything and refused to look at him, he wiped his hands on a towel and approached her.

Tessa's head shot up, and she took a step away. Her retreat was blocked by the island at her back. She cast her gaze down and worried her lower lip with her teeth until it was rosy red.

"Tessa, look at me."

She shook her head.

Sighing, he tipped her face up to his with a gentle finger and groaned when he saw tears in her eyes. His heart hurt. "Sweetheart, what's wrong? Am I that scary? Is the idea of dating me, getting to know me, that frightening? I'd never hurt you. I'll protect you with my life."

"Oh, no … it's not you. I really like you. A lot." She sniffled. "It's me. I'm not l-l-like Callie. I … I'm not a … good person." She reached for and squeezed his arm. "You're a hero. A good man. A man of law and order…" she trailed off and shrugged. "You deserve someone better."

"Bullshit." Earl moved into her body, forcing her to let go of his arm. She braced her hands on his chest and looked at him in shock.

His arms around her, he held her trembling body close to his. He took several deep breaths in an attempt to calm down. Not good enough for him? That was crap. She was so far above him, well … he could barely manage to hold back the full force of his anger at hearing her disparage herself in such a way. He'd like to meet the person who'd put those thoughts into her head; it was obvious she believed them.

He forced his voice into an even, soothing tone. "Tessa, you're everything that's good and precious in this world. Callie told me a little about you also." Tessa whimpered and shook her head. "Shh, hush, it's okay." He rubbed her back. "The past is just that … past."

"No, it isn't," she choked out. Tears streaked down her face.

Earl held her firmly with one arm and captured the glistening drops with his thumb.

Ahh, so whatever is bothering her originated in her past.

It had to have happened before Evan found her, during her abusive home life as Callie had called it. Tessa had never had any scandals attributed to her during her modeling career that he could recall. She'd become almost a hermit since she'd begun writing superb, best-selling thrillers as T.A. Parks.

Whatever the problem was, he'd take care of it. But first, he had to convince Tessa there was nothing that would ever put him off pursuing a relationship with her.

"The past *is* past," he kissed her forehead, "and it will remain the past if I have anything to do with it."

"What *exactly* did Callie tell you?" Tessa sniffed and rested her forehead on his chest.

"That you'd overcome an abusive childhood." She stiffened. "That Evan and Chad found you living on the streets of Chicago. That they took you to Callie and you became a loving sister to her and her brothers."

He stroked his hand up her back and kneaded the tight neck muscles at the top of her spine. The thick fall of her ponytail caressed the back of his hand like a silken veil. "I know all about your charitable work in third world countries. I also know you provided human intelligence to the CIA as an open source intelligence agent during some of your modeling assignments. The information you gathered, Callie said, saved a lot of civilians and US military personnel."

He smoothed his hand down her spine, from her

nape to the curve above her butt, soothing her as it also soothed him. "You used your travels for modeling assignments and your work for the CIA to plot your books, didn't you?" He wondered if something bad had happened when she'd collected information for the government. Was it coming back to haunt her now?

She nodded, the movement so slight he would've missed it if he hadn't been so in tune with her every move and breath. He pressed a light kiss over the top of her silky, dark hair.

"Your books are so realistic. I see myself in them. I've been in many of the places you write about. Been in many of the same situations." He tipped her head back and looked into her golden-brown eyes still awash with tears. "You're talented, loving … and beautiful, inside and out. You're a survivor. All of those things are good and outweigh anything that happened in the past."

Rescuing Tessa, is what Callie had told him. Evan and Chad had *rescued* Tessa. Evan and his partner were heroes in his book and had gained his undying gratitude and respect.

"You don't understand." Tessa shook her head and then lowered her face into his chest once more. Her tears soaked through Scotty's apron and the thermal turtleneck underneath.

Whatever had happened in her past—and whoever had resurrected it, because he'd bet everything he owned that was what was in the text messages that scared her so much—had to be bad.

Worse than an abusive home, worse than living on the streets, and those two things were bad enough. Maybe even worse than something she had seen or done for the CIA.

No matter what Tessa thought, Earl had to make one thing clear. "When I met Callie for the first time, I asked her if she had a sister. She told me no. So I asked her to find me someone just like her." He paused. "She introduced me to you."

Tessa stiffened against him and all but stopped breathing.

"Breathe, sweetheart."

Her breath hitched and the tears resumed soaking his clothing. He brushed kisses over her ear and down her elegantly long neck. He wanted to kill whoever had convinced Tessa she wasn't worthy, who'd put fear and shame in her eyes.

"Tessa, I want you in my life. Trust me to help you, protect you."

Tessa shuddered and leaned into the big, warm, strong body of a man far too good for her. She was tempted to tell him everything, let him take the burden, but she was afraid of what she'd see on his face if she told him all.

Callie couldn't tell him everything, because her friend

didn't know everything about Tessa's past. Evan and Chad had promised never to tell Callie or her twin brothers the whole truth as they knew it, and even they didn't know it all. The two men and the police had helped her obtain a new name, US citizenship, a new life. A life she loved, which was now being threatened.

The real story was far worse than an abusive home life.

From the age of thirteen through eighteen, Tessa's life had been hell on earth. When she'd managed to escape the Branhams, the couple who'd "adopted" her from a Shanghai orphanage, fate or pure dumb luck had Evan and Chad finding her before her captors could.

After two weeks in a hospital and a lot of reassurances from Evan, Chad, and a psychologist that she was safe, Tessa told her story to the police and took them to where she and other girls like her had been kept prisoner, slaves in an exclusive club for sexual predators.

But it had been too late.

Her former captors were dead. All the business records and the other girls, and some young boys, were gone.

Tessa had experienced tremendous guilt for not helping the police sooner. But eventually, with her new life in the Meyers' household, she'd found happiness, joy, ways to make a difference in the world, and a modicum of forgetfulness about that time in her life.

But Earl was wrong. Evan, Chad, the police, and her therapist were all wrong, too.

The past wasn't past—it had merely been sleeping, lying in wait until it could return and torment her, destroy her happiness and hard-won peace of mind.

Almost two weeks ago, she'd begun receiving strange and menacing text messages and e-mails. At first, she thought her cyberstalker was merely another crazed T. A. Parks fan; her publisher dealt with a lot of those as had she. The sender had raged about her most recent release.

But quickly the text messages and e-mails veered away from the book and became more personal, more specific, more explicit ... more threatening.

And, then, just before she'd left for Idaho, she'd begun to get e-mails with image and video attachments. Images and videos she'd never known about from a time she had hoped never to think of again.

Images of her ... naked ... bound ... men ... raping her ... hurting her—

Stop it, Tessa.

She fought the images bombarding her mind and forced them back into a dark corner of her brain. She couldn't lose control in front of Earl. He'd want to know what was wrong, and in a weak moment, she might tell him. She had to keep that part of her life hidden away from decent people.

Breathe.

Tessa took several deep breaths.

It was hard to regain control. Her heart pounded and adrenaline flooded her bloodstream. The images violently dragged her past to the forefront of her mind and reminded her of what she'd been—a sex toy, a receptacle, a less-than-human object.

Get control, Tessa. Breathe.

Sick, disgusted, and afraid some of the men who'd used her had resurrected the perverted private club, she'd reported her cyberstalker to the Chicago Police Department, and they called in the FBI. If she could prevent it, no other innocent girls would have to go through what she had. If the e-mails and messages she'd received could help the police stop evil from resurrecting in Chicago, then maybe she could let her past go once and for all.

If Earl saw those pictures, he'd see how filthy and tainted she was. She couldn't even stand to look at herself in the mirror since she'd received the perverted images. She found herself experiencing the same self-hatred she'd felt immediately after her rescue, and if truth be told, for several years afterward. Only intensive therapy and Callie's family, Evan, and Chad had helped her deal.

"Tessa? Come back to me." Earl rubbed her back. "Why are you so scared? Tell me what you're thinking."

Earl's voice was so deep, so soothing. She wanted to fall into it and never surface. If she'd been another person, had had even half a normal life, she'd jump at the chance for a life with him. She'd dreamed of a man like Earl for years, someone to hold her when she was scared, make her laugh, love her, give her babies.

Tessa's womb ached for a child. She wanted to be a wife, a mother, a lover, but it would never happen. No good man could overlook her past.

"Tessa?" Earl whispered against her ear.

"What?" She shuddered as his warm breath ignited a frisson of awareness in her pussy. He was the only man she'd ever met who made her pussy ache and her clit throb, and she couldn't let herself care for him, couldn't let him care for her.

"Whatever's bothering you, we'll handle it … look at me." When she shook her head, he tipped her chin up until she met his gorgeous, dark-brown eyes. "Ah, sweetheart, you're tired. I suspect the altitude is adding to your exhaustion and aches and pains. I'll help with your pancakes. After breakfast, you can take a nap. How does that sound?"

"You aren't going to let this go, are you?" She wanted confirmation she'd read him correctly—he was an alpha-dominant, over-protective, stubborn-as-a-mule male just like Risto Smith, the Maddox men, and all the Walsh men.

"Nope." He brushed kisses over her cheeks, taking away the few tears that still leaked from her eyes. "You like basketball?"

She tilted her head and blinked at the change in subject. Suspicious, she cautiously answered, "Uh, yeah. Why?"

"This Friday. I'll take you to the Bulls game." He grinned. "You can't turn down a Bulls game, now can you?"

Yeah, she could and would—once she got back to Chicago. She could never see Earl again, because once he got his foot in the door, she'd never get rid of him. And then he'd find out what she'd been, what she'd done to survive in a hell hole for five years. She couldn't allow that to happen, allow his look of attraction and liking change to disgust. It would kill her.

He frowned at her silence. But before he could call her on it, a sound at the kitchen doorway had her turning within the circle of Earl's arms. Jim and John Meyers stood there with big grins on their faces as they observed her and Earl.

Jim, the older twin by two minutes, laughed. "Doesn't look like you're making our *pannekuchen*, Tessie." He turned his bright gaze toward Earl. "Hey, man, you're interfering with greatness. You haven't lived until you've had Tessie's German pancakes."

Earl chuckled and released her, but not before he smoothed a hand over her rear end. A full-body shudder swept over her and then became concentrated as a pulsing ache just south of her belly button. The shock of the intensity of her reaction to what was only a slight touch had her heart racing with fear, or excitement, or maybe a bit of both.

Earl Blackhawk was a dangerous man, a man who played to win.

"Never let it be said I stood in the way of greatness in the culinary arts." He leaned over and whispered against her ear, "Make the boys their pancakes, baby. This conversation isn't over and will resume once you've had a nap and are at your fighting weight. Something's bothering you. You tell me, and I'll fix it."

She stepped away and wrinkled her nose. "I don't need you fixing anything for me. I'm fine."

"Little liar." He patted her bottom, and she had to bite her lip not to moan. "Go cook."

She glared at him.

He grinned and winked. The insufferable man knew exactly how much he affected her. God, if only she were normal. No, she couldn't think that way. If he knew all, well, he sure wouldn't hold her, kiss her, and lovingly pet her rear end.

Her resolve shored up once more, Tessa turned back to her pancake batter and began to fold the egg whites into the main mixture. She eyed the twins who stood on the opposite side of the island and the griddle cook top. They wore identical concerned looks.

She forced a smile on her lips and asked, "How many cakes, my little men?"

John grimaced. "Ahh, Tessie, we aren't little anymore."

"Baby boy, to me, you'll always be my little men. Now, cakes—how many?"

John looked at Jim, and Jim looked at John, and then the boys both looked at Earl who she sensed was right behind her, ready to step in if anything upset her further.

Yes, definitely a good man. Too bad she wasn't the right woman for him, no matter what Callie, or he, thought.

She turned and confronted the man who was far too close to her for her peace of mind. "Um, eggs? Bacon? Hash browns? Chop chop." She shooed him away.

Earl's serious expression disappeared as if it had never existed and his mouth broke into a heart-stopping smile. "Yes, ma'am." He saluted her smartly and turned back to assembling the main parts of breakfast.

It wouldn't be as easy to shoo Earl out of her life. The man had a mission—her. Her job was to convince him she was a waste of his time. In her mission. She. Would. Not. Fail.

CHAPTER 2

9:15 a.m.

Breakfast was over, and Tessa had just started the stock for the chicken risotto she'd planned for supper. Two soups for lunch were simmering on the stove and only would need a stirring now and then; the stock, some skimming.

Two large hands came around her waist. She inhaled sharply and barely managed to hold back a shriek. Her heart pounded. For a nanosecond she was thrown back into a distant past. Cruel hands. Pain.

Come back, Tessa.

She shook off the memories and took one calming breath, then another. These hands were gentle hands. There was no pain. Then she knew whose hands held her—

Earl!

Tessa hadn't heard him approach. Why she hadn't was a puzzle. Ever since the lessons she'd learned during her teen years, she'd always—always—been hyperaware of her surroundings, especially where men were concerned. Why in the hell hadn't she sensed Earl's approach?

There's a reason for that, Tessa. This is the man for you. Your body and mind recognize he's not a danger.

Oh, shut up. While the little voice in her head had been a savior many times, sometimes it was just a pain-in-her-butt, smart ass, know-it-all.

When I'm right, I'm right.

Shut up.

Tessa wiggled, but Earl's hands didn't budge. She heaved a sigh. "Earl, let me go."

"How did you know it was me?" The words whispered over her ear.

Tessa made another attempt to break away, but something in her liked his touch and her attempt was laughingly feeble.

Earl tightened his grip on her waist. "Don't move." He nuzzled her ponytail aside and pressed a light tease of a kiss on her nape exposed by the thermal T-shirt.

Goose bumps broke out over her entire body. She clenched her jaw to keep from moaning. His warm, firm lips felt so good against the very sensitive skin of her neck.

Um, how *had* she known it was Earl?

It had been his scent, all male musk and something citrus with a hint of spice. His aura. His magnetism. Only to herself could she admit she'd been highly attracted and attuned to Risto's hunky friend since she'd met him upon her arrival at Sanctuary. His large, muscular body had drawn her eye each and every time he entered a room. His thick, dark hair and dark eyes, his starkly masculine face, were attractive and all indicative of his mixed heritage of Native American and Scandinavian. The whole package appealed to her.

But she'd bite her tongue off before admitting any of that to him or anyone else.

What had Callie been thinking? She hadn't needed a maid of honor and a best man. This had been a setup from the beginning.

You know. Callie wants you to have a real man for a change.

Shut up. Just shut up.

Feeling Earl's stare on the back of her neck, she finally answered, "I knew because you're the only man here who has the audacity to grab me from behind." She shrugged and pulled away from another light touch of his lips on her sensitive neck.

He released her, but didn't move away. His warm scent enveloped her; it was delicious and made her mouth water. No, she wouldn't think about kissing his firm, sensuous lips to check if he tasted as good as he smelled.

Tessa turned within the small space between the counter and his body. "Um, could you give me some space, please?"

She stared at his chest, his very broad chest. If she looked into his eyes, she knew she'd find desire. She'd seen the hunger in his dark-eyed gaze each and every time she caught him looking at her. God knew, she couldn't afford to fall into those heated depths. Couldn't let him see too deeply into the heart of her. First, because he would see she was attracted in return, and second, because he would see the *real* her. It would hurt to see his warm gaze turn cold with revulsion when he realized Tessa was a complete fraud.

"Did you eat?" Earl asked. "And why aren't you upstairs napping?" He stroked a hand down her ponytail and gave it a gentle tug.

"I'm a big girl," she informed him in a snippy manner, "and I don't take orders from you."

Earl frowned at her response and tipped her chin up. His touch was firm, but also gentle. "Dammit, Tessa. You're paler than you were before breakfast." He took her shoulders and turned her toward the breakfast nook. "And since you don't seem to have any common sense as it pertains to your health, someone needs to take control. And, right now, sweetheart, that someone is me." He gently nudged her. "Go sit with Keely and the baby. I'll bring you some of my special oatmeal and an orange juice."

"Earl…" Her protest was cut off by a light swat on her rear. "Oww." She rubbed her bottom and angled her head to shoot him a glare. "That hurt."

"No, it didn't."

No, it hadn't. He was always careful when he touched her. But she had to make the point he couldn't go touching or kissing her whenever he liked.

Fess up. You like him touching you. Think of what his hands would feel like on your naked butt? On your breasts?

Shut up.

Earl eyed her up and down, his dark eyes glittering with emotions she was hesitant to put a name to. "It'll hurt worse if I put you over my knee and spank the stubbornness out of you." He nudged her once more toward a grinning Keely who was a highly entertained audience as she breastfed Riley. "Go sit, Tessa. Please. You're swaying on your feet."

Earl was correct; she was. And, she hated to admit it, but he was also correct in his earlier conjecture that she had altitude sickness on top of the exhaustion from a lack of sleep due to the stress of being cyberstalked.

"Hey, Tessa." Keely smiled as she cuddled her son, who fed hungrily from a breast. "Earl giving you a hard time?"

"Callie thinks we should date," Tessa blurted out as she sat across from Keely. "I'm not sure it would work. The man…" she shot a glare at his broad back, "… is bossy. Thinks he has rights over me just because my friend is trying to fix us up."

Keely laughed and said in a low tone that carried no farther than the breakfast nook. "You like him, huh?"

Tessa grimaced and replied in the same low tone, "Is it that obvious?" The petite blonde nodded, a broad grin on her face. "What gave me away?"

"Well, it could be that whenever he comes into the room, you stop what you're doing and stare at him hungrily."

Tessa moaned silently.

Keely continued, "Or, it could be that when he touched and kissed you just now, you leaned into him, instead of slapping him across the face. Or, it could be that you keep seeking him out as we're sitting here."

Damn, busted.

"So…" Keely's grin vanished, "…why won't it work?" As Tessa opened her mouth to tell the woman all the reasons why it wouldn't work, Keely waved a hand, stopping her. "Uh unh, don't lie to me. I've known you ever since you went to live with Callie—something's wrong. Is it about those frick-fracking e-mails you told Callie about?"

"What?" Tessa whispered, icy horror settling in her gut. Callie had ratted her out?

"Yes, she told me. She's worried about you and knew you wouldn't have mentioned them unless they really bothered you." Keely pinned her with a steely gaze. "I know Callie isn't available, but can I help? Or can the guys help? You've got trouble, SSI is here for you."

Even with the Chicago Police Department and the FBI on the case, it was so tempting to pass the problem to the SSI team. But there was no way she could show the recent e-mails to the SSI men, because Ren would show them to Earl.

Images of hooded men as they forced her to have sex … as they whipped her bloody … as they tortured her … made her less than even a whore. The images that showed her degradation.

Red, white, and yellow dots, then blackness encroached on her vision; she gripped the edge of the table so tightly her knuckles whitened, her fingers cramped in pain.

Breathe, Tessa.

In. Out. In. Out.

No, she couldn't show people she cared about those texts and e-mails. So, Tessa would have to rely on traditional law enforcement to find her stalker and stop him. Though they hadn't found him yet, which scared her.

"Keely, I can't…" She shook her head, her ponytail whipping wildly from side to side.

"Easy now. You're safe here." Keely nodded in Earl's direction as he stirred something on the stove. "Earl would be a good man to have at your back. He's Special Forces. Ren had a couple of black ops missions with him in the 'Stan and tried to recruit him for SSI."

Her temporary weakness had been unacceptable. Under control once more, Tessa turned more fully toward Keely, who now burped little Riley over her shoulder. The little burp, when it came, turned Tessa's insides to mush.

Prior to this visit to Idaho, she'd never thought so much about being a mother, but with Callie happily pregnant, despite the morning sickness, and seeing Keely with her six-month-old son—God, Earl Blackhawk and his pheromones were lethal.

Somehow his scent, his extreme alpha-ness, or whatever, had jump-started her maternal instincts. She now thought breast-feeding and burping were sweet and something she might want to do. She'd never had such feelings before, had no experience with babies.

Before she could halt the words, she said, "Tell me about Earl." She leaned toward Keely and kept her voice low so the man in question wouldn't hear. "Callie told me he lives in U.P. Michigan and is the mayor of Osprey's Point in the Cisco Chain of Lakes. And that he'd been an Army Ranger."

Keely snorted. "Well, that was the Cliff's Notes version. Guess Callie knew you didn't need much more than that to be attracted to the man. The electricity between you two could power the furnace for the Lodge. Hell, even my dense-as-a-brick husband could see it."

"Keely … talk … before he comes over here. Tell me about him, please?"

A crease appeared on Keely's forehead. "Hmm, where to start?"

At a low growl from Tessa, Keely grinned. "Okay, here's what I know, all of it is second-hand. Earl owns most of Osprey's Point. He's not only the mayor, but also the Chief of Police, head of the volunteer fire department, and is EMT-trained. He runs the marina, the year-round grocery store slash diner, and has a fabulous cliff-side home, designed by Risto's famous architect grandfather, overlooking Thousand Islands Lake. And, yes, he was an Army Ranger, but he was in Special Forces. SF are a whole nother animal. Most of what he and men like my husband did was classified."

The little blonde touched Tessa's hand and patted it. "But most of all, Earl is a good, decent man, and he really, really likes you … a lot."

"Well, shit." Tessa shook her head. "I knew he was out of my league, but this just underlines it."

Keely snuggled a sleeping Riley against her chest and aimed a narrow-eyed glance at Tessa. "What do you mean he's out of your league?"

"I can't tell you. I can't tell anyone." She shook her head. "Not even Callie knows the whole story, and Chad and Evan only know a part. I can't … just can't." She had to shut up. She couldn't tell anyone. Reporting the last bunch of e-mails to the police and the FBI had been hard enough.

Why the fuck not, Tessa Andrews? You're the wronged one.

Shut up. She fisted her hands on her lap, her nails digging into her palms.

They aren't going to blame you because you were powerless. Afraid. Alone in a strange land.

Shut up. Shut up. Her stomach roiled as the images forced themselves to the forefront of her brain yet again. Damn it, she was stronger than this. She'd beaten back the memories for years.

Let someone else share the burden. Isn't that what our therapist says?

Shut up, shut up, shut up.

You can't continue to keep this inside, or you'll never get on with your life. You want a baby. Earl would be a great dad.

She shoved away from the table, ready to flee. *Please just shut the hell up!* She screamed mentally, over and over, until the voice in her head went away.

God, was she going crazy?

"What did you do to her, Keely?" Earl's growled words came from over her shoulder. He set a steaming bowl of steel-cut oatmeal topped with brown sugar and raisins in front of her. He placed a large, warm, and oh-so-comforting hand on her shoulder, holding her in her seat. "Tessa, what's wrong?"

Before Keely could defend herself—and the little

spitfire would—Tessa turned and stared at Earl's angry face. Time to deflect. "You made me oatmeal from scratch? Ohmygod, are you for real?" She took the spoon stuck in the heavenly smelling concoction and took a bite. "God, this is so good."

Her words partially erased the glower from Earl's face. "I always make oatmeal that way. Callie likes it, too. I fed it to her at my diner."

"You can fricking cook," she muttered around a bite of oatmeal. "Unbelievable."

So out of my league.

"Yes, I can cook. I showed you earlier." He leaned over her shoulder until his bristly cheek rubbed hers. "Now, what did Keely say that upset you so much?"

The man had a mind like a steel trap. He wasn't easily deflected. She was in so-o-o much trouble.

Tessa wouldn't turn to glare at him. He was so close her lips would brush his and then she'd be in deep trouble. She bet he tasted as good as he looked and smelled.

"Um, she told me you're rich and the grand poobah of Osprey's Point." She took another bite of oatmeal and followed it with a gulp of the orange juice she hadn't even seen him place on the table. "I'm sure the women of northern Michigan have worn a path to your door."

Earl chuckled, his warm breath feathering across her cheek. The intriguing sound was a mixture of amusement and smugness. "Jealous?"

"No. Hell no." She put her spoon down carefully, leaned away from him, and then turned to look more fully into his glittering dark eyes. His nostrils flared as if he'd taken in her scent. His pupils dilated with what she knew beyond a shadow of a doubt was sexual desire. *Damn, damn, damn.* "You can fuck every woman in the Northern Hemisphere for all I care."

Liar, liar, pants on fire.

Yep, she was lying like a kid in a candy store with gummy breath and a pocket full of purloined candies. God, when had this happened? She was jealous and possessive of a man she'd only known since Saturday morning—less than three days.

Earl snorted and then leaned down to lick the corner of her mouth.

When she gasped and pulled away, he grinned. "Some brown sugar and oatmeal. Tastes good—especially off your lips."

Keely chuckled softly, her son sleeping soundly against her. "It's so much fun to watch you two dance around one another." She stroked her son's back. "It happened that fast with Ren and me, and from what I heard, with Callie and Risto. Face it, Tessa, you're attracted ... he's attracted. Might as well give in and enjoy the ride." She looked down at her son and smiled. "The end results are well worth the bumps along the way."

"Keely makes a valid point." At Tessa's disdainful

sniff, Earl chuckled and swept a hand down her ponytail and rubbed her upper back. "Don't worry about it now. Finish your food. I have the Walsh and Meyers twins signed up for kitchen duty. We can handle stirring soups, skimming stock, and getting the lunch service up and running. You go take a nap until I call you for lunch."

"Jesus Christ on a crutch! Would you stop telling me what to do?" Tessa took another bite of the oatmeal before she realized she'd done what he told her. She glared at Keely when the woman choked back a laugh. "You aren't helping, sista. We women need to stick together against the league of bossy men."

Keely shrugged, her eyes filled with laughter. "I like bossy men. I married one, grew up in a household filled with them. They take good care of me, and I still do what I want. It's fun to see how far I can push Ren and my brothers."

Earl choked. "Yeah, I heard some stories from Ren. Having a baby in a cave while being chased by mercenaries is pushing the envelope a bit too far."

"A cave?" Tessa shot the calmly smiling Keely a look of disbelief and awe.

Keely nodded. "Babies come when they come." She kissed Riley's head. "Plus, a doctor was present."

"O-o-kay." Tessa shuddered, shoved the suddenly empty bowl to the side, and then looked for something to do that would keep her at the table and in the kitchen.

She refused to get up and go to her room, didn't want to look as if she were following Mr. Bossy Pants' orders. "May I hold Riley? I haven't had much of a chance. That is, if it's okay?"

"Works for me." Keely patted the bench seat built into the nook. "Come sit here, and I'll hand him off."

Earl growled under his breath, "You are so taking a nap sooner or later, Tessa. Even if I have to put you to bed myself."

"Shut up, Earl." She shoved her chair back, just missing his legs. Then she went around the table and scooted onto the bench seat. "Will this wake the baby up?"

"No, Riley could sleep through Armageddon." Keely transferred the baby to Tessa.

God, Riley was a warm, little bundle, smelling uniquely of baby. Tessa cuddled him against her breasts. The ache in her heart and lower abdomen began again. She could almost feel her ripe eggs clamoring for fertile sperm.

But she couldn't even think of bringing a baby into her world, not with the way her life was now. She had to figure out how to deal with the past which had come back to plague her. She couldn't allow such evil to touch something so innocent.

Had she ever been this innocent?

Yes, before—them.

But even before the Branhams, her life had not been roses and happy childhood memories. Life in a Shanghai orphanage was far from idyllic, but at least she hadn't been abused.

Earl hadn't moved from his spot by the table. His dark gaze was fixed on her and the baby; his lips were curved in a warm, almost loving, smile.

"Go away, Earl." Tessa rubbed her cheek over Riley's head and rocked him. "I'll take a nap later." She looked at Keely. "Go take some time for yourself. Bet Ren would like some quality Keely time."

"Thanks, Tessa—you're sure?" Keely stood, staring down at her, her forehead creased and concern in her eyes.

"Yeah. Just leave the diaper bag. I'm betting the little guy will need a change before long. I watched you change him several times over the weekend. It's not rocket science. I'll deal."

"Thanks!" Keely headed for the hall, which led to the elevators that went to what the SSI men called the Bat Cave.

"You can go skim the chicken stock and stir the soups, Earl." She smiled sweetly and batted her lashes. "Since you said you would take care of those chores for me."

Earl chuckled and shook his head. "Sweetheart, you're asking for it." He leaned over, and because of his height, his nose practically touched hers across the rectangular farm table. "And I'm just the man to give it to you." He reached for and then caressed her jaw. "You look good holding the little guy. A natural."

Tessa's insides turned to mush. Yep, some strong pheromones the man had.

Earl swept a hand over Riley's head as it lay against Tessa's breast. His fingers lingered over the upper curve of her breast for a split second before he straightened and then walked back to the stove. His movements reminded her of a giant, predatory cat. Not an image she needed right now.

She closed her eyes and leaned back against the comfortable cushioned bench seat. The warmth and smells of the kitchen and the sweet powdery scent of the baby lying safely in her arms lulled her into a half-awake, half-asleep state in which she dreamed of what might have been if she hadn't been stolen by evil.

9:45 a.m.

EARL PREPPED A SALAD FOR lunch to go with the soup and chili Tessa had started. He'd been furious with her when he'd come into the kitchen and found her still on her feet and working when she needed to be horizontal in a bed.

Tessa had barely been able to stand without swaying. Plus, she hadn't even eaten. Yeah, the little darling needed a keeper.

So, he fed her. He liked feeding her. The oatmeal and juice had helped to bring some color back to her face. She'd been ashy under her beautiful, exotic skin tones. She was a perfect mix of Asian and European genetics and appealed to him in every way, even her mule-headedness.

It would take a stubborn woman to stand up to him on a day-to-day basis.

Earl chanced a glance at the nook area and smiled. She was asleep. She'd snuggled into the corner of the seating area and had Riley securely in her arms, lying against her full breasts. Breasts made for nursing babies, breasts made for his mouth—not necessarily in that order.

Hell yeah, he could see a dark-haired son with exotic skin tones cuddled against Tessa's naked chest. Before that dream could happen, though, he needed to convince her she was meant to be his. But she was skittish with whatever in the hell was bothering her. He might be ready, but she wasn't.

"Tessa's asleep." Tweeter, Keely's youngest and favorite brother, spoke from the entry to the kitchen. He sniffed the air and grimaced. "I think my nephew needs a diaper change, and Tessa needs a bed. What are we gonna do about that?"

"You can take diaper duty." Earl turned down the soups to the lowest setting and took the stock pot off the stove to let it cool a bit before he skimmed it once more and put it in the professional-sized refrigerator. They wouldn't use all the stock for the risotto Tessa had planned, and he could make a chicken noodle soup for tomorrow's lunch. Weather report had no one leaving Sanctuary until at least late Wednesday evening. "I'll tuck Tessa into bed. And steal her laptop so if she wakes up she won't be tempted to work instead of getting some rest."

Tweeter snickered. "You'll be in big trouble. No one touches Tessa's laptop."

"She'll deal." Earl took off the apron and laid it on the island. He walked quietly to the table. Tweeter followed. "I'll hand off the little guy to you, okay?"

"Gotcha." Tweeter pulled the table out so Earl could get to the two who slept the deep sleep of innocents.

Though, Tessa slept with a slight frown on her forehead and lips. What in the hell was bothering her? He really hoped it was a man, so he could punch someone's lights out. If it were something to do with her books—he wasn't sure what he could do to fix things, but he would damn well at least be a sounding board. Help her talk things through.

He gently tugged Riley away from Tessa. The baby's blue eyes had popped open upon hearing his Uncle

Tweeter's voice. The little guy smiled and gurgled at Earl. Once Earl had the little guy in his arms, Riley patted Earl's scruffy jaw, and his tiny body wiggled with joy.

God, he wanted a son, or a daughter, but only if Tessa were the mother. Yeah, Cupid Callie had filled his hide with arrows, but instincts as old as time had him yearning for a child of his own.

"Here, take the stinky little guy." He handed Riley to Tweeter, who expertly cuddled his nephew. Earl snagged the diaper bag from the bench seat and put it over Tweeter's shoulder. "You good?"

"Got it. Now put Tessa to bed. I don't think she's slept since she arrived. Too much excitement … and something's bothering her. She's been quieter than normal." Tweeter turned to go, then paused and looked over the shoulder the bag hung on. "This might be out of line, but bring her laptop back here. Keely told me Tessa had mentioned to Callie she'd been getting some e-mails that bothered her. Keely offered SSI's help, but Tessa ignored her and changed the topic. My sis backed off, but came to the Bat Cave and asked me to get Tessa to accept my help. Want to see what's going on?"

Earl grunted. "Fuck yeah. Her phone's on the island. Check it out too. She's been getting a lot of text messages and calls that are upsetting her. I'll take the flack if Tessa gets pissed." He looked at her, still leaning against the bench seat, sound asleep. She was so tired she hadn't even roused when he'd picked up the baby. "What if she erased the e-mails? The text messages?"

Tweeter looked somewhat insulted. "Damn, Earl, dontcha know? Nothing's ever *gone* gone, especially for someone like me or Keely. If there's someone cyberstalking Tessa, I'll find evidence of it."

"Don't need to know. Got you to do the geek work. I'll meet you back here as soon as I get sleeping beauty put to bed."

Earl leaned over and easily picked up Tessa. She was lighter than many of the packs he used to carry in the Army, but what weight she did have was in all the right places. She muttered something, but snuggled into him and sighed without waking up.

He carried her out of the kitchen and took the back stairs to the second level. Her room was two doors away from his. He nudged her door farther open with his foot.

Once in the room, he carried her to the bed. The bed was undisturbed. Just as he'd thought, she'd never gone to bed last night. He glanced at the desk in the room and found the task light on and her laptop open.

"Little fool," he muttered against her sweet-smelling hair. "What are you trying to do? Work yourself to death?"

Holding her, he bent and hooked the quilt in his fingers, dragged back the comforter, and placed her on the sheets. He removed her slippers and pulled the cover over her.

Tessa immediately turned onto her side and curled into a fetal position. Her ponytail tempted him, and he gently removed the torture device holding her hair up and stroked his fingers through the long, silky tresses. She moaned low in her throat, but didn't wake. He wondered if she moaned the same way when a man stroked her during foreplay.

The thought of another man making love to her, making her utter sexy little sounds, had him snarling. No other man would ever touch her again if he had anything to say about it.

Earl stopped stroking his fingers through her hair. He moved away and stood for several seconds, staring at her as she slept and fighting the urge to strip to his skin and crawl in next to her. He forced himself to turn his back on the temptation Tessa presented and stalked to the desk. He unplugged the laptop. It now ran on battery, but in sleep mode. He took the cord with him in case they needed it.

He'd let Tweeter do his magic. Earl, while not cyber-savvy, did recognize people like Tweeter, Keely, and Callie could do amazing things. If some fucker was stalking and terrorizing Tessa over the Internet or the phone, the bastard was as good as caught and in jail—after Earl paid a visit to the asshole first, of course.

CHAPTER 3

10:00 a.m.

Leaving Tessa sound asleep, Earl left the room and shut her door. Retracing his steps, he entered the kitchen to find Tweeter waiting on him, along with Evan and his lover, Chad. Evan looked better than he had last night when he'd retreated to his room with symptoms of altitude sickness. Chad looked tired and hungry. Must have been a rough night for both of the men.

"Hey, Evan. Chad. Do you want something to eat? Lunch won't be served for another two hours or so. I can make oatmeal, homemade, not instant. Or maybe toast and tea?" Earl placed Tessa's computer and its cord in front of Tweeter, who already had Tessa's phone in front of him. "Here, do your thing."

Evan frowned at the sight of the laptop, while Chad

answered Earl's questions. "We'll take the oatmeal and some juice. Evan also could use some more acetaminophen. We ran out."

"That's Tessa's laptop and cell." Evan looked at Earl and then Tweeter, accusation in his voice and gaze. "Why do you have her laptop, and where's my girl?"

Logical questions, but Tessa was now Earl's. Probably not the time to make that claim, though. He needed her to accept the new reality first.

"Tessa told Callie, who told Keely, she's having some trouble with a cyberstalker," Earl explained as he put water on to boil and pulled out the steel-cut oats to make the oatmeal. "Tessa's upstairs sleeping. She's exhausted. Since I'm darn sure it isn't a book deadline keeping her awake, Tweeter and I are going to see how bad the cyberstalking is and do something about it. You got a problem with that?"

Earl turned and glared at the couple, daring them to challenge him. He was surprised to see twin smiles of delight and what he read as relief on their handsome faces. He grunted with satisfaction and added the oats to the boiling water.

"Thank the Lord!" Evan looked to the ceiling. "Finally, a man who cares enough to take care of Tessa and not use her as arm candy or for sex or for her money and fame."

"Amen," Chad chimed in.

Tweeter said nothing. In fact the atmosphere in the large kitchen had gotten, for lack of a better word, ominous as the computer expert's face grew darker and darker. Keely's normally good-natured brother looked furious enough to kill.

"Tweeter? Talk to me, man." Earl divided his attention between cooking oats and the men at the breakfast nook. After several seconds without a response, he snarled, "Tweeter, what the fuck is wrong?"

Evan had scooted closer to the laptop to look at the screen. His face turned white and then flamed red. "Goddammit to hell and back! I thought this part of her life was over." The man responsible for Tessa being who and what she was today turned to Chad. "Look, love. Look at what they did to our baby girl."

Chad leaned across and instantly went ashen. He looked at Evan and Tweeter and then looked toward Earl. "God, we knew it had been bad. We went to the counseling sessions with her. Tessa had nightmares for years. But this? Hell, she kept *this* inside? I'll kill the bastard." He struck the table with his fist.

What the fuck?

Earl turned off the oatmeal and made it to the table in less than a second. "Show me."

Tweeter looked up and shook his head. "It's bad. God, it's bad." He turned to Evan, "Why didn't Callie tell us? We've known Tessa for years."

Evan shook his head. "Tessa didn't tell Callie or the twins. Didn't want them to know what had happened to her, where she'd come from. So we made up the story about abusive parents and running away from home. God, it was so much worse." He waved a hand at the laptop. "It's obvious she didn't share it all with us or the therapist, either."

As Tweeter scrolled through the images and played portions of the videos, Earl's breath stilled and his heart pounded as adrenaline flooded his system.

The pictures and videos were of a younger Tessa. Bound. Naked. Bloodied. Screaming. The images grew worse as she grew older in the horror montage. Gang rape. Whippings. Sodomy. Forced oral sex.

Earl's gut roiled, and the pressure from holding back his rage, from reining in the need to fight, threatened to blow the top of his head off—then the worst occurred.

What the—?

Earl covered Tweeter's hand and paused the image on the screen. That couldn't be true. He looked more closely. Hooded asshole. Hot iron. Close up of Tessa's naked bottom. Then—

His fury exploded. "Cocksuckingnmotherfuckingson-ofabitch. The bastard branded her. Hurt her. Fucking laughed as he did so. The fucker's dead. They're dead. Every. Fucking. One of them."

He let out a roar, turned, and hit the wall with his fist. And then he did it again … and again, shouting "fuck" with each and every punch. The wall buckled and dry wall dust floated on the air as he gave his fury and horror at what he'd seen full rein.

"Stop it, Earl." Tweeter halted Earl's arm in midpunch. "Don't break your hand—you'll need it for when I find the piece of shit fucktard who sent these to Tessa."

Earl shook Tweeter's arm off. "Yeah, find him. Find him fast."

He breathed through the madness and focused on containing an anger unlike any he'd ever felt before. He'd thought he'd seen the worst of man's depravity toward man in war zones, but this ... this ... fuck. The bastards hurt her ... no, he couldn't think about it. He couldn't erase what happened to her in the past. But he could stop anything similar happening in her future. He needed to stay in control and do what needed to be done to get the fucker who stalked her out of her life.

Earl slid onto the bench seat next to Tweeter who'd begun to do something to the e-mails containing the images.

"What are you doing?" He didn't recognize his own voice; it was low and feral, animalistic.

"Sending all this to my computer in the Bat Cave." Tweeter looked around the table and smiled, an almost evil look. "I'll have the fucker's name and address by lunchtime. Then we'll go get the sick asshole and find out where he got the images, who the sickos are in them, and who took them."

Chad coughed. Evan looked even paler.

"You know who took the pictures," Earl said. "Who filmed her, don't you?"

Evan nodded and his breath hitched. "The people who took her and some other girls from an orphanage in Shanghai and smuggled them into the United States. They were sex traffickers."

"Jesuschristfuckingsonuvabitch." Earl clenched and unclenched his hands. He ignored the pain in his right hand, which was swollen and bruised from hitting the wall. He really wanted to hit the wall some more, but Tweeter had made a valid point—he might need the hand later to beat up the cyberstalker and the people who'd violated Tessa.

"Tessa spent five years under the thumb of those depraved bastards," Chad added. "Somehow, she found a way to escape, and we found her before they could take her back."

Evan had gotten up, gone to the freezer, and brought Earl a frozen bag of peas, which he handed to him. Earl put it on his sore hand and nodded his thanks.

"You rescued her." Earl's thoughts were filled with murder and mayhem for the people who'd hurt Tessa. "You'll take me to them. I don't care where they're serving time. I'll only need a few seconds alone to beat the names of the others out of them."

Chad shook his head. "Can't. The two people who took her—Sylvia and Bob Branham—are dead. When

Tessa finally … um … could talk … the police went to the warehouse used as a private club. They found the Branhams dead in the basement dungeon and the rest of the club empty. All the records and the other girls and some young boys were gone. Place had been drowned in bleach, and every surface wiped. Chicago CSI got less than nothing from the site. The FBI techs also found nothing when Chicago called them into the case."

Earl cursed under his breath and hit the table with his fist, causing Chad and Evan to flinch and the bag of peas to slide off. He slapped it back on his hand.

Rein it in, Blackhawk. You're no good to Tessa in a rage. Save it for when you find the fucker terrorizing her.

Tweeter sat up. "I remember the case. Callie told us about it. The Chicago couple ran a club catering to sexual predators."

"Yeah." Evan choked and then swallowed audibly. "Tessa felt so guilty she hadn't been able to give the police details sooner, but she was so…"

Chad finished the sentence, his voice filled with unshed tears and anger. "…beaten up. Broken ribs. Vaginal bleeding. Anal bleeding. She had pneumonia. The, uh, brand was infected…" Chad stopped talking at Earl's feral growl.

"Then they're in hell where they belong." Earl stood. "Bet the cyberstalker is either the murderer or the murderer's accomplice. Could be some guy who bought the club's records from the murderer. The club's records would be ideal blackmail material. Don't really fucking care. Whoever the stalker is … he's history. The animals in the pictures? Are dead meat."

He stalked toward the back exit from the kitchen. "I need to check on Tessa."

Had to check on Tessa. Had to hold and kiss her. Kiss and caress the area on her hip where the bastard branded her. Had to tell her he'd never let anyone hurt her again. He'd kill anyone who tried.

10:25 a.m.

"OHMYGOD, OHMYGOD."

Tessa, her vision blurred by tears, her knees weakened by shock, managed to make it to her room without falling down the stairs or running into a wall.

Closing the door, she leaned against it for several seconds in an attempt to catch her breath. She was breathing so rapidly she was in danger of hyperventilating.

In. Out. In. Out.

She counted slowly through the mental exercise her therapist had taught her to control the panic attacks. After several seconds, she'd regained a semblance of control and could think again and not act like a frightened animal.

This wasn't the time to lose control.

When she'd awakened in her bed shortly after ten o'clock, she'd been pissed. She'd gotten up. And what had begun as a simple trip to the kitchen to retrieve her laptop, to ream Earl a new asshole for taking it, had turned into a scene from one of her more recent nightmares—the one in which people she respected, loved, discovered the revolting and degrading truth about her past.

God, they knew. Theyknewtheyknewtheyknew. They'd seen.

Con ... cen ... trate, Tessa. Breathe. In. Out. In. Out.

She moaned deep in her throat. The techniques weren't working. Sickening heat swept over her. Her stomach heaved. She covered her mouth and, on shaky legs, barely made it to the attached bathroom. Dropping to the floor by the toilet, she lost the oatmeal and juice she'd had for breakfast. After a minute of debilitating vomiting, she sank back on her butt and then leaned against the wall, thankful for the support since she'd lost all use of her muscles.

Tweeter, Evan, Chad ... Earl. They'd viewed what those people had done to her during her five years of sexual slavery. Seen the depraved acts that had taken her years of therapy to shove to the far recesses of her mind. The acts that, in recent weeks, had been thrust back to the forefront by her cyberstalker.

God, who was her tormentor? How had he obtained the images? Once again, she'd been reduced to an object to be used and abused. It was bad enough for her to relive the memories, feel the pain anew at seeing the images of her degradation, but for others to see?—ah, God ... no.

Tessa shuddered, choked, then retched air and liquid into the toilet bowl until she thought she might die. At the moment, she wanted to die ... just lie down on the cold tile floor and expire. Then she wouldn't have to think or worry about any of it ever again. Wasn't there peace in death? Infinite peace and no pain.

But she couldn't die ... refused to die.

She hadn't died all those years ago. She wouldn't give in now. But she also couldn't face any of the people downstairs—not yet. Maybe, not ever again.

She'd have to leave. Today. Now. This instant. Go back to Chicago and retrench.

While Evan and Chad had known the basics of what had happened to her all those years ago, had sat through therapy sessions with her, they'd never *seen* or *known* the extent. She had purposely left some of the more horrific acts out of her sessions, acts depicted in the videos and images on her laptop.

She felt dirty and worthless all over again.

None of it is or was your fault. The people who know and care for you will understand.

Maybe ... but she didn't want their sympathy or pity.

It's called compassion.

Same difference.

Tessa…

Shut up!

Tessa struggled to her feet, using the wall to brace herself as the world spun crazily around her for several seconds. When things settled down, she walked a few short steps to the sink. At the vanity, she picked up a wash cloth and scrubbed her face with cold water, then rinsed her mouth out. She glanced at her reflection in the mirror and cringed. It was the face from her past, the face of the weak, helpless creature she'd been during the five years in the hell the Branhams had created.

You survived. The Branhams didn't. You made something of yourself. Give yourself credit.

Ha! Credit for pulling the wool over everyone's eyes all these years. Deep inside she was still the pathetic loser who'd allowed herself to be subjugated for five years.

You were barely more than a child. You did what you had to do in order to survive. The therapist…

Nuts to the therapist! And nuts to you, too.

Tessa, I am you. You aren't thinking rationally.

No, she wasn't and wouldn't … couldn't until she was back in Chicago in the safe haven she'd made for herself. A place where she could shore up her defenses, regain her cloak of confidence. She needed to go home … now.

It's not Tweeter, Evan, or Chad knowing or seeing. You're running from him. From Earl.

Damn straight. And why was she arguing with the stupid little voice in her head?

Because I helped, you, us, survive, get away all those years ago ... and because I'm right.

Maybe, yes. Maybe, no. But instincts as old as time—fight or flight—had taken over her mind and body. She was tired, sick at heart ... too afraid to stay and deal with the fallout of what the men had seen. She could barely deal with her own emotions. How could she even begin to deal with theirs?

Tessa left the bathroom and entered the walk-in closet. She pulled on her fur-lined boots and then her shearling coat. She wouldn't, couldn't, take the time to pack. She grabbed her purse, making sure she had the rental car keys and her return ticket for the flight from the Boise airport. She left the bedroom and then fled down the stairs.

———

10:40 a.m.

TAKING THE STAIRS TWO AT a time, Earl swiftly made his way to Tessa's room and entered. She was gone.

Shit, shit, shit.

He checked the bathroom—she wasn't there. The smell of sickness was in the air.

Fuck.

He re-entered the bedroom and touched the bed. It was cool. He checked his watch; it was ten-forty. He'd brought her up around ten o'clock, so she hadn't stayed in bed long. But where had she gone? Not for a walk. The snow was blowing like a bitch, and it was well below freezing outside.

Then a horrible feeling struck. He'd taken her computer; she would've come after it.

Shit. Fuck. Damn. No!

Earl ran from the room and almost knocked over the Meyers twins who had their outside gear on.

"Hey, Earl. Tessa isn't there," one of the twins said. "She was heading down to the kitchen when we came up to get our coats fifteen or so minutes ago. Ren sent us back inside almost as soon as we got out there. Weather's a frigging mess."

"Fuck, just fuck." His gut had been on target. She'd overheard them talking in the kitchen. God, she'd run rather than confront him, confront the others. That couldn't be a good sign. She had to be hurting.

He had to find her.

Earl grabbed the boys' shoulders. "Keep your coats on and check the grounds closest to the house. Tessa could be outside and in danger."

"Why would Tessa go outside? What the fuck did you do to her?" one of the twins asked.

"She's being stalked by an asshole from her past. She overheard us discussing it." At their perplexed looks, he added, "Let's just get the fuck out there and look for her."

Earl ran down the hall and took the backstairs to the kitchen with the twins on his heels.

Ren, his brother Trey, Price Teague, and the Walsh twins were there, getting an update from Chad and Evan. Tweeter and Tessa's cell phone and laptop were gone.

The men gathered in the nook turned to look at them as they entered the kitchen.

"She's gone." Earl struggled to keep his fear at bay. He was furious with himself for not going upstairs as soon as he'd seen the first image. "She must've overheard us talking about the photos. The twins saw her around twenty-five after ten. She has a fifteen minute or so lead on us."

Chad swore and Evan moaned as he slunk weakly against the bench's back.

"What coat did she wear?" Ren asked as he strode to meet them.

"How the hell should I know?" Earl looked at the man he respected as much as anybody he'd ever met and frowned. "What the hell does that have to do with anything?" He waved a hand at the snow and wind outside. "She's out in that, and it's below zero without the wind chill."

"If she's wearing the coat she arrived in, then we're good." Ren turned to Trey. "Get to the Bat Cave. Pull up the security hologram and find her. We'll all grab Motorola headsets. You and Tweeter can direct us, if we don't spot her first."

Then Earl got it. "You planted a tracker on her. I'd totally forgotten you did that for all the guests."

The trackers were small GPS units that allowed the SSI security system to tell the good guys from the bad guys. The devices sent a location signal updated every thirty seconds and an ID to the SSI security system and created a holographic image map.

Ren could find anyone coming onto his property. But anyone without an ID was a bogey.

"Exactly." Ren smiled grimly. "Let's go. It's easy to get lost and turned around in a storm like this. If she took her rental, she can't have gone far. We didn't clear the road all the way to the state highway. Her rental SUV isn't off-road graded, so she's trapped on SSI land."

"Let's hope she stays with her vehicle when she finds she can't get through." Earl followed Ren and the others out of the kitchen toward the hall leading to the underground garage. Calmer now that he was assured they'd find her, he was still worried about her state of mind.

A premonition, a gut feeling, swept over him like a snow squall. *Fuck.* She was in danger. This second. He knew it. His gut was never wrong. It had saved him many a time during his stint in the Army; he wasn't going to disbelieve it now, not when Tessa's precious life was at stake.

Earl ran faster. "Hurry."

The others didn't question his sudden urgency, but merely increased their speed. Whether it was because of his tone of voice or how he looked, his sense of imminent danger had transmitted to the others, to men just like him who'd managed to survive hell on their instincts and training.

When Earl found her, and after he was assured she was okay, he'd spank her sweet butt for running and not confronting him and the others for invading her privacy. Not that he planned to apologize for the invasion, since she should have told him or someone.

Then he'd make love to every precious inch of her and make her his.

No effin' dating. No frickin' courtship. No fucking civilized rituals.

As Earl pulled on his winter gear in the mud room off the garage, a horrible thought struck him. Could she even stand to have a man's hands on her?

Don't think about it. He'd deal with that bridge when he came to it. He'd never hurt her. He'd cut off his own fucking dick first.

Then it hit him again … they'd fucking branded her.

Earl growled, and Tweeter backed off his position on Earl's left side, a wary look in his eyes.

"You okay, buddy?" Ren put a hand on Earl's shoulder. "What's wrong?"

"Later. We'll deal with what's bothering me later. Let's get the fuck out there before she freezes to death."

Nothing else was important now. Tessa's safety was paramount. He and Tessa would deal with her past later—as a team … with him as team leader.

She'd never have to deal with such shit alone again.

CHAPTER 4

10:35 a.m.

As Tessa drove away from the Lodge, the weight on her heart lifted somewhat from relief that she wouldn't have to face the men. They had still been in the kitchen as she moved quietly down the main stairs and to the front entrance. She had a head start on them.

Coward.

Shut up.

She drove with caution. While the driveway slash road was somewhat cleared, blowing snow had caused drifts over portions. Caution was also needed because the road had lots of curves and several deep drop-offs on one side or the other. Used to driving in rough, lake-effect winters in Chicago, Tessa was confident of her driving ability, and the all-wheel-drive SUV handled like a dream.

As she rounded a sharp curve which led to a bridge over a deep mountain ravine and stream, the road ended in a pile of snow that would reach the middle of the SUV's doors.

"Shit!" She pumped the brakes to slow her forward speed; she didn't want to throw the SUV into a wild skid. But it was too little, too late. The heavy SUV had too much forward momentum and not enough traction or time to stop. She turned the wheel sharply to avoid ramming into what looked like three plus feet of snow in the middle of the road.

"Damn. Damn. Shit." She gripped the steering wheel and turned sharply to the right to throw the SUV into a 180-degree-turn.

A sigh of relief hissed through her clenched teeth and jaw when the vehicle avoided the snow and was now aimed toward the Lodge. She pressed the accelerator and straightened the wheels, but the SUV instead of moving forward began to slide toward the steep drop off.

"No. No. No." She yanked the steering to the left, but the wheels had locked, had no traction. All she could do was hold on and pray the stone parapet would stop the vehicle from going over.

But it didn't.

The SUV's momentum and weight tore off the top of the low stone wall, and the vehicle plunged over the edge in a crunching of metal and whining of the engine, then fell into the steep ravine.

Tessa screamed and held the steering wheel in a death's grip. Her shoulder harness held her to the seat, but didn't keep her head from hitting the roof of the car and the windows as she bounced around.

She closed her eyes. She was going to die and didn't want to see it coming. She wished it were over already. But time had slowed down and seemed to stop.

God, when would this be over?

And then the sensation of falling vanished. The whine of the still-running engine was the only noise she could hear above the pounding of her heart.

She was still alive. How?

Don't question. Just thank God.

Tessa opened her eyes. She shut off the engine and looked around. She wasn't at the bottom of the ravine.

All of a sudden her neck refused to support her head. She rested her forehead on the steering wheel and breathed out a sobbing "thank God." It had been a close call.

You ain't home free yet.

Right. She lifted her head and began to examine the SUV's current status and how she would accomplish getting out of the vehicle.

Good news was a larger pine had blocked the SUV from falling farther.

Bad news was the SUV was lodged between the tree and the rocky incline at an awkward angle.

"Oh, shit." The driver's door was toward the mountain side. She wouldn't be able to open the door.

As she looked at the moon roof and wondered about getting out that way, a strong gust of wind hit the vehicle and the SUV teetered and tottered. A large creak and almost a groan came from the tree holding the SUV against the side of the ravine.

"Oh … my … God … no!" Tessa screeched as the SUV tipped even farther away from the solid rock. She held on to the wheel. "Hold, please hold."

Another jerking movement and the SUV groaned, right along with the pine tree.

Ohgod, ohgod, ohgod.

God has nothing to do with this. You do. Get your ass out of the car before it falls.

The SUV stopped rocking and the tree held … but for how long?

She had to get out … now.

Passenger side was out—it was a straight drop into the ravine on that side. Driver's side door was still mostly blocked. Driver's side window was her only safe possibility.

Turning on the ignition to accessories only, she powered down the driver's window. Her gut told her she'd only have one chance at this. Pull up and out. Reach and grab. And don't look down. And fucking breathe.

A quick glance upward showed her vertical granite rock walls with small cracks, crevices, and occasional jutting rock ledges. Her mind processed these as hand and toeholds.

You can do this. Think of it like the climbing wall at the gym. Just go.

The tree cracked ominously.

Move. Now.

Habit had Tessa pulling her purse over her head; it hung over her back. "No guts, no glory."

Tessa released her safety belt. She ignored all the bruises and aches. She could breathe and move and that was all she needed.

Carefully, she maneuvered until her feet were aimed toward the passenger door. She reached over her head and grasped the outside of the SUV's roof and pulled herself out of the vehicle in one smooth move like a reverse pull-up.

The SUV rocked at her movement. "Ohgod, ohgod." She froze and barely even breathed until the vehicle stopped rocking.

Too close. Her breaths came in gasps, and she was a sweaty, wet mess beneath her shearling coat.

She was afraid to move, afraid not to.

A gust of wind made the decision for her as the SUV groaned in chorus with the pine tree. She reached up and to her right. A small sapling anchored in the rock wall was just out of reach. She sobbed and stretched her arm even farther. The stress on her shoulders was torture.

Better than dead.

At that moment, the pine tree holding her SUV shifted away from the incline even more. A loud crack accompanied the root movement.

Tessa, grab now.

Tessa shoved against the center console of the SUV with her feet, giving her a few inches of boost, and grabbed at the sapling with both hands. Her body bumped through the car window as the SUV fell away, along with its former anchor, the tree.

She screamed and held on to the small sapling with everything in her, her torso and legs dangling in open space and hitting the side of the ravine as she swayed.

The subsequent crash of the SUV boomed and echoed off the ravine's steep rock walls.

Ohgod. Ohgod. Ohgod.

She gasped and shuddered at the close call. Her tears, a mixture of fear and relief, froze on her face in the gelid wind. She held on to the small tree and scrabbled to find footing. Her feet in their après ski boots slid and slipped off the icy, wet rock wall.

Calm down. You're wasting energy and your strength. Breathe.

Tessa stopped struggling to find footing. Then she breathed. In. Out. In. Out.

When her heart stopped fluttering like a hummingbird's wings, she chanced a look around and … ohmygod … down.

The SUV was crumpled at the bottom of the gorge. It had landed in the rushing waters of the mountain stream. It looked like a boat as it bounced and moved with the rapid current. It was hung up on the rocks … where she could have been.

Stop it, Tessa. Look at your feet. Find footing. And climb.

Her arms and shoulders ached; her body trembled from shock and the cold air. With concentration and effort, she managed to move her legs. But she couldn't find a place to put a foot.

Her upper body strength weakening, she chanced another look down and found a likely toehold. After several long, agonizing moments, she managed to get her right foot on a slight jutting of the rock face. The immediate relief on her strained shoulders and arms felt wonderful and gave her a small boost of confidence.

No resting on laurels. Keep moving.

She looked down long enough to find a place for her left foot.

"Thank you, God." With both feet now on solid bases and her arms still anchored around the tree as if hugging a lover, she took a few seconds to calm her breathing and rest. She wondered how much time had passed since she'd left the Lodge and gone over the edge of the road.

Would anyone miss her? Come look for her?

Not long. Rest later. Back at the Lodge. Move your ass now. Can't wait for rescue.

Right. The cold was getting to her. The shock. The pain. She had to keep moving. Resting on the side of a rock wall meant sure death.

Tessa raised her head and looked upward, toward her goal—road level.

Sweet Jesus. It had to be fifty feet. She sobbed. It might as well be fifty miles.

The climb looked impossible. Even with the ravine wall's many nooks, crannies, and small ledges, this wouldn't be an easy climb. It was nothing like the rock wall she climbed at the gym, the nice, dry, warm gym with ropes, a climbing harness, and a spotter. Here she had no gear, no buddy. Plus the elements conspired against her—besides the below-freezing cold and gusting winds, the snow had started again.

As if to prove Mother Nature was her enemy, the hold for her left foot broke away. No! She almost lost her grip on the sapling in her resultant panic.

"Tessa, get your ass in gear," she muttered between chattering teeth. Her arms and hands strained under her one-hundred-forty-pound weight. If she didn't do something proactive and do it soon, she'd lose hold and die.

She pulled herself up until she had her arms and legs around the sapling, which bowed under her weight and hung out over the chasm. The sensation took her back to a day in a Chicago park when she hung upside down on a jungle gym while playing with Callie's brothers. She hadn't liked the feeling then, and she sure as hell didn't like it now.

Forget liking. Look for another way up. This tree isn't going to hold your weight for long.

Yeah, yeah, as if I wasn't trying.

Quickly, Tessa eyed the areas above and around her. Between gusts of snow-laden wind, she thought she'd found a solution. But she'd have to use every inch of her long arm reach and legs to do it—and it meant letting go of her little tree.

Go for it.

Shut up. She only had one chance at this.

Accepting the necessity of moving, she found to her right a series of small, jutting ledges.

Giddy relief swamped her. She could do this. It would be like climbing a ladder, a very rough, slippery, and freezing-cold ladder.

Mother Nature taunted and tested her once more. A particularly strong gust of arctic wind hit her. Her tree held, but she shivered, a full-body set of shakes that indicated her body was attempting to stay warm. Her fingers, toes, and nose were so cold she soon wouldn't be able to sense her extremities well enough to climb. Hypothermia and all the attendant issues were mere minutes away.

Her next move was a swing and grab to an outcropping of rock almost six feet above her. And once she made it to the one outcropping, she'd have to do it all over, again and again, until she reached the road above.

Take one ledge at a time. Go.

After several deep breaths, she tested the sapling with a small swinging of her body. It held. Thankyougod, thankyougod. After several more breaths, she went for it.

When she let loose of the sapling on the upswing, she grabbed for the small rock ledge. She held on, digging her fingers into the cold rock. She let out a whoosh of air as she hit the rock wall with her torso, but managed to keep her grip. Her legs dangled for a second or so as gravity dragged at her. She finally found two crevices with her toes and took some of the pressure off her fingers, arms, and shoulders, which now all pulsed with pain from the abuse.

Pain is good. Use the pain. Pain means life.

With her right hand she latched on to a small tree which grew out of the side of the hill, then she moved her left hand. Using the sapling, she pulled her body up. Then, ignoring the pain from a new set of bruises, she scrabbled against the rocks until she found footholds, which allowed her to climb up and onto the ledge fully.

For a brief second, she lay on her front on the very narrow ledge, a safe haven in the storm swirling around her. She panted and sobbed and muttered prayers she hadn't used in years.

She'd made it and only had forty-four feet or so to go. God, how could she do it? She was tired, cold, hurt, and scared out of her ever-loving mind.

Just do it. Stop whining.

Tessa took several fortifying breaths. God, it was cold. Her lungs would freeze at this rate.

Not if you move. Keep moving. Keep warm.

Okay. She shoved the fear threatening to debilitate her to the corner of her mind where she shelved her nightmares. While some fear was good—it was part of the instinct to survive, the emotion that jump-started her primitive brain—too much fear was crippling.

Tessa needed to find the balance. She'd walked the same fine line in the past and had survived. She could again.

Then it hit her. Her panicked flight from the Lodge had been stupid, an over-reaction—too bad it had taken a life-threatening event to bring the truth home.

She was a survivor and nothing, not even a cyberstalker or a rock climb in crappy weather, would be allowed to defeat her.

And Earl? In another epiphany, she knew her attraction for the big alpha male and his for her was not a bad thing, but a wondrous connection. One she wanted to explore. Callie knew her better than she knew herself. Earl was exactly the kind of man Tessa needed; she'd been too scared to take a chance with him before. Now, it was all she wanted.

The wind and snow pummeled her, whistling and reminding her doom was near with every second that ticked by. She had a battle on her hands—against her body's limitations and the elements. But if she made it through this test, she could deal with anything, face anything her cyberstalker threw at her. She could face her past, because deep down she was a fighter.

Why … she could even take a chance at loving a man like Earl.

Now, you get it. Wish you'd gotten it before we landed in this mess. Yeah, well, she probably had needed a karmic slap in the face to bring it all home, but she wished it could have been a slightly more gentle hit than the one she'd been dealt. No use crying over bad choices. She had a climb to make and then a long walk back to the Lodge.

Tessa sat up and searched for the next set of hand and footholds she'd use to get herself to her next resting spot.

Over the next several minutes, she found enough accessible hand and footholds to climb about another fifteen feet closer to the road. The ledge she stood on now was stronger and much wider than the ones she'd used to get to this point. She still had about thirty feet to go—and she was exhausted. Her body was tiring; her strength, ebbing.

The altitude sickness, which had merely seemed irritating earlier that day, was now taking its toll. She'd thrown up several times during the climb, losing fluids she couldn't afford to lose and had no way of replacing. Eating snow would only increase her chances of hypothermia. The sickness also made her light-headed. Her exertions had caused her to sweat like a pig and her clothing was wet and sapping any heat her body produced. She was feeling for rocks with numb fingers and feet and holding on by instincts and sheer stubbornness.

Don't analyze. Move your ass.

Easy for the nagging little voice to say. Tessa's ass felt as if it weighed a ton by this point in the climb.

Her next set of handholds were just above her finger reach. Readying herself, she jumped for and managed to grab the jutting rocks with both hands, then she pulled up and up, digging into crevices in the rock wall with the toes of her boots.

Her fingers finally gave out, too cold, too sore, too swollen to grip any longer. She lost hold of first one handhold, then the other.

Screaming with rage and fear, she fell back to the ledge and hit her head on a jutting rock on the way down. Darkness came and went in her vision as pain wracked her head. As she landed on the cold, hard rock, some instinct had her roll away from the edge of the ledge and toward the mountain side.

Her breaths wheezed in and out of her laboring lungs. Her heart pounded rapidly, probably in an attempt to get blood to her brain; it had lost the battle to get blood to her extremities a long time ago. As the world spun around her in a kaleidoscope of blowing snow, fuzzy vision, and white and red dots, she knew she would lose the fight to remain conscious. All the aches and pains she'd sublimated during her short climb hit her all at once. As she slid into a nauseating, pain-filled abyss, her last clear thought was she wouldn't live to go to a Bulls game with Earl.

She'd really wanted to take a chance on Earl.

CHAPTER 5

"She couldn't have gotten very far," Ren said as he pulled out of the Lodge's underground garage.

"How so?" Earl sat in the Hummer's passenger seat and stared at the blowing snow; so much snow, it was almost a white out. The wind chill was well below zero. It wouldn't take long for a person out in this weather to lose body heat, get frost bit. At least Tessa was in a vehicle with heat.

"The boys had to come in because they couldn't see well enough to plow." Ren took the snowy curves at a steady forty miles per hour. "The drop offs on the lower part of the entry road are pretty steep."

"So, you're sure Tessa will run into deep snow and have to turn back?" Earl glanced at Ren whose posture was the picture of a man in complete control of his immediate surroundings.

Like Earl and his military experiences, Ren had served in some of the roughest, coldest, and most extreme conditions in the world while serving with the SEALs in Afghanistan. Winter in the Bitterroots was a mere walk in the park in comparison.

"Yes," Ren frowned and shook his head, "but she should've turned back by now. I hope she didn't run into the deep snow and get stuck." He spoke into his headset. "Trey, where's Tessa's tracker now?"

Trey's voice came back. "Just this side of the bridge. Not moving."

The sick feeling that had earlier lodged in Earl's gut like a big ball of ice grew worse. He turned toward Ren and asked, "Where, exactly, did the guys stop plowing?"

Earl pulled up a mental image of the twisting, torturous road that wound its way among the mountains from the state highway and the "official" spot in the road called Sanctuary up to the Lodge and the main SSI installation.

"Right before the bridge over the stream." Ren slowed to take a particularly sharp curve. "It's just around this corner."

Shit! Stopping the plowing on either side of the bridge presented a dangerous scenario. The berms on the approaches to the bridge were narrow, and the low stone walls were more for decoration than a protection against someone going over the side.

In fact, he'd bet Ren and the others had designed the road that way on purpose as a defense; with the knowledge of the terrain and proper skills, the SSI men could use the dangerous road to repel invaders.

But Tessa didn't have the knowledge or the proper defensive driving skills, and, for her, the road was a treacherous and potentially deadly obstacle course.

"I've got a bad feeling." Earl fixed his stare on the snow-covered road.

As they rounded the curve, he saw no car—only a deep drift of snow across the entry to the bridge. The bottom fell out of his world for a split second; an anguish so vast threatened to throw him into a deep well of despair and grief.

"Shit," Ren cursed. "Where is she?" He pulled to the side of the road, the Hummer's right-side wheels on the snow-covered berm, well away from the deep drop-off on the opposite of the road.

Earl was out of the car before it had come to a complete stop. The other Hummer, carrying Tweeter, Price Teague, and the Walsh twins, pulled in behind them.

"She went off the road!" Earl yelled as he ran to the skid marks which hadn't fully filled with new snow.

He approached the edge cautiously. The top of the low stone wall had been sheared off. The icy boulder lodged in his gut exploded and chilled him to the bone. He was scared to look, but he did so anyway.

The SUV lay on its passenger side in the fast-moving stream, hung up on a large rock. The driver's side had some damage, but was intact enough Tessa could've survived. But she'd be hurt. Alone. If conscious, scared and cold.

Unacceptable.

His gut urged him to leap over the side and climb down. His brain and experience told him he'd die before he ever got to the bottom.

Dammit, I need to get down there. Now.

Frustrated, he clenched and unclenched his fists. The pain in his bruised right hand reminding him of his earlier loss of control. Anger and fear had no place here. Tessa needed him calm and under control to rescue her. She wasn't dead. He refused to think of her as dead.

"The SUV is hooked on some rocks in the stream," he yelled over his shoulder as he studied the best and fastest way to get down the ravine. "Get climbing gear and a medical kit, now."

Someone, he didn't know who, ran for one of the Hummers. His gaze was fixed on the SUV tilted precariously on its side, the icy stream overflowing its banks pummeling the vehicle. *Fucking hell.* At any time, a strong current could dislodge the vehicle and sweep it downstream.

Hold on, sweetheart. I'm coming.

Loren Walsh thrust a full-body climbing harness and rope at him. "Here. Know how to use it?"

"Probably better than you SEAL boys." His time in Special Forces had thoroughly prepared him. At least this time he'd only be fighting the elements; no one would be shooting.

Tweeter suited up in similar climbing gear. "I'm going down with you. I have more climbing experience than the others. Price is attaching our ends to the Hummer for extra anchorage since we won't want to take the time to set pitons. My brothers will feed out line and send down the med kit when we need it. Ren's calling up to the Lodge to get them ready to receive Tessa."

Earl made sure his Motorola headset was on and secure, then he spoke into it. "Ren, tell them to set up my room to receive Tessa. I'll be taking care of her. Move her things."

"Earl?" Ren's tone had a "what the fuck?" aspect to it.

"She's mine, Ren. Just do it." Earl was feeling damn territorial right now and would fight anyone who attempted to keep him from holding her, warming her with his body—protecting her from the real and impending threat the pictures and e-mails promised.

"Your room," Ren said. "Gotcha. Just get her up quickly. If she's been down there since right after she left the Lodge…" He didn't finish the sentence. Every man there knew what cold and wet conditions would do to a body—and that would be on top of any injuries she suffered on the way down.

Earl growled. She was alive; she had to be. He could allow no other thoughts in his head. He needed to be on his A-game.

By rote, he checked and rechecked his gear as he walked to the puny stone wall and stepped on top of it. Tweeter matched his motions and stood next to him. Both men turned to face the others.

"Belay on," Earl said. Tweeter echoed the order.

Loren and Paul replied, "On belay."

Earl tested his rope—noted Tweeter did the same.

Loren said, "Climb."

They both affirmed, "Climbing."

He and Tweeter went over the edge. Then they began to walk and rappel down the craggy ravine.

Keeping an eye on what was around and below him, Earl watched in horror as a huge rush of water swept the SUV off the rocks and downstream.

"No!" he roared. "Fuck it, no!" At that moment, a darkness unlike anything he'd ever felt before settled over him. Numb, despairing, he almost let go of his rope.

"Earl! Fuck it, man." Tweeter grabbed Earl's rope and held him in place. The Walsh twins cursed over the headsets and took up the slack on the ropes. "Look down. She wasn't in the SUV."

Tweeter's words cleared the deadly feeling out of his mind. "What?"

Had he heard correctly?

"Look down." Tweeter angled his head as his hands were full controlling both ropes.

Earl looked where Tweeter indicated and spotted slender, jeans-covered legs on a ledge about twenty-five feet from the top. He closed his eyes and muttered, "Thank you, God."

He turned his head and said, "Tweeter—"

"I know. You okay now?" Tweeter asked. "You in control?"

"Yeah. Let's get to her." He took control of his climbing ropes.

"That's the plan, buddy. I'll tell up top." Tweeter spoke over the headset. The winds whistled and tossed them around on the slender climbing ropes. "She's on a ledge. She wasn't in the car."

Several relieved sighs and a couple of "thank the fucks" came over the com system.

"Climbing." Earl spoke into his headset. "I'm increasing my descent speed."

"Roger that," one of the Walsh twins said. "Climb."

As soon as Earl felt the slack, he kicked off the side of the ravine and covered the ten feet or so with one kick-off. He hung over Tessa's body for a second before making a controlled landing on the ledge next to her. The ledge was solid, thank the fuck.

"Tweeter, the ledge can hold us both," Earl said. "Come on down."

As Tweeter made his final descent, Earl tugged and received more slack and then bent over Tessa's still body. She lay on her front, her face turned to the side. Her eyes were shut, her lashes lined with ice. Her skin was whiter than the snow she lay upon.

"Tessa?" No response.

He brushed the snow away from her face with gloved hands. Removing one glove, he checked for a pulse and found it. He sighed with relief. "She's alive." He checked her neck and determined it wasn't broken as far as he could tell. "Neck doesn't seem to be broken, but I want a collar down here. Tweeter, a hat … need a hat here."

Most heat loss was from an uncovered head. He needed to get her warm ASAP. Hypothermia was the biggest danger at this point.

Tweeter hunkered down next to him and put his own stocking cap on Tessa. His climbing partner had on a balaclava just as he did and would be fine without the extra layer of wool.

"If you feel it's safe, then lift her," Tweeter said. "I'll get this solar blanket under her so we can wrap her in it."

Earl nodded. "Tessa, sweetheart? Talk to me."

Still no response, and she wasn't shivering. Not a good sign. Even unconscious her body would shiver to produce heat. Her lips were blue. Her skin looked dehydrated, and he remembered she had already shown signs of altitude sickness.

He felt under her coat and swore. "Godammit, she's soaking wet." He looked at Tweeter whose face was as grim as he felt. "Probably from the exertions of trying to climb out."

Tweeter nodded. "No matter how she got wet, it isn't good. We need to move, Earl." The man grabbed the collar sent down to them and gently placed it around her neck.

"Let's do it." Earl lifted Tessa's limp body into his arms and laid her on her back on the blanket Tweeter had spread on the ground.

"Fuck me." Tweeter's curse said it all.

Tessa's clothing was torn and bloody.

They quickly wrapped her like a mummy in the high-tech sheet which would keep her from losing any more body heat.

"God, sweetheart, look at what you've done to yourself." Earl lifted the edge of the blanket just enough to slide his hand inside. He quickly, by touch alone, checked her ribs, collar bone, and pelvic bones for breaks. Then he moved to her legs. "No obvious breaks that I can find."

SSI had a fully equipped medical facility run by Lacey Jones, a trauma nurse and the wife of Quinn, Ren's third in command. She could check Tessa out more fully later.

"She didn't climb all the way up from the stream bed." Tweeter looked over the edge of the ledge upon which they perched.

Earl retucked the blanket more closely around Tessa. He brushed the back of his fingers over her icy cold cheek. Her lashes fluttered—the first sign of movement from her since they'd gotten there.

Thank you, God.

"Looks like the SUV got hung up on a tree. I see an area where some roots are still hanging out from the side of the ravine. It's fresh damage." Tweeter turned to look at Earl. "She was lucky to have gotten out before the vehicle fell to the bottom."

She had to have been terrified, but she'd done what she had to do. His woman had grit.

"Yeah." Earl stroked her face once more before putting his glove back on. "We can find out exactly what happened later. Let's move."

The wind gusted even harder now than it had on their descent. Tweeter had to fight to stand upright on the ledge. Climbing out with an unconscious woman wouldn't get any easier the longer they waited.

"How do you want to do this?" Tweeter eyed the climb. "Sides of the ravine are too rough to haul her up. She has enough lacerations."

"I'll take her on my back." Earl began to fashion a rope harness with the extra rope he'd carried down. "You can tie her to me by my harness."

As Earl quickly fashioned a torso harness with doubled lengths of rope, Tweeter hunched down by Tessa and commented, "I did this with Keely when we went rock climbing one summer in Montana."

Earl put the make-shift harness on Tessa with Tweeter's help and tightened it.

"Keely sprained her ankle," Tweeter added. "She rode my back on the way up and out. But she was conscious and short and only weighed about ninety pounds at the time. Tessa's almost six foot and weighs maybe one forty."

"I can do it." Earl brushed his lips over Tessa's forehead. Other than the one fluttering of lashes, she hadn't made any other motions the whole time they'd been there. "I've carried wounded soldiers on my back, with sixty-pound packs, up the side of mountains in Afghanistan in worse conditions than this."

Those times hadn't been a walk in the park, but they had been crucial and necessary. Carrying Tessa to safety fit into the same category—life and death.

He pulled the wool neck scarf off his neck and wrapped it around her lower face to give her more warmth. "You'll have to get her on my back and then make sure she's tied to me securely. The wind's vicious." He didn't want her torn from him with a savage gust.

"I can do that." Tweeter double-checked all the harness knots. "Knots I'm good at."

At Tweeter's last words, Tessa blinked and slitted her eyes open. What little body heat they'd managed to salvage for her had helped her rouse a bit.

Earl murmured, "Hey there, sweetheart. Welcome back."

"Cold. Sick…" she muttered and moved her head from him to Tweeter and then back. "Where—" Her voice trailed off and she closed her eyes.

"Tessa! Stay with me, baby. Where do you hurt?" Earl sat and gathered her into his arms, adding his warmth to the solar blanket.

Her eyelids fluttered, but remained closed. She licked her lips, which were tinged blue and very chapped. "All … over. Sick … threw up." She coughed, and Earl tilted her body so she could breathe easier. "Do I have … flu?"

Earl groaned. "No, baby." She wasn't completely with them. Delirium wasn't good. He looked into Tweeter's worried eyes. "Let's haul ass."

Then Earl spoke into his head set. "Ren, have someone get an IV ready. She needs fluids."

She'd been sick before she left the Lodge; he'd smelled it in her bathroom. If she'd been sick again on the mountain, she was in danger of not only hypothermia, but hypovolemia and possibly hypovolemic shock. A deadly double whammy. He'd lost men that way on forced marches at high altitude in a war zone. He wasn't losing her.

"On it," Ren's calm voice replied. "Price is setting it up now in the Hummer. We have heat packs ready to go also. Just get her up here. Weather's deteriorating. A new storm front is moving in with blizzard warnings for the rest of today and tonight."

"Roger that," Earl replied. "Hold her up for a second, Tweeter."

Tweeter took over bracing Tessa as Earl stood. "Okay, I've got her." Earl pulled Tessa up and held her against his body, her front to his front. She was as limp as an overcooked noodle. "Can you hold her upright while I turn and take her on my back?"

"Got it. Go." Tweeter encircled Tessa from behind and braced her against his body.

Earl turned his back to them and stooped. "Lean her on me and brace her. I'll pick her up and then you can tie her to me."

"Got her, Earl," Tweeter confirmed.

"W-w-what's … happening?" Tessa slurred the words.

"Shh, it's okay, Tessa. Earl's giving you a piggyback ride." Tweeter's explanation was spoken in a gentle voice as he positioned Tessa for Earl to pick her up.

"Yippee." Her tone held no inflection, and her voice was breathy. She could speak, but aphasia wasn't far off. Without warmth and proper hydration, her brain would shut down unnecessary systems in order to protect the crucial internal organs to maintain life.

Earl reached for her legs, hooked his arms under her knees, then lifted her onto his back. Tweeter immediately began to secure her rope body harness to Earl's climbing one. Tessa's head lay on his shoulder, her cheek turned toward his neck. The scarf he'd wound around her face must have slipped, because he could feel her labored breathing against his neck.

"Tweeter, we're gonna lose her," Earl rasped. His fear for her well-being tinged his voice.

"She's on," Tweeter said. "Let go. I need to secure her legs to your waist, so they won't impede your climbing."

Earl straightened, and once he was sure her body was tied to him, he let go of her knees one at a time. Tweeter fashioned a sling to support her bent legs and attached it to her rope harness and then to the D-rings on Earl's climbing harness.

"Her torso and legs are secure, but what about her arms?" Tweeter had come to stand next to him. "She can't hold on. She's unconscious again. Do you want me to tie her arms around your neck?"

"Yeah, but tie her wrists to the D-rings on my shoulder," Earl suggested. If he were on level ground, he would've just held her arms around his waist, but he needed both arms for climbing.

"Gotcha." Tweeter quickly tied Tessa's wrists to D-rings on each of Earl's shoulders. "I made sure the ropes were around her gloves and loose enough not to cut off circulation."

Neither man spoke the thought Tessa might not have any feeling by this point in any of her limbs. Paresthesia had probably set in once Tessa had gotten cold and then been exacerbated by her loss of fluids.

"Yo, on belay," Earl informed the men on top.

"Belay on. Climb," a Walsh twin said.

"Climbing," Earl replied.

When he felt the tightening of the slack in his ropes, he found a foothold off to the right of the ledge and stepped off the ledge, first his right foot and then his left. He found his balance at a slight angle from the rock wall, and then, using all his upper-body strength and training, began to climb up the wall. The men on top picked up the slack and assisted, but much of the work was still on him. He used natural footholds when he could, but relied on the men at the top to make sure the rope stayed taut as he walked his way up the side of the ravine.

Tessa's extra weight, coupled with gravity, made the climb a challenge. The wind didn't help the situation as the gusts shoved him around on the unforgiving, cold, wet wall.

Earl ignored the strain on his hands, arms, and shoulders and concentrated on using all the skills he'd learned in the Army. He'd be sure to drop his trainers a thank you for pushing him to his limits during Mountaineering School. Failure had not been an option then, and it wasn't one now.

Tweeter climbed easily and effortlessly at his side, using a hand to keep Tessa's head from flopping around even with the neck brace.

The computer geek brother of Keely Walsh-Maddox might never have served in the military, but Earl would take the man climbing in a war zone any damn time. The man was a cool customer under pressure, and if Earl hadn't been here, he didn't doubt the youngest Walsh son would've gotten Tessa up the side of the ravine all by himself.

A slurred "sorry" was murmured against his neck. Tessa had roused again as she was jostled about on his back. Her bruised and lacerated front had to be hurting. He wanted to howl at the pain he was causing her.

"Shh, we'll talk later, sweetheart." Earl paused long enough to turn his head toward her face. Tessa had somehow raised her head and was looking at him through slitted lashes covered in ice crystals. He smiled with what he hoped was reassurance. "Close your eyes, Tessa. You're safe with me."

She blinked and buried her face against his neck with a deep sigh. She went even limper against him, and he began climbing faster.

Ren looked over the edge, his facial expression fierce, and spoke over the headsets. "You're close. Price, Paul, and I have you. Tweeter, Loren has you. Let us do all the work once you get to road level."

"Roger that." Earl kept climbing. Tweeter echoed him a second later.

When he and Tweeter reached road level, two sets of hands pulled him and Tessa over the edge and onto the top of the small stone wall. Earl let Ren and Price unhook Tessa and take her off his back while he held on to the wall.

His body was wracked with shudders as the combination of fatigue and stress hit him. His rasping breaths showed as little puffs of white in the frigid air. He took the short respite to regain control over his body after the arduous climb in blizzard conditions. Even now, he could barely see ten feet in front of him, and the storm was getting worse.

Once Tessa was freed from his back, he swung over the wall and stood. Shoving the effects of the climb aside, he held out his arms to Ren. "Give her to me."

Ren handed her over, and Earl jogged toward the Hummer they'd come in. It was barely visible through the sideways sheets of snow.

Pacing him, Ren said, "We set up the back seat. Lay her on the reclined one. Get the IV started, and then we'll head back to the Lodge. Short clock, guys. The storm front is moving through now."

"Roger that." Earl lifted Tessa into the back of the Hummer. Price had beaten them to the vehicle and was ready to take her inside. Earl followed quickly and began to strip the wet clothing off Tessa.

Price moved to help, but Earl glared. "I got this. Thanks. Get the IV started, okay?"

Price nodded and began testing for a vein on the arm closest to him. He swore like the SEAL he'd been. "Shit, her veins are sunken. She's too dehydrated. Her blood volume sucks. Butterfly it?"

"Do it." Earl grunted as he wiped the chilled dampness off Tessa's skin with one of the extra blankets in the Hummer and began to stuff Tessa into a man's thermal long-sleeved shirt and long johns. "Somebody get some dry socks on her and warm gel packs on her extremities."

He wasn't sure who responded, but soon Tessa had on two pairs of men's thermal socks with hot gel packs between the layers on the soles of her feet.

Tessa moaned in pain. He knew how it must feel— like hot pokers stabbing her feet—but she needed to get warmed up. He took care of the hand Price wasn't working on, using two more socks with a hand warmer between them. With the butterfly stick going into the vein on the top of her hand, the IV fluid should help warm that hand up.

"Any more blankets?" Earl sat next to Tessa on the side that didn't have the IV. He opened his jacket and the heat he'd built up climbing almost created mist in the cold air coming from outside the Hummer. He pulled Tessa with Price's help into his arms and pulled his jacket over her as much as he could.

Price wrapped two more blankets over Tessa and tucked a larger warm gel pack under the blankets at her waist to help with the warming. "Best we can do for now. You all set?"

"Yeah, let's go." Earl rubbed his cheek over the top of Tessa's head as it lay on his shoulder. He angled his face and kissed her cold forehead. "Hang in there, sweetheart."

Price nodded, shut the rear passenger side door, and climbed into the front next to Ren. The other men had already started back to the Lodge to make sure all was ready to receive Tessa.

As Ren sped up the road, the Hummer's heating system began to pour out its heat.

Earl was hotter than hell, but he could care less. Tessa had started to moan and shiver. The heating packs and the fluids and electrolytes were doing their job. He only hoped they'd gotten to her in time and had managed to forestall any permanent damage.

Price looked over the back of the passenger seat. "How's her face? Any noticeable frost bite?"

Earl tipped up Tessa's head and looked. He let out a sigh. "Looks okay. She must have just fallen unconscious right before we reached her. She climbed for a ways, so she had some circulation and heat production while she was exerting."

"It was hard." Tessa's eyes remained closed and her voice was weak, but the slurring was almost gone.

"Thought I was gonna croak. So sick. So tired." She let out a sigh and snuggled into Earl's chest. "Warm. Nice. Smell good." Then she yawned like a kitten who'd tired itself out and relaxed bonelessly into him.

"God, baby." Earl kissed the top of her head.

Price looked from Earl to Tessa and then back. "You claiming her?"

"Yeah." Earl glared at the too-handsome man. "You got a problem with that?"

From what Earl had heard from the other SSI men, Price had nailed every eligible female over twenty-one and under thirty-five in Idaho County and points north to Coeur d'Alene. The man wasn't getting anywhere near Tessa if he could help it.

"I don't poach." Price turned to look out the front as they approached the Lodge's underground garage area. "But it's her choice, ya know. I'll be around in case she decides she doesn't want to be claimed."

Ren shook his head. "Price, do you have a death wish?"

"Nope, just sayin' little Tessa hasn't agreed to take on Big Earl." Price sounded smug.

"She will." Earl kissed her cheek and nuzzled her ear. "She likes how I smell."

That admission had set it in stone as far as he was concerned. She recognized him on some primal level just as he recognized her. She was his, and he was hers, and all that was left were the details of how soon she'd move in with him.

CHAPTER 6

6:00 p.m.

Tessa swam up through the layers of what felt like a deep sleep. First, she noted the solid warmth all but surrounding her. Second, she realized she was naked, and she never slept naked. Then aches and pains made themselves known and pierced the fogginess that had taken over her brain. Her hands, arms, and shoulders throbbed and cramped as if she'd done a thousand pull-ups, and the front of her body seemed bruised as if she'd taken several kicks during Krav Maga class.

As her mind cleared, the memories hit her.

The men seeing the horrific images on her laptop. The overwhelming need to get home. The frantic flight from the Lodge. The snow wall she missed hitting. The fall over the edge of the road into the ravine. The perilous climb to save herself. Finally, the fall to the ledge and unconsciousness.

"Shit," she muttered into a pillow that smelled like something she recognized as safety, but couldn't put a name to.

"Tessa? You in pain?" A low baritone whispered over her ear.

The calming scent on the pillowcase was Earl's. It was his solid warmth aligned against her back. It was his bare, muscled arm which encircled her waist and held her to him. He swept a hand over her front from just under her breasts to her lower abdomen where he massaged her stomach just above her mound in what was both an exciting and soothing motion.

She angled her head to meet Earl's emotion-filled, dark eyes. "Um, I'm okay."

A frown creased Earl's forehead, and he muttered in a snarling tone, "Bullshit, sweetheart. You're bruised from head to toe. You've got some nasty lacerations. Your head has to be throbbing like a heavy metal band."

"Are you mad at me?" Tessa struggled to sit up, to get into a better position to defend herself.

"Shh, easy," Earl murmured against her cheek. His hand now massaged circles on her hip as his body cocooned her even more, his front to her back. "I'm not mad. Still trying not to be scared."

He nuzzled her neck and kissed her jaw where it met

her ear. "You scared the shit out of all of us. We barely got to you in time to stave off hypothermia and hypovolemic shock. You could've died."

Tessa nodded. God, she had been so stupid. Tears slid from the corners of her eyes. What little strength she had completely disappeared, and she sank back onto the bed and against Earl's naked body.

"Shit, sweetheart." Earl hugged her closer. "Don't cry. You'll be fine. You're killing me here." He rubbed his hand up and down her side from rib cage to hip and back, again and again.

Tessa sniffed, but the tears, a combination of release of her pent-up fears and relief she was alive, continued.

All the while, Earl held her, swearing creatively in a low, grumbling tone. "Dick-cheese, douche-bag, pecker-headed son of a bitch."

The profane combinations struck her as funny, and her sobs became intermingled with half-laughs and snorting chuckles.

God, she was losing it.

No, you're fine. When have you ever allowed a real man to hold you, naked skin against naked skin, and let go? All your emotions hanging out there for him to see?

She'd slept with men. Had sex with men.

Not naked—and not like Earl. Those guys were pretty boys looking for bragging rights. Earl is a real man. The kind of man you need to protect you from your past. To cherish your tender feelings.

She flash-backed to the epiphany that had gotten her up the mountain to the safety of the ledge. She'd sworn she wouldn't miss the chance at being with Earl—and she wouldn't. From this second forward, she'd accept the man to whom fate, and Callie, had led her.

"Sweetheart, you're tensing again. Stop thinking. Just feel." Earl kissed her ear and leaned his cheek against hers.

Tessa luxuriated in the sensations of the moment. Earl's strength surrounded her; his scent permeated the air and soaked into her very pores. She'd never felt this safe in her entire life; the only other time that came close was the night Evan and Chad had found her in the gutter, bleeding and near death. They'd saved her from a world of cruelty; Earl's presence promised to save her from a lifetime of being alone.

"I'm thirsty." She angled her face back and kissed the underside of his bristly jaw. "I need to pee, too."

Earl stiffened against her as she licked and nuzzled the spot she'd kissed.

He turned her to face him.

The strength in the maneuver both amazed and aroused her. The emotions sweeping over his face astonished and humbled her—and excited her. Her pussy clenched, and she moistened at the enormity of what she saw in his dark eyes.

The snarky little voice in her head had been right—Earl was the man for her. He cared; it showed in every touch, every action since she'd met him, and every emotion that crossed his face, glittered from his eyes, and tinged his tone of voice.

He cared for her and—she could admit it now—had since he first met her. She'd been the one to run from the chance at finding a true partner, a mate.

It had taken the "aha" moment on an icy ledge and then seeing the emotion in Earl's eyes for Tessa to see what had been in front of her from the moment she'd met him. While she might have been slow on the uptake, she wasn't dumb. She planned to grab this chance at love and hold on tight.

But first, she had to deal with an Earl whose feathers were ruffled over her running away, instead of facing the problems from her past and the potentiality of her future.

That he was pissed was evident in the frown-line on his forehead, but none of his anger touched her physically. This man, unlike others she'd known, knew his strength and had it under control.

"What are you thinking, baby?" Earl touched his nose to hers. His hands were warm on her back, holding her close to him. His large erection pressed against her stomach; her pussy throbbed and grew wetter. No man had ever made her wet just by holding her. She shivered, and Earl pulled her even closer to his heat.

"You're naked." She licked her lips and tasted mint. A hazy image of Lacey Quinn washing her face and swabbing her mouth flashed across her mind. "I'm naked." Had Earl stripped her, or had Lacey?

"Your clothes were wet, sapping your heat. You were half-frozen. So I stripped you. Plus, skin-to-skin is more effective in warming a body up."

Earl brushed a kiss over her mouth, his tongue tracing the path she'd just licked. "Do you want me to get dressed?" he asked between nibbles of her lips.

She thought for a few more seconds, testing her freak-out meter, and found his nudity, his kisses, his touch, and his very large cock throbbing against her mound were just fine with her. "Uh, no, don't think so. Nope, not scared of you at all."

Tessa leaned back within the circle of his arms. She found his dark, serious, and very intent gaze fixed on her. "I'm not afraid of you, Earl. I feel this … um, us … whatever it is or could be … is right. It feels right."

"That's good, sweetheart." Earl smiled and cuddled her head against his chest. "Then why did you run? Those pictures are nothing you need to defend or explain. You were a child, a precious and fragile teenage girl who should've been protected, not abused. Didn't you think we would understand that? That I would understand that?"

Tessa swallowed past the lump in her throat, tears falling down her cheeks unchecked. God, she didn't deserve this good man, but she was going to keep him any way she could.

She sniffled. "I was scared. Humiliated. It's one thing for you all to know I was abused, but to see it." She sighed. "Can I claim temporary insanity and let it go at that?" She kissed the base of his throat, and he rumbled a purr like a large, contented cat.

Earl kissed the top of her head. "Yeah, as long as you understand you never need to be scared of me. I'll never hurt you. I'll protect you with my life."

"I knew that inside. Maybe that was one of the reasons I ran."

"What?" He tipped her head back and scowled down at her. "Why?"

"Because I knew as soon as I met you that you were different than the other men I'd had um, well, you know."

"Damn right I am," he growled, and she giggled.

"To them I was nothing but arm candy and maybe a quick lay."

"This—you and me—is more than a quick lay, trust me on that, baby." His expression was serious, solemn.

"Exactly. I recognized right off you are a forever kind of guy. But I never expected to find anyone like you, never expected you to want me and be willing to accept me and my garbage."

"Listen up, Tessa Andrews. You are not garbage. No one, not even you, is allowed to slander you. Understand?" He cradled her head and massaged the base of her neck with his thumb. She relaxed into his supportive hold.

"Yes … no … I'll try."

"Do more than try." He kissed the tip of her nose. "But I'll be here to remind you of how precious you are. Okay?"

She nodded, tears streaming down her face again. God, she was so lucky.

"So, you ran because you were afraid of what we'd think? Not because you were afraid of me?" Earl massaged her jaw with his thumb.

"Uh, yeah … I needed to go home to the haven I'd created for myself. Regroup, so I could think."

Earl nodded. "I can understand that. Osprey's Point is a place like that for me and some other war vets. A place where you can control your surroundings and you feel safe."

"Exactly." She rubbed her cheek against the hand supporting her head. "I would've called you … eventually. I really wanted to go to the Bulls game, ya know."

Earl laughed and kissed the corner of her mouth. "Well, sweetheart, you can go to every Bulls game this season once we get this ass-bastard off your case and out of your life. I promise."

"Yay." She wrinkled her nose. "Now can I go pee and get a drink?"

"Yeah." Earl laid her back down, released her, and then rolled out of the bed on the opposite side, his back to her.

Even in the dim lighting, she could see every detail of his muscled torso. The man was huge and had to outweigh her by a hundred pounds. She licked her lips and imagined all that yummy mass over her, thrusting— then he turned to move to her side of the bed.

Oh, my God! His huge cock stood at attention, and the tip of it touched his navel. She whimpered in arousal and, yes, a slight touch of fear.

Yes, he is definitely more man than you've ever had. Yowza!

"Tessa, you scared?" Earl came around to her side of the bed and leaned over her prone body, his arms caging her. "I can put on some clothes. I don't want you being scared of me physically. I'll never hurt you. We can take our relationship as slowly as you need. The nudity was only to get your body temperature up since I didn't want to risk putting you in a hot bath."

"Not afraid. Impressed is more like it." She licked her lips and assessed her body and mind's reaction to his maleness. "I'm aroused, sort of." *Be honest.* "No, not sort of. A lot."

Earl groaned, and his cock twitched and seemed to seek her like a dowsing rod looking for a source of water. "God, sweetheart. Don't say that if you don't mean it, because I've had a hard-on since the first minute I met you on Saturday. Lying next to you has been a lesson in restraint. Restraint isn't something I'm used to when it comes to sex." He lifted one hand from the bed and swept some of her hair behind her ear. "But for you, I would, and will, do anything you need."

"I want you." Tessa touched his chest, swirling a finger in the smattering of dark, silky hair that covered his chest from nipple to nipple. "Very much."

Earl groaned. "Baby, you were very close to death. I'm not sure the kind of sex I need is something you're up for at the moment. And with your past … I'm worried—"

"Shh, it's okay. I'm fine." Tessa took one of his hands and placed it on her abs just above her navel. She hesitated and looked at his expression and found only desire and something even more precious in his dark eyes. She slowly pulled his hand down her body, her gaze never looking away from his.

"Sweetheart, do you want me to pet your pussy?" His voice was husky and low. "Make love to you?"

She nodded and placed his hand over her very wet slit and aching clit. "After I get cleaned up a bit and have something to eat and drink, will you try?"

Earl swept a finger through her wet folds and growled. "God, sweetheart, you're drenched."

He lifted his fingers to his face and sniffed and then licked her juices from them. His gaze never left hers, and she about died at the desire and love she saw there. He liked her, maybe even more than liked. She was something more than a body to him. She choked back a sob of relief.

She'd done enough crying in front of this special man.

"You want me to love you, baby? You sure?"

"Yes. I want this. I want you." Tessa took his hand once more and held it firmly over her pussy.

"I promise to make it good for you, but only if you're up to it. You took quite a beating on the mountainside." Earl's lips twisted into a slight smile, and then he swept her up into his arms and carried her to the bathroom in what she now saw was his room and not hers. "But first, let's take a bath together, relax a bit. Then we'll get some chicken noodle soup and some more fluids into you. If you're still awake after all that, we'll revisit this discussion in bed. Okay?"

Tessa leaned her head on Earl's shoulder and sighed. "Sounds good to me." She caressed the nape of his neck. "Just so you know—sex doesn't bother me. I've had a lot of therapy." She hesitated and buried her face in his neck.

Earl stopped and looked down at her. "What is it? You got all stiff on me. If sex doesn't bother you, why are you upset again?"

"I've never had an orgasm with a sexual partner—ever. I can get myself off with a vibrator, but I never, well … I don't want you to be disappointed if I don't respond the way you need."

"I'm not worried about that. How you respond will be on me … and I'm very patient and goal-oriented. I just don't want to scare you."

"*You* won't." Tessa nuzzled and kissed the side of his throat.

"God, I love it when you kiss me." Earl walked to the toilet and sat her on the closed seat. "Do you still need to pee? I'll turn my back."

Tessa blushed. God, the man had already seen her naked. She'd placed his hand on her pussy. But she couldn't be totally exposed in that way … not yet. *They* had never given her privacy, had controlled her every—

Stop it, Tessa.

She shook off the ties to the past. "Uh, could you start the bath and then wait outside?"

"Sure, sweetheart." Earl leaned over and kissed the top of her head. "Never be afraid to ask for what you want or need." He turned and opened the taps to fill the Jacuzzi tub. He looked over his shoulder. "If you feel dizzy, yell for me. I'd rather you be a bit embarrassed than get hurt from a faint."

"I promise." She smiled. "If I need you, I'll holler."

Earl left the bathroom and shut the door until only a crack was left. Tessa took care of her more urgent bodily needs, then moved to sit on the edge of the tub and tested the water. She added more hot water.

"Tessa?" Earl's voice came from the other side of the door. "You ready for me to come back in?"

"Yes." Her heart pounded, but with excitement, not fear. This man was her future, and she intended to embrace it, and him, fully.

Earl walked to the tub. His gaze swept over her. "You moved without me. Any dizziness? Nausea?"

"None. I feel weak, sore, but other than that, I'm fine," she reassured him. "Looking forward to the bath and the food and … uh, later, in bed … with you."

"Let's talk a little bit more about later, about going to bed." He turned off the taps and put some bath oil into the water; it smelled like him, lemon and something musky. "What did your therapist say about your inability to orgasm?"

Tessa touched his arm, and he turned toward her. She gasped at the look of deep concern mingled with desire and something more in his eyes. No man had ever looked at her in that way. She looked away from his intense gaze and watched the swirling water and inhaled the scent of the bath oil mingled with his scent as she decided how to express what she'd learned after years of therapy.

She cleared her throat. "Um, the doctor said I had bottled up my sexuality in response to the abuse I'd suffered. Her explanation was since I had no control over what those people did to my body, I did have control over my response to what they did. So-o-o … when I started dating and having sex…" Earl growled at the mention of her having sex with other men and she had to smile, "…well, my mind refused to allow me to react even with my chosen partners, even though I knew they weren't out to hurt me. I continued to repress my sexuality to protect myself."

"What did your therapist say about that?" He swept a hand through the water and added some cold.

"She said I didn't trust them with my heart, my emotions, my mind. While they didn't hurt me physically, I still couldn't allow myself to feel." Tessa sought Earl's hand and squeezed it. "I trust you. I have since I met you, and that kind of scared me." She scrunched her nose. "I wondered how I could see a big, strong man like you and trust you so implicitly from the first second I met you. Was I nuts?"

She smiled to lessen the sting of her initial doubt. "Then, in that ravine, I realized I wanted to stay alive for all sorts of reasons…" she traced his mouth with a finger, "…but the main one was you." He kissed her finger and smiled. "I wanted to go to the Bulls game and take a chance that date would lead to more."

Earl captured her hand and kissed the palm. "It will, baby. I've had a lot of women in my past. But I've never met one I wanted to see in my home, in my bed, having my children before. Only you."

This wonderful man had just put himself out there. His words were a declaration of commitment, of love. He might not have said the words, but his intent was clear.

God, she could have it all … all she had to do was reach for it and hold on.

Tessa began to cry from relief and happiness.

Earl cursed under his breath. "Damn me all to hell and back. I made you cry again." He pulled her onto his lap and rocked her. "Stop it, honey. I can't stand it. You make my heart hurt."

Tessa snickered against his chest and slipped a hand down to enclose his cock. "I think I make something else hurt more."

Earl squeezed her gently. "Behave, you minx. Bath. Food and liquids. Then bed, and then we'll see if we can take care of each other's needs." He slid one arm down her front and cupped her mound. "Deal?"

"Deal." Tessa blushed and turned away from Earl's searching and heated gaze. "Tub's full. Can we have the jets on full?"

"You can have anything you want. Just ask."

From the tone of his voice, she knew he meant it. Her heart beat faster, and the future looked ever brighter.

Fate, in the form of her best friend, had brought her this strong, wonderful man. She would owe Callie a big damn favor.

Name your first-born girl after her.

What a good idea.

Earl lifted Tessa and placed her in the tub. The water was warm, and she sighed as the heat soothed aching muscles and eased any remaining tension. She accepted a wash cloth from Earl. Then he got into the tub and settled himself behind her. He encircled her with his arms, his long legs lying parallel outside of hers.

She leaned back into his chest and sighed. "I could

get used to this."

"Plan on it." Earl took the cloth from her and soaped it up, and then began washing her arms. "I'm darn sure I'm gonna want to give you lots of baths. Jesus, baby, you've got bruises and scrapes all over you." He growled under his breath as he sought out each and every injury. It was the most thorough and gently intimate bath she had ever had.

"There, all clean." He kissed the top of her spine. "Now, lay your head back on my shoulder and relax. Let me just hold you for a bit."

And that was what she did—and he did.

CHAPTER 7

7:00 p.m.

E arl had leashed his libido while bathing Tessa.

It had been a fierce battle, especially when with each stroke of the cloth she'd emitted little moans and sighs that made his cock flex against her bottom and lower back. It would have been so easy to lift her and slide in from behind in a reverse cowgirl position, but he'd promised her a relaxing bath and then food.

He also kept in mind she'd been minutes away from death when they'd found her. If not for the immediate first aid in the Hummer, she could've gone into shock. Her core temperature had been dangerously low. The fact she hadn't died he chalked up to her excellent physical conditioning, a strong will to live, the well-stocked medical kit in the Hummer, and plain dumb luck.

It had been too close of a call.

Bath over, Earl sat next to Tessa on the small sofa in front of the fireplace in his bedroom suite. He liked watching her eat. Her color was much better now that she was warm both inside and out. She was still somewhat dazed from her adventure; her movements were slower and she would stop and drift into a sort of fugue state for a few seconds before eating another spoonful of the chicken noodle soup.

But, on the whole, she recalled most of what happened, was oriented to time and space. More importantly, she was receptive to his attentions and, in fact, seemed as eager as he to explore the more physical side of a relationship with him.

In the back of his mind, the rage he'd felt at what had been done to her younger self still burned; it was a steady simmer, ready to boil over at the first sign of threat to her person or her mental and emotional well-being. He kept the anger caged. He refused to allow any of his darker emotions to touch her; she'd had enough darkness in her life.

Tessa deserved to be loved and pleasured—and assured she'd never be harmed in their bed.

Her ready acceptance of his personal care after her close call had pleased and humbled him. She'd been wet and ready for him before the bath. She'd openly shared her sexual past. How she could ever think she wouldn't please him, that he would be disappointed in their love-making, he'd never understand.

"Earl, you're frowning." Tessa placed the empty bowl on the cocktail table and then traced his lips with her index finger. He nipped the tip, then kissed it. She smiled. "What's wrong?"

"Were the men in your past all stupid or what?" He mentally groaned. He hadn't meant to ask that, but it was out now. "I mean, no real man leaves his woman hanging and takes all the pleasure for himself."

Tessa shook her head, a slight twist to her lips. "Are you jealous?"

"Fuck, yeah." He brought one of her hands to his lips and kissed it. "You were meant for me. But I'll get over it—eventually."

Like hell. It burned in his gut. The only way to douse the flames was to make sure she was in his bed and pleasured by him for the rest of their lives. Any man who touched her or even looked at her wrong was toast.

A glint of laughter in her eyes, she stroked his tense jaw. "Earl, they were nice guys. Most of them were models." She shrugged and wrinkled her nose in a self-deprecating manner. "Some of them, I think, just wanted to demonstrate their masculinity by having me on their arm at a nice restaurant. Some of them just wanted the attention being with me brought them. None of them could hold a candle to you for pure, unadulterated masculinity."

She leaned over and inhaled against his neck. "And none of them smelled right. I could find you in the darkest cave on the darkest night by scent alone." She licked the line of the throbbing pulse in his neck and smacked her lips. "Yummy. You taste as good as you smell."

Earl let out a low growl and pulled her from her place on the couch and crosswise onto his lap. She twined her arms immediately around his neck and nestled her head on his shoulder. He sensed no fear in her at all, just acceptance, complete and total.

Slowly, he untied the robe he'd loaned her and swept the folds back to expose her breasts. Unlike many models, she was naturally well-endowed. Her breasts were tear-drop shaped, full and lush, when compared to the rest of her bone structure and lean musculature.

As he stroked the under-curve of her breasts, testing their weight in the palm of his hand, she purred against his throat.

"Like that?" His voice was harsh, guttural with his need to make love to his woman.

"I love your touch." Her voice was husky, sensuous. "Earl, kiss me."

Tessa lifted her lips to his and he took them. The kiss was all hot tongue, lip-eating, and low groans—on both sides. She tasted of chicken soup and another flavor that was all Tessa. Sweet and spicy—and fiery.

When he became more aggressive, taking the kiss

deeper, Tessa twisted into his body, her fingers holding his head to her.

God, thank you. His Tessa wasn't afraid of his strength.

Earl groaned into her mouth. He moved his hand to cup her bottom and rubbed her against his hard-on. He demanded her complete surrender to his will. And she responded beautifully. Her moans turned to whimpered gasps into his hungry mouth.

As he held her to him with the hand on her sweet ass, his free hand moved over her satiny, rosy-from-her-bath skin with sweeping strokes along her side from her breast over her lean mid-section to her hip. Sliding his hand over her thigh, he cupped her pussy. She moaned low in her throat.

He broke off the kiss. "You okay, sweetheart?" He needed to make sure she was with him and he wasn't scaring her with the strength of his ardor.

"God, yes," Tessa moaned and arched her lower body into his hand. "More."

"With pleasure." He bent to take her lips once more and held her steady as the hand on her pussy began a pattern of tracing and then rubbing.

After firmly massaging her clit with the heel of his hand, he tested her opening with a finger. *Oh, hell yeah.* She was wet; she'd responded to him instantly.

Earl needed to take his loving of her to the next level, but he didn't want to do it on the too short couch in the drafty high-ceilinged sitting area. Tessa deserved the warmth and comfort of a bed for their first time together. He attempted to break away from their kiss, but found himself going back for more, reluctant to lose the taste of her on his tongue and her grasp on his neck. It was several long minutes before he could finally tear away from her too-tempting mouth and touch.

"Angel, we need to take this to the bed." He kissed her nose and cheeks, unwilling to lose contact with her completely. "I want to pleasure you." He cupped her mound and claimed with his hand what he would soon take with his hard-as-granite cock.

"Can't we do it on the couch?" She licked and kissed a spot under his ear he'd never before realized was a hot spot for him. He trembled and brushed a kiss over her shoulder.

"No. Bed. Now." He released his hold on her pussy and gathered her more firmly against his naked chest. He stood. "You have bruises on top of bruises. I'm not gonna be the cause of any more."

"Okay." She nuzzled his neck and smoothed a hand over his chest hair from nipple to nipple and then traced a teasing finger up and down the midline of his abs. "I love how strong you are."

His cock throbbed, and he swore he might come from her petting alone.

"Tessa, sweetheart," he muttered as her hand found the tip of his cock sticking out of his boxers' waistband,

"I'm ready to explode. You might want to leave my cock alone until I can get you ready for me."

"Here's a little secret." She nipped his earlobe. "I'm ready now. Readier than I've ever been in my life. You do it for me, tough guy."

"Baby, that's just it—I'm tough and big and ... I don't want to—"

Tessa grasped his cock within her hot, delicate hand. "Yes, I would agree this is a prime example of a big cock." She muttered against his ear, "And I can't wait to have it in me. I'm not a virgin, Earl. I can handle anything you want to give me. I'm not afraid. Really."

She read him too well. He was anxious about not only hurting her, but also scaring her because of her past violent sexual experiences. He also wasn't a prissy-assed model. When he made love to a woman, he was all in—pleasure for her and him was the name of the game—and he went for it with gusto. He was afraid he'd be too rough, too demanding.

"Tessa—" Earl stopped by the bedside and gently lowered her onto the already turned-back bedding.

"Hush." Tessa sat up and covered his lips with her fingers. "Earl, I won't break. I've never balked at intercourse. During my modeling years, most of my sexual partners went at the act with enthusiasm and energy. They all had a very good time, at least they said so. They just never did it for me. You do."

She smiled; it was a look of pure, sultry sex and all for him. His balls tightened and a spurt of precum covered his glans.

"I can't be any more blunt than this—don't hold back." She swirled a finger around one of his nipples. He inhaled sharply at the pleasure one little sweep of her finger gave him. "You can't hurt me as long as you care about me."

Tessa leaned forward and rubbed her cheek against his abs; her breath wisped over the head of his cock. He had to tighten his hold on the reins of his driving need to push her back on the bed and plunge his aching cock in her hot, tight depths.

"You see..." She straightened and looked into his eyes. Her gaze was filled with faith and what he read as love. "...those men never cared about me. They had sex with me, but you'll be making love. I see it in your eyes, feel it in your touch. Felt it when you risked your life to carry me up a rugged ravine in a blizzard."

"You remember that?" He cupped her chin and gently caressed her jaw line with his thumb.

"Uh-huh. You came for me. No other man has ever risked his life for me before."

"Tweeter was there, also." Earl felt it only fair to make sure she knew her rescue wasn't on him alone. Not that he would let the computer geek come within touching distance of his Tessa. "And Ren, Price, Loren, and Paul were aiding us."

Tessa got to her knees. She placed her arms around his neck and laid her head on his chest. She nuzzled the area over his heart and took a deep breath and let it out on a sigh. "But they don't smell right." She leaned her head back and looked him in the eye. Her gaze was serious and intent. "You would've come for me whether they'd helped or not. I know this in my heart."

"Yes," he brushed a kiss over her lips, "I would have. Nothing and no one could've kept me from finding you and bringing you back safely."

"And that's why I love you, Earl Blackhawk." She kissed him back, a gentle teasing of her lips over his.

"I love you too, Tessa Andrews." He took her lips, a kiss of promise and desire. A kiss of fealty and protection. A kiss pledging his love and utter adoration for the rest of their lives together.

Tessa moaned into his mouth and then pulled away, a mere breath separating their lips. "Make me yours, Earl. I can't wait another second."

"Oh, hell yeah." He peeled the robe off her and tossed it to the floor. "Lie down, sweetheart. Let me love you."

Tessa smiled, her desire evidenced in the glitter of her eyes and the rapid pulse beating at her neck. She looked him up and down and licked her lips. "I don't think you need those shorts, do you?"

"No." Earl's voice was raspy with his need for this

beautiful woman. His beautiful, precious woman. "Lie down. Let me look at you."

Tessa reclined; her arms lay loosely at her side and her legs were slightly apart. Her breasts rose up and down rapidly. She watched him avidly, her gaze aimed at the bulge in the totally unnecessary boxer briefs.

"See what you do to me?" He took her hand and placed it on his cock. Even through the cotton of his underwear, her touch was hot and erotic.

"Hurry, Earl." She stroked a shaky finger down his thigh.

He stripped off the boxers and let them drop to the floor. Then he climbed onto the king-size bed at her feet and gently pulled her legs farther apart. He sat back on his knees between the V of her legs and caressed first one leg, then the other, from knee to outer thigh and then down her inner thigh.

As he sensitized her skin to his touch, he hungrily eyed her exposed sex. Her pussy was beautiful just like the rest of her. She had a cloud of neatly trimmed dark curls above her opening. The labia, though, were free of hair and glistened lushly pink with her juices.

Under his gaze, her vaginal opening contracted and dilated. He could actually see her sex get wetter.

Tessa moaned. "You make me ache by just looking at me. I need you to make the aching go away." She reached for him with a hand that trembled.

"You ever have a man go down on you, sweetheart?" He licked his lips as the aroma of her heated sex reached his nose.

Her arm dropped to the bed. "No, um … I never let them … you don't…" She bit her lip and closed her eyes. Pink touched her cheekbones and a flush of excitement colored her chest.

"I want to eat you out, Tessa. Need it." He swept a finger around her opening and over her clit, then back again, before inserting it into her tight, moist sheath. She groaned and arched from the bed, thrusting her hips toward the invasion. "You'll like it. I promise."

Her eyes flew open and were dilated with her need. Her nipples were taut, rose-colored buds and begged to be kissed, suckled … and bit. Later, he'd spend quality time tasting those delicate nips, but first he wanted to taste her. Had to taste her. Needed to give her pleasure.

Leaving his finger in place inside her tight channel, he leaned down and traced with the tip of his tongue the path his finger had taken. Tessa's response was all he could hope for from his woman. She made the sweetest sounds of pleasure as her hips moved to meet his touch.

When he reached her clit, he lightly, teasingly, flicked it with the tip of his tongue before resuming his path around her labia with the flat of his tongue. As he warmed her up orally, he stroked her vaginal walls and opening with his finger, loosening her up for his entry.

When he thought she could handle it, he added another thick finger to stretch her even more.

At the addition of the second finger, she let out a low guttural moan that had his cock shooting a spurt of precum. He liked making her moan, knowing he was giving her pleasure.

But he was still concerned about taking her with his cock. She was tight, too tight to take his girth comfortably. He wondered just how long it had been since she'd taken one of her metro-sexuals inside her sweet body.

Earl rumbled low in his throat. He needed to get past the other men she'd had before meeting him. It figured when he finally fell for a woman, he'd get all cave man about her, and he wouldn't apologize for the knee-jerk reaction either. She was his and his alone.

"Earl ... so good ... need ... need ... harder. More." She swept her fingers through his hair, clutching at his head, and urged him closer to her clit. She whimpered and gasped with little sexy hitches of her breath.

Yes, harder. Harder was good and what instincts urged him toward.

Permission given, he let his libido off the leash he'd placed upon it. He added a third finger to the two inside her and reached with the pad of his middle finger for the fleshy bunch of nerves on her vaginal wall. As he stroked the ultra-sensitive spot, he suckled her clit with deep, strong pulls of his lips.

Within a few seconds, Tessa arched off the bed, her feet planted into the mattress. This position threw her hips up into his touch and mouth. She screamed, high breathless sounds, mingled with whimpers and pants as her orgasm took her over. Her vaginal muscles squeezed his fingers tightly, and he almost came at the thought of how his cock would feel inside her, massaged by those same strong muscular contractions.

Her climax was so intense he caught sight of her full breasts bouncing. So intense, she dug her nails into his scalp.

He growled low in his throat with male satisfaction at making his woman wild. He savored her body's response to his love-making. Her pleasure was his—so much so, the sounds and sight of Tessa climaxing did trigger his own. He huffed and groaned his pleasure into her sex as he soaked the bedding beneath them with his cum. The vibrations from his groans over her engorged clit sent Tessa over the cliff of another climax.

"Earl! … oh my God … good … so good … ahh!" Tessa arched into his mouth once again. She released his head and grabbed at the bedding as if the sheets were a lifeline holding her to earth.

His seed spent, he nuzzled her mons and licked delicately over the top of her clitoral hood. His fingers still inside her vagina, he felt another series of smaller contractions as her orgasm ebbed. He gently stroked her vaginal sheath as she came down and until she relaxed bonelessly into the mattress.

Earl kissed a spot above her dark curls and slowly, carefully pulled his fingers from her opening.

Tessa moaned, "Oh God," and shuddered as another small climax swept over her body.

More than pleased with her reaction to his love-making, he idly licked his fingers as he watched his precious woman become reoriented to the world around her. When her golden-brown gaze fixed on him, it was filled with the dreamy satiation of a sexually fulfilled woman.

"You liked that." Earl moved to lie next to her. He pulled her into his arms and held her head on his chest. He stroked his fingers through her long hair.

"Yeah, I liked that." Tessa swept a finger over his spent cock as it rested on his lower abs. "Um, why didn't you come inside me?"

"Because this time was for you." He kissed the top of her head, loving the heated scent of her.

"When's your turn?" She stroked the same finger around one of his nipples. His cock jerked and unbelievably began to harden. He hadn't recovered this quickly since his early twenties.

"If you keep doing that, sooner than you'd think." Earl placed his hand over her finger and stopped the movement. "Sleep first. You need the rest. My cock isn't going anywhere." He pulled the covers over them. "We've lots of time to explore each other. Weather report has us snowed in until late Wednesday."

"Goody." Tessa yawned and snuggled into his body; she moved her hand to his chest and covered his heart.

"Sleep, sweetheart." He anchored her with an arm at her waist, wanting her as close to him as he could get.

"Don't go anywhere." She clutched at him as if she were afraid he'd disappear.

"Not planning on it," he whispered over her hair, "and when I do, you'll be right there with me."

Another "goody," another yawn, and then Tessa was sound asleep.

Earl smiled and pulled her even closer. He'd never felt this kind of contentment before in his life—and he'd hold on to it with everything in him.

With that vow, he let sleep take him over.

CHAPTER 8

Tuesday, December 6th, 6:30 a.m.

Tessa woke to the gentle throbbing of her clit.

The cause?

Earl circled the tiny taut bud with his finger—his body aligned against her back and the arm attached to the teasing digit around her waist.

"What are you doing?" *Dumb question.*

Her breath hitched as he nibbled her shoulder lightly and increased the pressure on the bundle of nerves at the apex of her thighs.

"Getting you warmed up," he whispered against her ear, "so I can come inside you this time."

She moaned and recalled the intense sensations this man had caused with just his fingers and his mouth. She wasn't sure she'd survive having his big, beautiful cock inside her.

But she damned well wanted it there.

"Okay." Suddenly a small orgasm swept through her, and she arched her back away from his body, her head resting on the strong shoulder behind her. "God," she gasped and moaned, "you're good."

The pleasure ebbed to a gentle flow. She relaxed into his body once more and then angled her head to look over her shoulder.

The look of fierce concentration on his face as he continued to pet her clit brought happy tears to her eyes. This man was into her unlike any man she'd ever known. Contentment glowed in her heart and mind. She was loved and felt blessed.

Luxuriating in Earl's gentle, arousing touch, she looked around the bedroom. It was dark, but that could be merely because Earl had the shutters closed. "Um, what time is it?"

"More like what day. You slept like the dead." He never stopped tracing patterns on her clit and her labia with that devilish finger.

"Okay, I'll bite," she gasped as he pressed his finger on the hood of her clit and firmly rotated the skin over the bundle of nerves, "um … what day is it? … Earl! I'll come if you keep doing that."

"That's the idea, baby. It's Tuesday." He kissed her neck where it met her ear as he inserted a finger, stretching her oh-so-sensitive and needy vaginal opening.

"Uh…" What had been the other question? Her pleasure increasing, she couldn't think. Then it came to her. "What time is it?"

"About six-thirty in the morning. More importantly, it's time for me to make love to you fully." He pulled his finger from her and then pulled her top leg up and back over his thigh. "Hold your leg there, please." Then he notched the head of his cock in her opening from behind, slowly fed his thick length into her partway, and then stopped.

His thickness throbbed within her, making her ache. She wanted to move to soothe the sensation, but was afraid to. She wasn't sure she could handle him going any deeper.

"You okay, Tessa?" Earl kissed her neck. "Am I hurting you?"

"No-o-o, not really."

"Are you sure?" He nuzzled her shoulder. "You're tense."

He was correct. Her muscles had almost seized when he'd entered her. She took a couple of deep breaths and concentrated on opening herself up to his cock. The discomfort eased as her body adapted to his thickness. "It's better."

"Yeah, it's more than better." His hand on her mons, he played with her clit as he thrust in and out in small movements; with each inward motion, he went a little deeper.

"I feel so full … I like it." She especially appreciated the heat of his body all along her back. It was nice being close, connected.

His slow, rhythmic push-pull built her pleasure gradually.

"If I hurt you, let me know." He slid the hand on her mons up to cup the lower curve of a breast and caressed it. He kissed her shoulder and slowed the thrust of his cock to almost a stand-still. "God, baby, you feel so tight and moist around my cock."

"You aren't hurting me. It feels different, a good different." She thrust her butt at him, moving him more fully into her sheath. "I like how you feel inside me. All hot and throbbing."

His cock was really deep now and rubbing on a spot in her vagina that doubled her excitement. She thrust back again, seeking the sensation. She needed to come, but his slow push-pull and light, teasing touches were keeping her on the edge.

Tessa took the hand on her breast and moved it back to her clit. "Um, I need more. Are we gonna make love, or are you gonna tease me?"

She shoved the heel of his hand on her clit and moved it in a circular motion. "I need this … harder … and I really need you to move."

"And I will." He scraped his teeth along the length of her neck. Her pussy clenched at the rougher caress. "I'm such a dumbass. I forgot to ask about protection. Are you on birth control?"

"Yeah, that's covered … um, on the pill." She wiggled, and he thrust his cock in farther. "I haven't had intercourse for over a year. I'm clean."

"I haven't had sex without protection ever. So—" Earl groaned when she tightened her vagina around him; he nipped her shoulder.

A frisson of pleasure zeroed in on her clit. Who knew she liked biting?

Earl trailed nipping and licking kisses over her shoulder and up her throat. He then tilted her head back and took her mouth in a deep, biting kiss that had her grinding her bottom against him. His reaction was to seat his cock fully inside her so the tip touched her cervix and his balls nestled against the curve of her bottom.

Tessa broke away from the luscious kiss and groaned. She then licked his lower lip and sucked it into her mouth, letting it go with a slick *pop*. "So…" finishing the talk of safe sex so they could get on to the good parts of the program, "…you don't need to use a condom."

"God, bareback. Never, ever done it this way." He began thrusting again. In. Out. In. Out.

His slow hip action had her moaning low in her throat as each move rippled his cock along the ultra-sensitive nerve endings in her sheath. He was conquering and claiming the intimate territory as his own.

And she was so okay with that.

With her arm up and behind, she reached for his head and stroked his hair and whatever else she could reach. The hair on his chest rasped across the overly sensitized skin of her back as he undulated against her in the slow dance of love-making.

And always, always, he kissed her face, her neck, her shoulders, and his fingers fondled her clit and the labia spread wide by the girth of his cock.

The pressure within her built until she couldn't hold back the whimpers and mewls of the pleasure-pain of the slow and excruciating buildup. She recognized what he was doing, and God knew, she loved him for taking special care with her this first time.

But enough was enough.

"Earl. Let go, darling. I need you to move." She pinched his hip to make her point.

"God, baby…" Earl groaned and rested his sweaty forehead against her shoulder. His rasping breaths were warm and damp against her skin. "…if I let go, it'll be rough. I don't want to hurt you."

Scare her or remind her of her past, he meant, but he was too loving and kind to say it out loud.

She smoothed a hand over the arm holding her to him as he thrust slowly, maintaining a snail's pace that was frickin' driving her nuts. "I trust you. Now, let go and make love to me. I want it hard and fast and … frickin' now."

"God, I love you." He lightly bit the juncture of her neck and shoulder.

She hissed at the sharp sensation. He chuckled against the smarting spot and increased the speed of his cock until he thrust rapidly in and out of her aching depths.

Tessa threw her head back and moaned. "God, that feels … so … effin' amazing. I can feel your cock throbbing."

Earl grunted. "Fucking perfect. You're … fucking … perfect."

And then her lover took it up another notch. As he moved faster and faster, she held on to the arm around her waist, the arm whose hand flicked and teased her clit, driving her crazier and crazier with pleasure. The sounds coming from him became more and more animalistic the faster and harder he thrust.

His excitement became hers.

"God … baby … don't let me hurt you." The pleading in his tone couldn't be mistaken. He was still worried.

"You aren't." She nipped the underside of his chin. She let go of his arm and reached back to cup his buttock. "Take me. Harder." She shoved him into her as she thrust back to meet his pistoning hips. "Harder."

"Goddamn. Fuckin' wonderful." His groan of pleasure made her pussy contract.

Earl surged inside her harder and faster. Pressure increased. The ripples along her sheath built until they became waves. His cock throbbed more rapidly and seemed to thicken. The sensation was more than wonderful. But she needed more.

"Earl ... I need to come."

"Hell, yeah. Come for me."

Earl's words rumbled like thunder around her, a sexual storm front.

The sounds were so low, so rumbling, she felt the vibrations from his chest against her back. His body was coated with sweat and moved slickly against her own heated skin.

A quick glimpse of his face showed his masculine features contorted into a rictus of pleasure-pain as he took her steadily, denying himself as he worked to give her pleasure.

All Tessa could do was hold on and pray the pressure Earl built inside her wouldn't kill her before it released.

She kissed, licked, and bit his chin and jaw as her head lolled against his shoulder. She whispered words of love amongst the moans and whimpers and animalistic sounds coming from her throat.

"Let go, baby. Come." Earl growled and ground the heel of his hand over her clit. "Fucking now."

And that was what she'd needed. Her climax blew through her like the leading winds of a thunderstorm, sweeping her into the sky and tossing her around as she screamed her pleasure and Earl's name amidst the tempest of his taking.

The pleasure of her release was painful. Euphoric. The best sensation she'd ever felt in her entire life. She made noises she'd never made before as she gasped for breath. Grunts. Mewls. Moans. Raspy harsh groans. And finally, a stream of "oh Gods."

Earl's hips never stopped moving, pummeling her butt, thrusting so deeply inside her his cock head hit her cervix as he fed the storm inside her body.

Then he roared, "God, yes, Tessa."

The world seemed to stop moving along with his hips for one infinite second—after which, Earl shouted her name once more and exploded into a rougher, faster, more erratic motion, pounding her hips as his cum filled her depths and sent her soaring even farther into the storm-filled plane of existence created by their coming together.

For what seemed like forever, she floated on zephyrs of pure pleasure as Earl's hips slowed the intensity of the in-and-out movement. His still-hard cock nursed her through mini-climax after mini-climax.

But she wasn't afraid of this new plane of existence, because Earl held her safely in his arms.

She was so safe. So happy. So very loved.

As she finally settled down to earth, felt the mattress beneath her, Earl whispered against her cheek. "Sleep, sweetheart. I've got you."

She managed to utter one "love you" and a yawn before sinking into the deep sleep of satiation. All worries of what would come later shoved to the far recesses of her mind by the pleasure she'd shared with Earl and the security of his arms.

CHAPTER 9

Tuesday, December 6th, 9:30 a.m.

This time when Tessa woke up, she was alone. She turned over and felt the depression in the sheets where Earl had lain next to her and found they were cold.

Dammit, she had plans for the man, and he'd sneaked out and left her sleeping. The next time they were intimate, she intended to explore a bit, beginning with his cock.

Tossing aside the covers, she sat up and swung her legs over the side of the bed. She winced when areas that had taken a beating in her fall over the edge of the ravine made themselves known, along with the more sexual tenderness of having taken Earl's big cock.

God, she wanted him again.

But before that could happen, she needed a shower, some ibuprofen, and food. Tessa noted her things had been moved from her guest suite to this one. Earl's doing she was sure. The man had claimed her and was making his possession clear. She giggled. She liked being possessed by Earl; it showed how much he loved her. Then she sobered as she wondered how many women in his past he had moved into his space. A sharp pang of jealousy made her wince.

Get over yourself. The man hasn't been a monk waiting for you to come along. Enjoy the moment.

Overthinking things was one of her issues; always had been.

Tessa entered the bathroom. Her personal items were mingled with Earl's on the vanity. The sight looked and felt right. She could live in this kind of moment for a very long time.

With a happy sigh, she took her shower and washed her hair.

Once her hair was reasonably dry and in her favored high ponytail, she took the backstairs to the kitchen hallway.

She inhaled deeply as she descended the steps. The aroma of bacon and eggs had her stomach grumbling again. Quickly, she walked the hallway toward the kitchen, ready to eat, and more than ready to see Earl again, to touch him and see his reaction. To reaffirm he loved and wanted her.

Then she hesitated, ugly thoughts pushed their way

to the front of her mind. What if last night had all been about booty call?

Geez Louise, Tessa. The man loves you. What happened to live in the moment?

She couldn't help her insecurity. She was still in a state of shock at the thought this wonderful man wanted her, could overlook her sordid past. In the light of day, had he looked at her and seen a slut, an easy lay?

God. I'd wash my hands of you, but we're sort of inseparable. Go in there. You'll see. Earl loves you.

She took a deep breath and entered the kitchen. When she was less than two feet into the room, she stopped.

The gazes of the seven men, none of them Earl, sitting around the breakfast nook table turned her way. Each of them looked grim—and shamefaced.

The reason for their guilt was her opened laptop in the center of the table. Her stomach clenched. She backed up, ready to turn and run.

"Tessa, come here, sweetheart." Earl stood by the stove and held his hand out. The concerned look on his face told her he could read her fear. His eyes held love and affection … and understanding.

God, when would she stop being such an idiot?

See? I told you so. Go to him.

Tessa must not have reacted quickly enough, because Earl started for her, muttering things she couldn't hear, but probably didn't need to. Obviously, she'd interrupted a planning session about her problem. She needed to gain some control over this knee-jerk reaction to the others knowing about her. Best to start now.

"Earl?" She met him halfway. She walked into his open arms and twined hers around his lean waist. "What's going on, tough guy? Did you forget to invite me to the powwow on my cyberstalker problem?"

Earl's warm—and what she read as proud—gaze swept over her face, twice. A fine trembling traveled through her. She hadn't dreamed any of the previous night or this morning—Earl Blackhawk loved her. Tessa was glad for the support of his arms, since her knees went weak at the desire in the depths of his eyes.

God, the man could make her want, no, need him with just a look.

"You're okay then?" His voice was husky and loving.

"I love you," she whispered. "I'm fine."

"Love you, too, sweetheart." He brushed a kiss over her flushed cheeks.

Several male snorts and grunts from the interested onlookers had her face heating up even more. She couldn't believe she just blurted her love for Earl in front of an audience.

Earl shot a nasty look in the direction of the noise, and the men shut up. He pulled her with him toward the stove where he took some scrambled eggs off the burner.

Then he leaned down and kissed her on the mouth—several warm, firm brushes of his lips. He placed his mouth near her ear and spoke in a low monotone which would carry no farther than them. "Did I hurt you this morning?"

Tessa's cheeks had to be fire-engine red by now. But his words, his husky, caring tone of voice, had her pussy clenching in need. She wanted him now.

"I'm fine." She stood on her tiptoes and kissed him, adding a sharp little nip to his lower lip. His pupils dilated and his nostrils flared at the provocation. "I understand why you let me sleep, but this is my life, tough guy. I think I should be involved in figuring out how to handle the bastard."

Earl's face darkened. He obviously wanted her out of it, but then he nodded. And if she hadn't already fallen in love with the man, that acceptance, reluctant though it was, and especially because it was grudging, would've done it.

"Fair enough. We haven't started yet, so you haven't missed anything." Earl moved her to his side and placed an arm around her waist. He ushered her to the table and pulled out a chair for her. "Sit, sweetheart. What do you want to eat?"

"Bacon, definitely, with some eggs." She looked up. "What else did you cook? And where in the heck is Scotty? He can't still be hung over."

"Scotty's taking care of Riley this morning, so Keely can sleep in," Ren offered with a warm smile. "My wife didn't sleep well last night."

The choking coughs of his men and Ren's naughty grin said it all.

Keely was sleeping the sleep of a sexually satisfied woman. Just as Tessa had after both intimate interludes with Earl. She'd never slept so well in her life.

"I made biscuits." Earl leaned over and kissed the top of her head as he stroked her back. "Want one?"

She smiled. "I want two."

"Whatever you want, Tessa, I'll always get it for you."

She was fairly sure he was talking about more than just food. More than sex. His next words confirmed her supposition.

Earl looked her in the eye. "No one here is judging you, baby. Understand that. We want to get this asshole out of your life so you and I can make a new one together. Got it?"

Tessa smiled through the tears forming in her eyes. This man not only loved her, but also had her back. If she had to go through all the hell in her life again to reach this moment and find this man, she would do it in an instant. He was worth it.

"Got it, tough guy. Now feed me."

Earl chuckled and flicked the end of her nose lightly. "Yes, ma'am."

Tessa turned to face the men at the table. Besides Ren, there was Tweeter, Paul, Loren, Price, Evan, and Chad. "Hey guys. Sorry about yesterday. I sort of freaked.

Thank you for saving me."

Evan, sitting on her immediate right, shoulder-bumped her. "Tessa, sweetie, you know Chad and I have always had your back. You should've told us about this stalker. About what he had on you." He turned her face to meet his gaze. "Please tell me you at least reported this to the Chicago police."

She leaned over and kissed the weathered cheek of the man who'd saved her life and her sanity at a time when she'd feared to lose both. "I did. Detective Roebuck of CPD—remember him?—and Detective Wayne in CPD's Cyber-Crimes division are on this, as is Special Agent Garcia from the FBI."

The men seemed to grunt with approval in unison. Well, at least, she'd done something right.

Earl, still behind her, squeezed her shoulders.

"The most recent e-mails and, um, images came right before I left Chicago for Sanctuary. The CPD and the FBI already have them. I forwarded them from O'Hare while I waited on my plane. These were an escalation over the previous ones I received. They're all there, on my laptop, if you want to see the pattern."

"I looked at them all, Tessa. I found the bastard," Tweeter spoke up. "I was going to tell the guys about it over breakfast."

"You have?" she squeaked and stared at Tweeter with shock—and respect. He'd done in less than one day more than the law enforcement types had done in weeks.

Earl's warm hands massaged the tension from her neck and upper back, calming her immediately.

"Who is he? Where is he?" she asked.

"Eat first, sweetheart, and then we can talk about all this. You need fuel to deal with the remnants of the altitude sickness." Earl rubbed his cheek over hers. "Do you have contact numbers for the detectives and the Feds? We'll need those for later."

"Yes. They should be in my address book on the laptop."

"I'm on it." Tweeter typed and moused. "Got them. Earl's right. We all could use some food before we make plans to nail the mother-fucker. I know I'm starved."

Loren shoved his brother's arm. "You're always hungry, geekazoid, that's why mom called you her bottomless pit." Tweeter shoved him back.

Ren laughed. "Stop it, you two." The leader of SSI looked at Earl. "We gonna let the CPD and the Feds take this guy down or…?"

"Fuck no." Earl growled and his hands tightened on Tessa's shoulders. "I'm taking the bastard out. The law can have what's left of him."

"No, Earl…" Tessa started to turn to plead with him to let the law handle it, but he stopped her with another squeeze.

"You're mine. I protect what's mine. We'll talk about

this after we eat." He nuzzled and kissed the tip of her ear, and then moved away.

Ren grinned. "Well, looks like Earl and I are on the same page, Tessa. The cops had their chance. And from the way they've dragged their feet, I figure they were using you to draw the bastard out on something bigger than cyberstalking. Tweeter found the guy awfully damn fast. And even though the CPD and the FBI might not be at my brother-in-law's caliber with computers, they aren't chopped liver either."

Earl spoke from his place near the stove. "I agree. They've got a deeper game going and are using Tessa. The cops have some explaining to do."

Ren nodded. "My thoughts exactly. But the longer this guy is on the streets, the more he'll escalate in his stalking of Tessa. We don't want him making physical contact."

Tessa shuddered. "No, I don't want that either."

Evan hugged her, sharing his warmth and providing comfort. "Bastards. I hope Earl beats the ever-loving shit out of the asshole and reams some cops and Feds new assholes."

Tessa had to laugh. For Evan to wish violence on anyone and use vulgar language while doing so demonstrated just how upset he was.

"Tessa, from what I've found, this guy is dangerous to not only you, but other unsuspecting women," Tweeter said. "Earl has a theory."

"What?" Tessa asked.

Earl placed her food in front of her. "He's a sex trafficker."

Tessa couldn't stop the whimper that escaped her mouth.

Earl swore something so foul she gasped. "Sorry, baby. But the bastard had to have been involved with the Branhams' business. Probably a silent partner or maybe a financial backer."

He leaned over and kissed her suddenly wet cheek. "Don't cry, baby. You know it kills me. I promise he won't get his hands on you. I swear it on my soul."

Tessa turned and kissed his lips. "I know. I know. I'm fine."

"Like hell you're fine." He swiped the tears from her cheeks with his thumbs as he cupped her face. He looked around at the interested onlookers. "Breakfast is served. Help yourselves."

Tessa half-smiled as there was a mass exodus from the table as the men moved to the island and swarmed the buffet servers.

Even with Earl's reassurances and the end potentially in sight, her stomach was knotted with anxiety. She forced herself to eat the fluffy eggs. After a couple of bites, her hunger beat out her nerves and the food went down more easily. Her man had a magic touch with eggs. She took a bite of the thick-sliced bacon and moaned. He was a wizard with bacon. It was crispy, just the way she liked.

Earl went to the kitchen island and came back with his own loaded plate. He sat down on her left side. "It's good?"

With a mouth full of bacon, she could only nod.

He smiled. "I like feeding you. Juice is on the table. Want me to pour you a glass?"

She swallowed and said, "I can get it, Earl."

The man was taking the "taking care of her" thing too far.

Tessa placed her fork on the plate and looked at him. She found concern and love in his eyes. His stubbornness was there in the tension and angle of his jaw. The man was over-protective to the nth degree. If Earl didn't want to let her pour her own juice, he sure as hell wouldn't allow her to help take down the bastard.

And did she really want or need to?

Let's not. He's the one that branded you.

The stalker-bastard had been happy to claim that little act of torture in the e-mail which had accompanied the video and images of the "scene" as he'd called it. When she'd first viewed the video and the stills, she'd barely made it to the bathroom where she'd lost her dinner.

The day she'd been branded had been the day she'd made the decision to take control of her life, the day she decided to escape or die trying.

And now was the time to assert some more control

over her current life situation. It would be so easy to let Earl and the others handle it all. She couldn't be powerless again and live with herself.

Tessa rubbed her cheek against Earl's shoulder. "You know, I'm not helpless. I can pour my own juice. Dish up my own eggs. And I was taking care of this problem before you came into my life. I reported the threat to the proper authorities. I did the right and smart thing."

At his frown and snort, which she decided had been aimed at the proper authorities part of her little speech, she added, "Detective Roebuck is really eager to get whoever this guy is, because his gut says my stalker is the man who killed the Branhams. *He* called in the FBI because of the cybercrime nature of the stalking."

Earl took her chin in his hand and massaged her jaw with his thumb. "The police and the FBI don't love you, I do."

Her heart fluttered with happiness.

He went on, "There's no way in hell I'm letting the police use you to draw this bastard out for whatever bigger fish or case they have in mind, or maybe a promotion for one of the cops or the Fed."

Her insides turned to mush at the intensity of his need and desire to protect her from all comers.

He kissed her lips, tasting her leisurely, before breaking off at the coughs of their audience. "The bastard needs to be taken out now. From what I could see in your

278 | MONETTE MICHAELS

correspondence with the law, they're definitely dragging their damn feet."

Grunts of "oh yeahs" came from some of the SSI operatives.

"Which means," Earl continued, "(a) they can't find their asses and don't have a fucking clue what they're doing, or (b) and the most likely, they're using you. Ain't gonna happen. We'll move on the stalker as soon as we can get to Chicago."

He's right, you know. The wheels of justice had gone to slo-mo on this case.

Tweeter said, "The fact they didn't nail this guy weeks ago is criminal in my mind. What if the stalker decided to try to get into your condo and attack you for real?"

Earl snarled like a pissed-off tiger, and Tessa petted his shoulder. "I have excellent security on my home. Plus, when this all started, I upgraded it. I hired the security firm Callie used on her place and had my house wired for video and audio security and also added new digital security to all my windows and doors. I even changed out my front door to solid steel."

Tessa pulled her laptop away from Tweeter and toward her. She hit a few keys and then entered a series of passwords. She pointed to the monitor. "There ... see, that's my condo. And since I've been gone, the system was set to send a silent alarm to not only my security company, but also the police, if my perimeters were breached."

Tweeter came around the table and viewed the monitor over her shoulder. He reached over, keyed in a few things, sped through the feeds from the past several days, and then snorted. "Tessa, that picture is looping. Note the clock, it keeps going back to the same time in ten minute intervals. Someone has messed with your system, and what's really happening in your condo is anybody's guess."

"But the alarm?" Tessa had a sick feeling in her stomach.

"Turned off," Tweeter replied.

"Fuck!" Earl turned to look at Tweeter. "You mean the bastard has been in her place and has corrupted her security?"

"Someone has." Tweeter picked up the laptop and took it with him to his seat at the table. Ren moved Tweeter's half-eaten breakfast out of the way so Tweeter could put the computer down. "I can reset the system to live feed over the Internet since you have the program open. Let's see what real time looks like. I'll also check the alarm and lock settings."

Tweeter hummed under his breath as he typed and clicked the mouse. His face darkened and he said, "Fuck."

Ren echoed the sentiment, anger turning his eyes stormy.

Tessa's stomach knotted. "What is it?" Her voice was strained.

Earl pulled the monitor around. "Mother-fucking, sonuvabitch, sick-ass bastard."

Tessa's great room was a shambles. Her Italian modern couches were shredded. Everything that could be broken was. Those items that couldn't be broken were dented or torn apart.

Tweeter shifted the view to the kitchen which looked as if a tornado had sucked out all the contents of the cabinets and refrigerator and tossed them all about.

But it was the bedroom that had Earl and the others swearing the loudest. There was no destruction—but the bastard had attached shackles to the platform bed all around the edges and at all four corners and then had laid out the instruments of torture he planned to use on her.

A frightened sob escaped her throat. She clenched her jaw, halting any others. But she couldn't stop the tears streaming from the corners of her eyes. She took several breaths, appreciative of the men's silence, their sensitivity in allowing her to regain control over her emotions.

Tessa shoved her plate away with a trembling hand. She was no longer hungry. She shivered and wrapped her arms around her waist, hugging herself.

"Fuck this." Earl shoved back his chair and then pulled her into his arms until she sat across his lap, his arms around her.

She twined her arms around his neck and rested her

head on his shoulder, inhaling his scent and letting it and his warmth and strength soothe her.

"Bastard is going down, baby. Down hard." He kissed her forehead. "Just hold on to me. I've got you."

"I know." She kissed the side of his throat. "Whatever you decide to do, please be careful. I can't lose you now that I've found you."

"Not gonna lose me. Won't happen." He tightened his arms. "Relax into me."

Tweeter, his lips thinned with anger, looked up after several minutes. "Good system. It's back up and working properly now. I had it send an e-mail with a report to this laptop and to the e-mail address of the cops and the Feds. Gave them your Skype address. We should hear from them soon, I would think." His lips twisted into an evil grin. "I sort of insulted them."

A chorus of "fuck yeahs" and "damn rights" traveled around the table.

"It's lunchtime in Chicago," Ren drawled. "We might have a wait. Why don't you show Tessa the asshole stalker and the data you pulled on him?"

"What I want to know," Price said, "is why did he wait for almost seven years to use the info he had on Tessa? It's not like Tessa isn't famous. She was all over the place as a model, and it isn't all that well-kept of a secret she stopped modeling to write thrillers as T.A. Parks."

"I have a theory," Chad spoke up. "Her last novel

used some of what's in those photos and the, uh, video. The book was about sex trafficking. Evan and I knew she wrote the book as a catharsis."

Evan nodded. "Her therapist had always told her to write things down and get them out of her head. Our little gal just took it a step further and made money off the cathartic act."

Tessa nodded. "The earlier e-mails began with him raving over the book. Then the tone changed and became more about ... me and ... his sexual perversions. Maybe he's afraid I figured out who he really is, and so he decided to scare me to keep silent. To keep me from revealing his perfidy to the world."

"It's as good a theory as any." Earl rubbed her arm. "I'll be sure to ask the son of a bitch when I'm beating the shit out of him."

The men chuckled and Tessa grinned at the image. "That would be nice of you, Earl. Thanks."

Tweeter shoved the laptop toward her. "I've opened the file I created on the bastard. There are several news articles and photos and even a bio. See if the man is someone you recognize."

Earl released his tight hold on her and let her lean forward.

Tessa clicked a folder titled "Bio." She read out loud. "Dion Denuccio. CEO of Denuccio Investment Fund, Ltd." She looked up. "He's not even an American citizen. His company is incorporated in England. He has branches in London, Chicago, Rio de Janeiro, Shanghai, and Moscow."

"Bet he kidnaps or falsely adopts girls from the other places, and at least seven years ago anyway, he took them to the club in Chicago. Probably moved his operations after killing off the Branhams." Ren looked at his brother-in-law. "Can you start a search using our NSA connections and see if you can find this guy's travel patterns over the last couple of years or so?"

Tweeter grinned evilly. "Already set that search up. It's been running since last night. The guy travels a lot. I have my analysis program plotting patterns, then I'm cross-checking with criminal activity reports of dead bodies, missing women, and the like in the places he frequents."

"Good idea," Earl murmured. "Try the next folder, Tessa. It has his picture."

Tessa opened the image folder. A picture of a smiling, dark-haired man in his middle forties stared out at her from the screen. "I've never seen him before in my life. The men who…" she choked and then swallowed, "…hurt me always wore masks and never talked." *Just grunted and groaned.* "So, I can't say if he is or isn't the man. But if Tweeter says this is the guy sending the e-mail, then it must be him since he acknowledged he'd branded me as his property."

She choked over the last words, fear tightening her throat.

"You're mine." Earl tipped her chin up and whispered against her lips, "You are mine."

Then he kissed her, branding her more permanently than any piece of hot metal ever could.

CHAPTER 10

Later on Tuesday afternoon.

Earl sat on the leather sofa in the Lodge great room with Tessa snuggled next to his side. Ren sat on the companion sofa.

After the beautiful, intimate interlude with Tessa that morning, the day had been filled with one bit of bad news after another about Tessa's stalker, Dion Denuccio.

The man was in the wind, and even Tweeter, now with Keely helping him, couldn't find the bastard. The man either had some computer skills, or had hired someone to blur his trail since he'd left his London home over two weeks ago, right before Tessa began receiving the threatening texts and e-mails.

The worst of it was, the asswipe had been spotted in Chicago two days ago. The FBI and the cops had known that fact and lost him.

Turned out, they'd traced Tessa's stalker's identity weeks ago. The FBI had known of Denuccio's many crimes, as had Interpol and several other major law enforcement agencies in the world. The fucker was wanted for sex trafficking, murder, kidnapping, and money laundering. They'd rationalized leaving him free to pursue Tessa as a path to the greater good.

"So," Earl gritted out as he faced the large-screen television being used for the teleconference call among several of the law enforcement agencies pursuing Denuccio, "let me summarize. You concluded Denuccio, a murdering, predatory sexual offender who'd eluded you for over seven years would make a mistake in his lustful need to regain control of Tessa. But you didn't tell her or give her physical protection. Is that the gist of it?"

Tessa trembled against him. She hadn't uttered a word since the Chicago cop and the FBI agent had detailed their reasons for not including her in the loop. He hugged her and pressed a kiss against her too-cool cheek.

Detective Roebuck had the grace to look embarrassed. The Interpol and MI-6 reps just looked uncomfortable.

The FBI agent, Garcia, glared and said, "We had protection on her until she took the notion to go to O'Hare without letting us know and fly to the fricking middle of nowhere Idaho."

Earl smiled, and he was fairly sure it wasn't a pleasant one if Roebuck's audible gulp said anything. "Good thing she came here then, isn't it? With her security being compromised and you guys unable to find your asses with a GPS."

Garcia stuttered. "That …that's an inaccurate representation."

"Shut up, Garcia," Ren said. "Did you catch the current live feed we sent from her apartment? Did you see what the animal did to her place? He's a sick fuck, and your people saw him and did nothing."

"We don't have enough evidence…" Garcia began.

Earl growled. "Shut the fuck up. We don't want to hear any more lies. You've been chasing this guy for over seven years. How can you not have enough evidence?"

"When would you have stepped in?" Tessa's breath hitched. "When he was in my apartment raping me? When he'd taken me to wherever his new *playroom* is and branded me again? When?"

Earl massaged her shoulders and brushed a kiss over her tear-stained cheek. "I've got you, sweetheart. Not gonna happen ever again."

"We wouldn't have let it go that far." Roebuck spoke over the mumbling of the other law enforcement representatives who also denied they'd ever let such a heinous act occur. Garcia sat and said nothing as he stared stonily at Earl.

"No, you sure as hell won't," snarled Earl. "Tessa's under my and SSI's care now. We'll handle her personal protection. If Denuccio comes anywhere near Tessa, he's dead."

"You can't just take the law into your own hands," Garcia blustered, his face brick red.

"You'd be surprised what I can and will do to protect Tessa from the bastard." Earl stared first at Garcia and then Roebuck. "Tessa's mine, and no one touches what's mine. Understood?"

Roebuck nodded and a glimmer of respect for Earl's words appeared in his eyes.

Garcia's lips thinned in anger. "Then we'd have to arrest you for interfering in an ongoing federal investigation and murder."

Earl snorted. "Try it. But note, I never said I'd kill the bastard. I'll merely make sure he's in no condition to ever touch another unwilling woman." He looked at Ren and nodded. "Tell the nice FBI man what we'll be delivering with Denuccio's slightly damaged body since they haven't managed to find enough evidence to arrest the fucker before now."

Ren smiled, a particularly nasty smile which Earl had to appreciate. "I'd be happy to, Earl." He turned and stared at the men on the screen. "Courtesy of my brother-in-law, Dr. Stuart Walsh, and my lovely wife, Dr. Keely Walsh-Maddox, you'll be getting the proof needed of not only his sex trafficking business, his clientele lists, and the places he launders money for his own and other crime organizations, but also what he launders for known terrorist groups. You can say thank you now."

"Will it be legal?" the Interpol agent asked. "To use in the World Court and other countries' courts?"

Ren snorted. "It's legal in the United States, and as far as I'm concerned that's all that matters. You gentlemen sat on your thumbs while the man laundered terrorist money."

Visibly restraining his rage, Ren continued, "We had two Federal judges sign off on the warrants last night before we began looking into Denuccio's bank records and holding companies."

"How did you get that kind of access?" Roebuck asked, a frown on his face. "Garcia said it couldn't be done. We didn't have enough evidence."

"My wife has access as a contract employee for NSA to pursue terrorist money wherever it lurks. This is legally obtained evidence pursuant to several terrorism laws, and the case will be tried in the United States. Y'all can fight it out with the US Attorney General for Denuccio leftovers."

Earl fixed Garcia with a narrow-eyed stare. "If the FBI had taken the initiative to reach out to its fellow agencies in the US Intelligence community, you would've learned of the CIA's and NCS's long-time interest in the movements of Denuccio as it applied to terrorism money laundering. If the FBI had shared its information with Homeland Security or even Interpol, Denuccio would've been picked up years ago."

The "then he couldn't have terrorized my woman" he left unsaid. If the asshats hadn't picked up what was most important to him by this point in the call, then there was no help for the idiots.

Tessa choked on a sob and turned her face into his chest. He smoothed her hair and cuddled her shuddering body as she wept. He reined in the anger that his angel had been reduced to tears by the callousness and disregard of the law enforcement agencies that should have been protecting her.

"When we informed the Director of NCS last night that their money-laundering Denuccio was also under suspicion of being an international sex trafficker, a sexual predator," Earl spit his words out like bullets from an automatic weapon, "the Director consulted with the AG and they decided it was time to pull him in."

"*They*," Earl stressed the word, "wound up a multiple-year communications intelligence gathering and human intelligence gathering terrorism investigation in order to get this piece of human excrement off the streets. That's real law enforcement."

The "unlike you two pieces of garbage" also went unsaid.

"I'm sorry, Tessa." Roebuck's voice was raspy. "If he's still in Chicago, we'll find him. He won't hurt you."

"Damn right, he won't," Earl rumbled, "because he has to go through me first." He shot a nasty look at Roebuck and Garcia. "Go take care of the other fine citizens of Chicago, you boys missed your chance on this one."

When Garcia opened his mouth to say something, Earl snarled, "Shut it, Garcia." He turned to Ren. "I think we're done here, right?"

"More than." Ren nodded. "The Director of NCS in conjunction with Homeland Security acting on the behalf of the US Intelligence community and the US Attorney General has contracted SSI to bring Denuccio in on the terrorist money laundering charges. Other charges, including sex trafficking," and he now addressed the international agencies, "can be brought after we bring him in."

The international law enforcement representatives smiled and murmured their thanks and support.

All but Garcia, who opened his damn mouth to speak, but was cut off by Tweeter, who'd just come upstairs and had, Earl knew, been following the call on a monitor in the Bat Cave.

Tweeter looked at the Fed. "Garcia, I just sent copies of what NCS and Homeland have kindly told us to share with the FBI. Your boss has them. He also has a detailed analysis by my sister, Dr. Walsh-Maddox, of the evidence in this case from the intelligence community perspective. She also details that under the new anti-terrorism laws, you failed to share your Denuccio case reports with the other boys and girls in the IC. That's a big no-no." Tweeter grinned. "If they don't can your ass, you'll be looking at a permanent assignment to Fargo."

"We're done here." Ren pointed a remote at the screen and terminated the feed. He turned to his brother-in-law. "What's up, Tweeter? I know that grin."

"I know where the bastard is." Tweeter's lips thinned grimly. "He's in Chicago in a condo not two blocks from Tessa's condo on Oak Street. He bought it just about the time he began sending the e-mails. The FBI and the Chicago cops thought he was staying in the apartment where the transmissions came from, but that was his smokescreen and how they lost him. They checked hotels and motels, but never bothered to look for another private residence. Tunnel-visioned idiots. Denuccio's using public Wi-Fi within two to three blocks of this condo."

Tessa lifted her head from Earl's chest and sniffled. "How did you find him, Tweeter? How did you find the condo?"

"It wasn't hard." Tweeter frowned and muttered under his breath, but Earl heard him say, "It was easy. The cops must have had a blind spot. Need to see why the cyber-crimes guy didn't tweak onto it."

Earl stiffened and wondered why also.

In a louder voice, Tweeter continued, "Denuccio bought it under your pen name, T.A. Parks. Keely had an idea that if he was so fixated on you and, if as we suspected it was the novel you wrote that turned his eyes back on you, we should try character names and then your pen name with recent real estate purchases. Your pen name did it."

Tessa shoved out of Earl's arms, ran to Tweeter, and hugged him. "Thank you ... thank you." She turned and smiled through her tears. "It's almost over. I need to go hug Keely now."

"Tessa?" Earl called out; he didn't like her out of his sight, even here where she was as safe as she would ever be.

Paranoid much?

Fuck yeah.

Tessa turned and ran back to him. She leaned over and kissed him on the mouth. Tongue was involved. When she pulled away, he wanted to pull her back, but the others were grinning, and he decided to wait until later when they were alone to take the promise of that kiss further.

"I'll be back, tough guy. Meet me in the kitchen. We'll throw Scotty out and make something special for dinner. Okay?" She stroked his face. "I love you."

"Love you, too." He took her hand and pressed a kiss to the palm. "Steaks, you think?"

294 | MONETTE MICHAELS

"Yeah, steaks. See you in the kitchen in fifteen minutes. I want to cuddle little Riley after I hug Keely." She whispered, the barest sound for his ears alone, "I want to practice for the day I hold our child."

Earl pulled her to him for a deep, hungry taking of her mouth. Letting her go, he whispered, "I look forward to that day."

CHAPTER 11

Thursday, December 8th, 9:00 a.m., Chicago.

Earl stood among the shambles of Tessa's condo. He didn't know what to do for her. He'd never felt so helpless in his entire adult life.

"Sweetheart…" he began as he reached for her.

"Shh, we knew it was bad from the live feed. So I was prepared." Tessa turned and placed her head on his chest. "They were just things. Things can be replaced."

Her calm acceptance of what the fucknut had done made him even angrier. "Screw that. They were more than just things."

He tipped up her chin and looked into her sad, sad eyes. Not as unaffected as she wanted him and the others picking through the mess to think. "This was your haven. The place you were supposed to feel safe. The place where you created all those wonderful books."

"Yes, it was…" she kissed his chin, "…but now I have you. You're my haven. You make me feel safe, loved."

She looked around, and a bittersweet smile touched her lips. "This was my past. My old life began in Chicago, and it ends here." She relaxed more fully into his body and rubbed her cheek on his chest. "My new life is with you—in Osprey's Point. I can live—write—anywhere, Earl, as long as you're there also. I've learned since Monday, I really need you close by."

"And that's where I'll be." Earl kissed her, taking her mouth with hunger. He'd never get tired of kissing or loving this woman. "I've found I need you just as close. We'll have a wonderful life in Osprey's Point, I promise."

"I know we will. From the moment I met you, I knew, deep inside, I'd waited my whole life to find you … the one man who would love and care for me. The one man I could trust with all that is in me." She shifted to stand at his side, her arm around his waist. She kicked a piece of broken pottery. "Let's get out of here. We can't stay here." Her voice echoed in the destroyed room.

Earl snarled low in his throat as someone approached. He placed Tessa behind him and turned to see who dared to interrupt a personal moment with Tessa.

Detective Roebuck coughed as he stood in the entrance to the great room.

"What is it, Roebuck?"

"I … um … couldn't help but overhear. But Ms. Andrews is right. She can't stay here. It's a crime scene." Roebuck looked around, a fierce expression on his face as he took in the extent of the destruction. "Whatever your computer tech guy did, the security is running now. From what the CSI techs are telling me, Denuccio did this right after Ms. Andrews left on Saturday to fly to Idaho."

The detective sighed and looked as if he had aged since the teleconference on Tuesday. "If Denuccio comes back, we'll see and get him."

"Fuck that, he won't come back here, and we all know it," snarled Earl. "This," he waved his free arm around the space, "happened on your watch. You and Garcia dropped the fucking ball. Denuccio should've been arrested as soon as you tracked the e-mails and text messages."

Roebuck's face darkened. "I know CPD fucked up. And while it doesn't totally excuse me, Garcia was running the case. We got big-footed by the Feds, okay? I didn't like it, but I had to eat it and do what he said. Todd in our Cyber-Crimes Division looked over the shit both Dr. Walshes sent and agreed we should've found Denuccio's lair a while ago."

Roebuck ran a shaky hand through his thinning hair. "My boss knows all this now. He's talking to Garcia's boss. That Fargo field office mentioned on Tuesday looks like a real possibility for Garcia. He screwed the pooch, and we're all paying for it."

"I'm sorry about all this, Ms. Andrews." Roebuck shook his head. "I want justice for you and all those girls this freak's harmed all these years. It bothers the hell out of me we have to use money laundering of terrorist money to put him away. He should be going away for multiple murders, kidnapping, and sexual deviant acts. Crimes against persons always trumps crimes concerning property in my book, but we'll take what we can to get him off the streets."

Tessa trembled within Earl's arms, but she held it together in front of the cop.

"Shut it, Roebuck," Earl said, feeling feral. "Tessa lived it. You don't need to stand here in her destroyed home and tell her what she already knows."

"It's okay, tough guy." Tessa petted him. "Detective, you were very gentle and patient with me all those years ago." Her voice was strained. "I've never forgotten. You treated me like a human being and not as an object of pity. I don't blame you or anyone for what happened now or back then other than the person responsible. Denuccio will be caught and will serve time for his criminal acts."

Earl was not as forgiving, but damn, he was so proud of Tessa. Her voice and demeanor exhibited none of the trembling he felt as she snuggled even closer to his body.

"Damn right, the man will be caught and soon." Earl kissed the top of her head. "Paul and Loren are scouting his condo now. Keely and Tweeter are keeping eyes on his accounts." The locals didn't need to know the two were also using spy satellites to keep an eye on Denuccio's hidey-hole from the sky. "We'll know his every move."

"And the Chicago police are providing backup as requested by SSI acting as agents for Homeland at the request of the National Clandestine Service," Roebuck said. "The FBI's nose is way out of joint."

Earl snorted, "Well, if *all* of the alphabet intelligence agencies would've shared intel before now like they're supposed to, the FBI would've known their stalker suspect was a person of interest in international terrorism and acting within the US." He glared at Roebuck. "Homeland should've taken over the case and surveillance as soon as Denuccio had been identified as Tessa's cyberstalker."

"Yeah," Roebuck looked around and sighed, "would've prevented this, that's for sure."

Earl said nothing else. Nothing and no one would ever violate Tessa's world again and live to tell about it.

——

11:00 a.m., Chicago Fairmont Hotel.

TESSA LEANED INTO EARL AS he gave her another kiss. They sat on the bed in the beautifully appointed, lake-front-view suite at the top of the Fairmont Hotel. When she'd complained about the cost, he'd just kissed her and made love to her until she was too exhausted to even think about it.

The man's love-making had been both hungry and tender. Already she missed his touch, but he had work to do.

"Now, Tessa baby, you don't leave this suite until I, Loren, or Paul come back for you. You go with no one else. Not even the cop Roebuck stationed at the door. He's there to keep people out."

"I understood that the last two times you told me, Earl." Tessa smiled and petted his chest.

"I'll be at Denuccio's condo, but always reachable by my cell. Call if you need me."

"Yes, Earl. I'll be fine." Her man really didn't want to leave her, but then again he did. She knew he wanted to be in on the take-down of Denuccio.

He kissed her forehead so sweetly it brought tears to her eyes. "The warrant from the US Attorney General's office should be coming through any second now. It should be over soon." He smiled and rubbed his thumb over her lower lip. She sucked it and his eyes heated. "Hold that thought, baby. After it's over, we'll take the guys and celebrate at Gibson's this evening. Then," his voice lowered to a sexy growl, "we'll come back here and burn up the sheets, get a good night's sleep so we can head home tomorrow."

Tessa kissed Earl's lips. "I'm good with all that, but I have no clothes. Can we stay an extra day before going home so I can shop for something to wear? I can always shop for more stuff online once we get to Michigan. I assume UPS or FedEx deliver to Osprey's Point?"

Earl nipped her lower lip and then licked it. "Yes, they deliver. We'll be living in the U.P., not the Arctic Circle."

"Same difference from what the Walsh twins told me." Tessa giggled. "I can't wait to see your home."

"Our home," Earl corrected instantly.

Warm and gushy feelings settled in her stomach and she nodded. "Our home."

Tessa eyed her man sharply, taking in his dark clothing and winter gear which reminded her of what she'd seen SWAT officers wear. "You do have on a bullet-proof vest, right? I don't want…"

"Shh, sweetheart." Earl kissed her mouth as if he couldn't stand not to. "Ren and the guys outfitted me fully. Loren has my weapons. I'll be fine. If the Taliban couldn't kill me, this fuck sure as hell isn't gonna. Okay?"

"Okay." She smiled. "Just think, instead of e-mailing or calling the Walshes for military details, I only have to turn over in bed and grill you."

"Sweetheart, if you think I'm going to talk war games and tactics in bed when you're naked and lying beside me, think again." He rubbed his nose alongside hers. "I have much better ideas for our bed than that."

"Okay, I'll save the research for the dinner table." She rubbed his nose back with hers. "I'll research the sex scenes in bed."

Earl grunted, his dark eyes turning smoky with leashed desire. "Much better plan." He stood. "Now … order room service and eat something. You need to keep up your energy. You almost died on Monday. You need fuel, liquids, and rest."

"I am hungry." She frowned. "It's not safe for me to go down to the restaurant in the hotel?" She got out of bed and pulled on Earl's T-shirt to cover her nakedness.

The heat in her man's eyes flared and seared her. He'd told her the first time she'd attempted to pull on her pajamas she was always to be naked in his bed. The dictatorial, dominant pronouncement had made her instantly wet, and the sex afterward had been incendiary and kinky.

Tessa found she could do kinky with Earl, but only with him. No flashbacks at all.

Earl was her miracle.

"I think I made it clear you weren't to leave the room at all." Earl took her in his arms and hugged her to him, his hand fondling her naked bottom under his shirt. "I have to know you're safe, or I'll go nuts. I need to keep my mind on the take-down."

"Okay. Just call me when it's over, so I know you and the guys are safe." She peeked at him through her lashes.

"I'll be going just as nuts stuck here, not knowing what's going on."

"Just as soon as it's over. I promise." He kissed her once again, this one a deep, tongue-thrusting, hungry kiss that had her moaning. He broke off with a groan.

Tessa smiled because she could feel his cock against her stomach. He wanted her again. The man had some serious stamina.

"Hold my place."

"Oh, I have it memorized, book-marked, and noted." Tessa followed him to the door.

Earl turned in the open doorway. "Lock it. Use all the security locks. No one in, not even room service, just have them leave the cart outside the door and let the guard ring you. Okay?"

"Okay. Now go, or you'll miss out on all the fun." She pasted on a teasing smile, but inside she wanted him to stay here, be safe with her.

But she knew Earl well enough, even after knowing him for less than a week, to know he had to be there. Had to eliminate the danger to her. She'd never deny him his revenge, especially since he was doing it for her. All for her.

She said "hello" to the uniformed cop who sat on a chair in the reception area for the four suites on the top floor. She closed and locked the door, then headed for the bathroom to take a long, soaking bubble bath with the luxury products the hotel provided.

All the recent Earl-type sex had taken a toll on her body which was unused to such vigorous love-making. Her man was definitely in a league of his own when it came to sex. All the men she'd dated in the last seven years had been in the minors, no, less than that, they'd been bush league.

Tessa had herself a real man now. So, she'd needed to make sure she could keep up with him.

After the bath, she'd order in a light lunch. She'd need to save room for Gibson's, her, and as it turned out Earl's, favorite local steakhouse. She'd use the time after she ate lunch to use the computer in the hotel room to get a head start on replenishing her wardrobe and have the items shipped to Earl's—now her—home.

God, she couldn't wait to start her new life in Michigan with Earl.

CHAPTER 12

11:45 a.m., Outside Denuccio's Oak Street Condo.

The wind off Lake Michigan whistled down the residential street as a winter storm front moved into the city. Already the snow swirled around the law enforcement teams camped outside Denuccio's condo. A blizzard warning was in effect with six inches of new snow predicted along with gusting winds upwards of sixty miles per hour.

The urgency to get the take-down done was palpable in the atmosphere. No one wanted to go head-to-head with Mother Nature at her worst. Getting Denuccio off the streets was piece of cake when compared to Chicagoland's fierce weather patterns.

Earl wanted to get back to Tessa. Being snowed in, in a penthouse suite, wouldn't be a hardship.

"Are you sure he's in there?" Earl asked the SWAT team leader.

"Someone's in there," the man said, pointing to the infrared sensor. "CPD officers said they saw him go in with a cup of Starbucks and a bag from the bakery down the street around eight-thirty this morning, and he hasn't come out since then."

Loren and Paul came up to Earl.

Paul said, "The situation doesn't feel right. The blinds are all shut as if he knows we're watching."

Earl looked at the twins. While he'd been Army Special Forces, he had a healthy respect for SEALs, who attended many of the same training schools. When a SEAL said something didn't feel right, it wasn't.

"We need to get in there. Now." Earl shoved past the SWAT leader who grabbed him. Earl looked down at the man's hand. "Move it or lose it."

"You just can't go barreling in there. He's considered armed and dangerous."

"Your orders are to support SSI. We're going in." Earl shrugged the man's hand off. "He's not there. I'm betting whoever is, isn't even alive. Look at the infrared again. The pattern is too even. Humans' heat patterns aren't uniform, and they move, even when sleeping."

The SWAT leader's ego had just taken a hit, but Earl had seen terrorists use the same trick. A dead body wrapped in an electric blanket would show a warm human-shaped form.

"Don't beat yourself up, Captain." Earl waited at the condo entrance, really a row house, while Paul picked the locks. "I've seen this trick before. Now, so have you. You'll never get caught by it again."

"What happened the first time you were fooled?" Paul asked as he turned the handle on the door and shoved it open.

"I spent two weeks in the hospital and have scars and no spleen." Earl went in low while Loren and Paul covered him and entered high. Two SWAT guys moved in behind them to cover the front and rear entrances once the main floor was cleared.

Earl checked out the first room, a home office. "Clear."

Paul and Loren made their way down the central hallway to the back of the condo. Their "clears" echoed in the empty condo, empty except for what he suspected was a blanket-wrapped corpse on the second floor.

If there had been a live body upstairs, they should've been shot at by now or heard the man fleeing. All he heard was the lake-whipped wind howling through the front door.

Earl made his way up the stairs, keeping his eye out for any booby traps. He registered Loren speaking to the SWAT captain over the head sets. Loren remained downstairs to cover his and Paul's asses as they cleared the second floor.

Paul shadowed him. They moved together as if they'd trained together. In a way they had; Special Forces training in all the service branches covered clearing a building as part of modern urban warfare. Just because Earl suspected the body showing up on infrared was a red herring that didn't mean another person masking his body heat wasn't secreted somewhere on the premises.

"So? Who's the body upstairs? Denuccio?" Paul asked *sotto voce.*

"Maybe." *Maybe not.* "There could always have been more than one silent partner. And bad guys have been known to get rid of partners." Earl practically snarled the words. "I counted at least ten different men hurting Tessa in the photos and videos. Any of them could've been in on the filthy business."

"Gotcha," Paul said.

"Ren and I had a long talk as we studied the…" Earl swallowed past the knot of anger lodged in his throat, "…uh, what those fuckers did to Tessa. We're planning to get them all, sooner or later. Your genius brother and sister are looking for clues to the men's identities on the images by cross-checking the client list they found for the Chicago club."

On Tuesday night, after viewing and reviewing the evidence of Tessa's torture, he'd been sick to his stomach—and to the very depths of his soul—at the depravity.

Before he'd joined a sleeping Tessa, he'd gone and done a few rounds of hand-to-hand at the SSI gym with Ren and Price to work the rage out of his system. He refused to let his madness touch Tessa. She'd had enough violent emotions in her life; he wanted to show her only his love and passion.

When he'd gone to his and Tessa's bed, she'd moaned his name and snuggled into his body. That unconscious trust had wiped out any remnants of his wrath the hand-to-hand hadn't. He wasn't ashamed to admit, tears had formed in his eyes. He'd been in awe of the miracle of Tessa. She'd survived hell and come out of it well enough to take him into her body and let him love her. He planned to thank God every night for that blessing for the rest of his life.

Signaling a stop, Earl looked into the room where a very dead man lay on a bloody bed. Then he saw the wires and a ticking timer counting down seconds. Fifty, forty-nine—

"Bomb! Get the fuck out of here!" he shouted over the headset. "Get back! Get back!" he warned those outside the condo.

He turned and followed Paul. Both men used the railing and the wall to make a quick, sliding descent. In his head he mentally counted down the seconds remaining. Thirty-six, thirty-five—

As they hit the bottom floor and raced out the front door and down the steps, time ran out.

The bomb exploded.

The percussion of the blast threw him and Paul toward the street. Earl tucked and then rolled farther away from the heat of the flames chasing him. He continued to roll in the snow-covered lawn toward the street until he could no longer feel the heat of the fire which roared like an animal in the residential neighborhood.

Loren helped Earl up and away, as one of the SWAT team grabbed Paul.

Earl and the Walsh twins turned to look at the burning building as SWAT team members went to double-check the neighboring houses they'd cleared earlier. This time for pets. All humans were accounted for.

"What the fuck happened?" Loren asked as he visually checked his twin and Earl over for any injuries.

"Dead guy on a bomb." Earl swore and swiped at the snow on his clothing. "Someone watched and waited until we breached the house, then started the timer. Probably done remotely. They wanted to make a statement."

"And what statement was that?" Paul asked.

Earl growled and looked at the two men. "That he's smarter than us. And right about now I have to agree with him." He strode toward the rental Hummer he'd parked two blocks away. "We need to get back to Tessa. She's not safe. Denuccio's out there, plotting, planning."

A sense of urgency had him break into a run and ignore

the SWAT commander's shout. He hoped Denuccio was a long way from Chicago, but his gut wasn't buying it.

He ran faster. Loren's and Paul's pounding feet behind him told him they were on the same wave-length.

He tried to call Tessa. No answer.

———

12 noon, The Fairmont Hotel.

TESSA HAD JUST LEFT THE tub when she heard a thud and then the ringing of the suite's doorbell. She pulled on Earl's T-shirt since the bottom of it covered her ass and just because it smelled like him. Then she pulled on the fluffy bathrobe the hotel provided over it.

She left the bedroom and walked into the suite's main living area. She hadn't placed her room service order. The bell could be the guard with an update or the maid wanting to clean the room. She didn't have to open the door in either case. She could talk through it.

Earl had said not to open the door to anyone, and she wouldn't.

Putting her eye to the spy hole, she spotted Special Agent Garcia whose face filled the entire view.

"Damn," she swore under her breath. She didn't like the man, had never liked the man.

Earl had also expressed his thoughts about the Fed, and none of them were repeatable.

"What do you want, Agent Garcia?" She spoke loud enough to be heard through the door.

"Let me in, Ms. Andrews. I need to talk to you," Garcia shouted.

Something about his voice, his insistence, his being here and not at Denuccio's condo with the others, set off alarm bells in her head. Denuccio would've been arrested weeks ago according to Earl if the Fed had done his job. Garcia's incompetence now seemed sinister.

Go with your gut.

"Go away, Garcia."

Her heart pounding, Tessa hurried to the phone in the room and entered Hotel Security's three numbers with trembling fingers. Her gut screamed at her to run, but where could she go?

She heard the operator speaking loudly over the open line. She left phone off the hook on the table next to the sofa. She figured an unanswered emergency call would get her help faster.

Good, you're doing good, Tessa. Call Earl.

Then Tessa, her breaths coming in erratic gasps, hurried to her cell phone which was in her purse on the bar separating the kitchen from the main living area of the suite. She pulled out her phone and pressed Star 2, Earl's phone.

The click of an electronic key card snicked loudly in the room.

She stifled a scream; the resulting sound came out as a whimper. Garcia had a master key.

Ohgod, ohgod, ohgod. She was trapped.

Breathe, Tessa. Breathe.

Garcia would have to break the door open to get past the extra security locks. She had time, maybe a minute or so at the most, to alert Earl, hide, and prepare a defense.

"Tessa!" Earl's roar came over the cell.

"Garcia's here and trying to break in," she whispered, her breathing erratic, into the phone as she moved to the bedroom. "What should I do? I think he did something to the cop." The thud she'd heard.

"Sweetheart…"

Tessa winced and gasped as she heard more and even louder thuds from the outer room. The Fed was trying to knock the door down.

Ohgod, ohgod, ohgod.

"Tessa, baby…" Earl's voice centered, reassured her. She could hold on until he got there. She wouldn't let him down.

Then she heard, "…Denuccio might be with him. We're on our way. Loren is calling hotel security."

Denuccio and Garcia?

Icy fear froze her in place. No … no … she couldn't

face her tormentor. Memories of what he'd done to her threatened her sanity.

Stop it. Move your butt. Survive. Earl's coming.

"Tessa, sweetheart, did you hear me? Security has been—"

She took a deep breath, then another, and whispered, "I already called them. I left the line open. The phone is sitting in the living room. They'll be able to hear everything that happens." She swallowed past the lump of fear and said as calmly as she could, "Hurry." Her voice cracked at the end.

"Leave the line on the cell open also. We'll need to know what's happening."

"O-o-okay." Tessa held the phone between her shoulder and cheek and then pulled on some sweat pants. She didn't want to be, couldn't be, bare-assed under the robe and T-shirt if she had to face Denuccio.

"We'll be at the hotel in a few minutes and upstairs ASAP." Earl mumbled something she couldn't hear as more and louder thuds came from outside the suite. Or was that her heart threatening to pound its way through her chest?

She shook her head and listened carefully. "Sounds like someone is using the fire ax on the door."

"Fuck, baby, hide. The cops are on their way. All entrances to the hotel will be blocked. They can't take you anywhere."

"I'm not leaving this suite. You said not to, and I'm not." She went to the bag Keely had packed for her and pulled out the small ladies' Ruger.

As soon as she had the gun in her hand, a preternatural calm settled over her. She could defend herself. Keely's dad had taught her how to shoot. She recalled his words: *When you pick up a gun, Tessa, be prepared to use it. An unused weapon ain't worth fucking spit as defense.*

Or, in other words, shoot and worry about the fallout later.

"Earl…?" She flicked off the safety and chambered a round.

"Yes, sweetheart?"

"I've got a gun." She heard his sharp inhalation over the crystal-clear connection.

"Good. Shoot to kill, baby."

Could she kill a man? She looked at the gun in her hand, her shaking, cold hand.

Hell yeah, you can. Defend yourself. Do. Not. Hesitate.

Tessa gasped as a loud crash sounded from the main room. "Oh, God. They're in. Hurry."

Tessa put the cell phone on the floor by the bed and hit the speaker button. Then she hurried to the wall behind the slightly open bedroom door and waited.

She could almost feel the evil emanation from Denuccio. Remembered how he smelled like sour sweat and blood. Her blood. How cruel his hands were on her skin. How he'd laughed as she begged.

Ohgod, ohgod, ohgod, he was here.

Stop it! Remember Earl.

Earl *was* coming. The knowledge calmed her. She adjusted her grip on the gun. It felt better, more natural.

Thatta girl. Stay alive.

"Ms. Andrews." Garcia's voice was loud, calm, and very smug-sounding.

Smarmy son of a bitch. The man thought he was hot shit and irresistible to women. He'd even hit on her when she first reported the stalker.

Well, Tessa had hot shit with Earl; Garcia was dog crap in comparison.

"Shut up, Garcia," Denuccio ordered.

While he hadn't spoken much as he tortured her, something primal in her knew this was his voice. His next words verified her instincts.

"Tessa, my pet. Come to your Master." The voice of evil had a high-class British accent. It churned her stomach.

Breathe. In. Out. In. Out.

Tessa breathed and swallowed the nausea.

Then she realized Earl was hearing this as he raced to get to her and she got mad. More than mad. She felt the burn of a rage unlike anything she'd ever felt before. A cleansing rage like a wildfire preparing the forest for new growth … new life.

Pet? Master? My ass.

She gripped the Ruger as she'd been taught and waited. She'd let them make the first move.

"Tessa, you should never have shared our little sex games with the world. I'd forgotten all about you, my little pet, and then you reminded me." He laughed. "I knew as soon as I read the branding scene … it was a sign we should come together again."

Over my dead body. Tessa shuddered and controlled the urge to scream at her abuser.

"When I went back and viewed the good times we had, well, little slave, I just got the urge to relive them … forever. I've already prepared your room, pet."

She knew in that moment Denuccio's elevator didn't go all the way to the top. The man was nuts. Of course, she was still gonna have to shoot him.

He was in the bedroom doorway. She saw him pass through the crack of the partially open door. He couldn't see her, but the instinct of the hunted had her shrinking away from his presence, making herself a smaller target.

Garcia. Don't forget about him.

Where was the Fed? Couldn't the SOB hear how crazy his employer was?

Denuccio moved into the bedroom and headed for the closed bathroom door. Thank God. She'd counted on him heading that way. Now, if he would just go into the bathroom and take his time, she might be able to get away.

Where in the hell is Garcia?

Tessa didn't care. She'd take her chances with Garcia over Denuccio any day. She wasn't as afraid of the Fed as she was Denuccio, the bogeyman from her past.

Could she shoot Garcia if he tried to stop her?

Damn right, you can. No second guessing. If the Fed is between you and freedom, shoot his smarmy, crooked ass.

Yeah, she could.

She barely breathed as she kept a sharp eye on the open area of the bedroom as Denuccio moved cautiously, silently, toward the bathroom where he thought she hid. Did he have a gun?

Yes. There.

Denuccio raised his arms in a shooter's double-handed grip. The gun was matte black and had a silencer.

"Tessa, are you in the tub? Hiding? Silly girl, you can't hide from me. Didn't you learn anything all those years ago?" Denuccio continued to move slowly, stalking her like the predator he was. He opened the bathroom door and entered.

No guts, no glory, Tessa.

She raised her gun and kept the door of the bathroom in sight as she walked sideways around the bedroom door. A quick glance showed her Garcia was positioned by the door to the hallway, his back to her as he kept an eye on the elevators and stairs.

Tessa entered the main room quickly and as quietly as she could, but Garcia heard something and turned toward her. He raised his gun, and she didn't even think, she brought her gun up and fired.

Amazingly she hit his gun arm, and he dropped his weapon. "You fucking bitch."

Tessa ran at Garcia. "Get out of my way."

"No!" Garcia charged her and knocked her to the ground. He tried to get her gun away from her, but she refused to let it go.

"Don't hurt her, Garcia, or you're a dead man!" Denuccio shouted.

Tessa kicked and bit at Garcia. The only reason he hadn't gained the upper hand and subdued her was because he was bleeding like a stuck pig.

"Give me the gun, bitch," Garcia screamed in her ear. He got his hand on the wrist of the hand holding the gun and squeezed.

"No." She gritted her teeth and held on to the Ruger for all she was worth.

"Let her go, Garcia," Denuccio yelled. "I have her covered."

Out of the corner of her eye she saw Denuccio approach. She used all her strength and pointed the gun in his direction and pulled the trigger.

Denuccio dived to the side. Whether he had intended to or not, he shot at her and Garcia.

Garcia groaned and stopped struggling. His body pinned her to the floor, and she couldn't get enough leverage to move him off her. She was trapped and couldn't see her remaining enemy.

"Ahh, now I have you, my pet." Denuccio's voice came from above her and to her right.

"I'm … not … yours, you freak." Tessa still had the Ruger, in her hand and hidden by Garcia's body. If he got within sight, she'd shoot.

"Ahh, but you are mine. You wear my mark." He gloated.

"I have no mark. I'm not yours." The mark had been gone for years. Only a tattoo of a phoenix existed where the brand had once been. And like the phoenix, she'd risen from the ashes. And she planned to stay that way and begin a new life with Earl.

She freed her hand from under Garcia's arm, pointed her gun in the general direction of Denuccio's voice and pulled the trigger.

"Bitch! You shot at me!" He screamed, a wild maniacal sound that chilled her to her bones. "You'll pay, little slave. You don't need a knee cap for what I want to do with you."

His thudding footsteps came closer. When she turned her head, she didn't have a shot. Couldn't see him. He'd be on her before she could shoot. God, she was dead.

Then more pounding of feet came from the open doorway. She turned her head toward the new sound, the sound of rescue. "Earl! Watch out, he has a gun!"

Denuccio growled and turned away from her and headed toward the door.

God, no, Earl was a sitting duck. She raised her hand and took the shot she had, getting the bastard in the leg.

Denuccio turned and aimed at her. "Bitch. You're dead."

A shot and Denuccio fell to the floor next to her. Half his head blown away. Blood and unspeakable gore splattered Garcia's body and dripped onto her.

Tessa screamed and screamed as she tried to get out from under the dead weight on top of her. Get away from the dead creature who would've enslaved her.

"Goddamn, baby. Fuck, just fuck." The dead weight was suddenly gone. She was pulled against a warm body smelling of sweat, musk, citrus, snow, and Earl.

"Tessa. Baby. Shh. I'm here." Rocking her in his arms, Earl's voice finally broke through the image of what was left of Denuccio's face.

Tessa sobbed and tried to curl into his body even more. He caught her up in his arms and stood in one fluid showing of strength. He headed for the bedroom. She buried her face in his chest as she wrapped her arms around his neck.

"God, sweetheart. I almost died inside. I couldn't get here fast enough." Earl rubbed his jaw over her hair. He held her as if he'd never let her go.

She could live with that.

Someone tried to pry the Ruger out of her hand. She half-whimpered, half-growled and held on to it. Keely's "just in case" foresight had saved her life; she wasn't letting go of the damn gun.

"Tessa, sweetie, give me the gun." Loren's voice sounded over the rapid beat of Earl's heart where her head lay on his chest.

"Tessa," Earl whispered against her ear. "Give Loren the gun, baby. I need to get you checked over. Cleaned up."

She released the gun and then dug her fingers into Earl's back. He didn't complain a bit.

"Loren, you coordinate with the cops," said Earl. "I'm going to take care of Tessa."

"Take your time," Loren replied. "Paul and I can handle the locals."

After Earl carried her through the bedroom and entered the bathroom, he attempted to put some distance between their bodies.

"No, hold me." She held on to him as if she'd fall into nothingness if he let her go.

Earl was having none of that. "God, sweetheart, I'm not leaving you. But you need to let me look at you." He stroked a trembling hand over what parts of her body weren't plastered against him. "Are you injured? Did he touch you? Baby, please let me look."

His bordering-on-frantic voice finally penetrated the haze in her mind.

Tessa lifted her head, looked into his dark eyes, and saw his fear. Her strong man was scared for her.

"I'm fine." Her breath hitched as she stifled a sob threatening to erupt. She stroked his face with blood-spattered fingers. "I'm fine. Denuccio didn't get near me. I shot him."

"So did I."

Tessa saw a satisfied gleam in her man's eyes. "Yeah, you did. Thanks." She kissed his chin. "I hid and got away from Denuccio. But Garcia stopped me." She swallowed as her throat threatened to tighten up on her again.

"Just take your time." Earl turned on the shower, efficiently stripped her, and put her under the warm spray. He climbed in and stood behind her, fully clothed, and held her in his arms as he washed blood spatter off her. "How'd you get under Garcia?"

"I shot his gun arm. He came at me and we … struggled for my gun." She stopped and took a couple of shallow breaths. "I fought him. I had to get to you. Then Denuccio came, and it all went to hell after that. God, he was going to shoot you. So, I shot him."

"You did good, sweetheart." He turned her to face him and kissed her. He muttered against her lips as he stroked her back with shaking hands. "Fuck, I couldn't get here fast enough. I heard shots and noises and … fuck, baby."

He cupped her face and stared into her eyes. "You did very, very good." He kissed her again and then gently nudged her head onto his chest. He rested his cheek on the top of her wet hair. "You stayed alive. No thanks to me. God, I should never have left you alone."

He was blaming himself? Why? He'd provided a guard and a secure place. No one could've predicted Garcia being in bed with Denuccio. It had only made sense to her when she'd seen the Fed's face through the spyhole.

"I'm fine. We're fine." Tessa rubbed soothing circles on his back under his now sopping-wet jacket and kissed his chin. "This was where I needed to be. You did nothing wrong." She angled her head to look at him and grinned. "Please note, I followed instructions to the letter. I didn't open the door, and I didn't leave the room."

Earl half-chuckled, half-groaned. "So noted. Plus you were smart and held it together. The hotel security had already called the cops and the paramedics. We all hit the penthouse floor at the same time."

Tessa shuddered. "Thank God you did. The man was crazy. He was going to take me with him at first, but when I shot him … he decided I wasn't worth the effort."

Earl growled. "Crazy fucker." His fierce expression eased. "Sorry you had to see me kill him. But I couldn't chance he might get a shot off at you. I had to go for a head shot."

"No apologies. You saved me." She massaged the nape of his neck. "I love you, Earl."

"And I love you." Earl kissed the tip of her nose. "Now, let's get you dry and dressed before the authorities descend like locusts to question us."

He turned off the water and helped Tessa out of the shower. When he would've wrapped her in a towel and begun drying her, she put her hand on his arm. "I think we need a bath … together. To relax us both." She unzipped his sodden winter jacket which he shrugged off and let drop at their feet.

Earl shook his head and smiled. "You are amazing. You *will* marry me."

She noted it was an order and not a request, but she didn't care. She wanted to belong to this man.

"When?" She stopped unbuttoning his shirt at his words. Her heart pounding, she smiled through tears of joy.

"As soon as possible."

"I'm good with that time table." She threw him a naughty grin. "But after our bath, okay?"

"Deal." Earl picked her up and carried her to the tub. He started the bath water and placed her in the tub. "Be right back."

Tessa adjusted the water temperature and added some bath oil as Earl locked the door. As he walked back toward the tub, he stripped off his clothing. The man could make a living as a male stripper. He was yummy … and all hers.

A naughty grin on his lips and a gleam in his eye, he approached, his cock leading the way. "Ready for some clean relaxation, sweetheart?"

"Oh, yeah." Tessa laughed and scooted forward so he could climb in behind her.

Earl aligned his legs outside of hers, his arms circling her waist, and then placed a kiss at the top of her spine. "We'll fly to Vegas once the winter storm lets up. But tonight, I plan on getting an early start on the honeymoon."

Tessa relaxed against him, surrounded by his scent and his warmth. "Sounds good to me, but I think we need to move to another hotel room. They might have to re-carpet this one."

Earl laughed. "I'll get right on that, baby, immediately after our *bath*." He lifted her until his cock could enter her from behind.

She moaned as he filled her emptiness. "Um, is that what you're calling this now?"

His breath was warm on her shoulder as he kissed her there. "I call it loving you, Tessa."

As she settled even farther onto his thick cock, his hands urging her gently down, she whispered, "Yeah, love me, Earl."

"Forever and ever, baby." He whispered against her ear. "Forever and ever."

THE END

ABOUT THE AUTHOR

Monette is a lawyer/arbitrator living with her retired pathologist husband in Carmel, Indiana. She also writes under the pen name Rae Morgan. You can visit her web site at *http://www.monettemichaels.com*.

OTHER BOOKS BY THIS AUTHOR

WRITING AS MONETTE MICHAELS:
Death Benefits
Green Fire
Vested Interests

GOODEN AND KNIGHT MYSTERIES:
The Virtuous Vampire (Case File #1)
The Deadly Séance (Case File #2)

SECURITY SPECIALISTS INTERNATIONAL:
Eye of the Storm (#1)
Stormy Weather Baby (#1.5)
Cold Day in Hell (#2)
Storm Front (#3)
Weather The Storm (#3, coming in 2013)

PRIME CHRONICLES TRILOGY:
Prime Obsession (#1)
Prime Selection (#2)

"Tate," a short story in Lucky's Charms anthology.

Writing as Rae Morgan:

Coven of the Wolf Series:
Destiny's Magick (#1)
Moon Magick (#2)
Treading the Labyrinth (#3)
"No Secrets" (#4), in the *Zodiac: Pisces*

A Terran Realm Book:
Earth Awakened
Terran Realm Anthology, Vol. I,
containing *Earth Awakened*

Enchantress, a novella

"Evanescence,"
in the *Edge of Night* anthology

"Once Upon a Princess,"
a short story in *Ain't Your Mama's Bedtime Stories*

Made in the USA
Lexington, KY
31 July 2013